SOMETHING HAPPENED

SOMETHING HAPPENED

ARTHUR AVALOS

To my mother for always believing in everything I do. You are forever in my heart, I love and miss you.

Theresa "Tina" Avalos
4/9/1962 - 11/22/22

CONTENT WARNINGS

The following book is a work of fiction and deals with sensitive topics. The book works through themes of rejection, revenge, and redemption, among others. There are discussions around depression, anxiety, and narcissism. Check the list of content warnings below for more.

Anxiety / Panic Attacks
Explicit Language
Kidnapping
Mention of abortion
Passive Suicidal Ideation
Rejection with Sexuality (homophobia)
Talk of Physical abuse (past tense)
Talk of Substance Abuse
Violent Content (it's a horror Slasher)

PROLOGUE

JAYSON

With flashing lights and the sound of the ambulance sirens off in the distance, I stand relieved that we are finally going to get out of here. Powering on the phone didn't result in an immediate call, so I had to wait for the phone to catch a signal. I pace back and forth with questions running through my mind, my adrenaline at its peak. When the dispatcher's voice came on the line, all I could get out was, "Not everyone made it." It came out in choked syllables, the lump in my throat restricting the few words I had left.

Looking around, I see there are only a few of us left. Thinking to myself, I try to answer the question, *How did we get here?* This was supposed to be a family vacation. A time filled with fun, not a trip full of terror and nightmares. Trying to calm my breathing, I sense eyes on me like I have the answer to everything that's just happened. I gaze over at Ale; she's still coughing and spitting up blood. She's been through a lot. We've all been through so much.

1

I reach into my pocket and pull out a napkin, and notice it's stained with someone's blood. I quickly scan my body, checking my arms, and see it's not mine, as I don't have any visible cuts. There are bruises from the struggle and I feel like I might have a broken arm, but there are no open wounds and no broken skin. I'm tempted to get in the car and drive off, but I need to wait for help to arrive, and with them in the distance, I know I don't have to wait much longer. Although it will be hard, I need to explain what happened, even though I don't even know for myself. The only thing I know is it was supposed to be a fun family vacation.

Walking over to her, I hand her a napkin to help her clean herself off. She takes it from me and wipes at the blood. Looking into her eyes, I lean in and whisper, "I'm sorry."

She looks up at me, confused. I've seen this face on her before and I know she wants to ask me about a million questions. I know she is wondering what do I have to feel sorry about? She knows I didn't do this. I didn't cause this. Her eyes tell me everything she is thinking, and then she leans in and embraces me. Her grip around me growing tighter the longer we stand there.

I always wondered why we still went on these trips. I stopped having fun a long time ago and I am not sure I see anyone enjoy themselves anymore. Mom said it was to keep us together as a family. "Family" was a word she liked to throw around every time she wanted us to feel an ounce of guilt or make us stop behaving badly. Her troubled upbringing caused her to spend her entire life trying to create the perfect family. For starters, we never acted like a family, so how could we be the perfect family? We were all so different, complete opposites of one another.

We stopped being a family a long time ago. I can't pinpoint when it happened, but I can think of many instances where it might have started, or where maybe it should have caused cracks. The last time one of us seemed truly happy was the last time we went camping. This was before Dad's business became successful and the company took off. That was decades ago, when we were too young to understand the dynamics between all of us, before the toxicity of the family reached alarming levels.

Every year, we would take a trip somewhere. Each trip somehow ended in chaos. Someone's unfinished business or someone's ego getting in the way. This time, the unthinkable happened. This time, some of us didn't make it home and there would be no more family vacations. If we ever went on another family trip, it would look a lot different. The people standing around me are the only family I have left.

I don't know how to make sense of it all and how much of a part I might have played in it. I'm questioning why it happened to us, and if we could have prevented it had we been more in sync with each other. Could we have avoided this if I would have just done what I planned to do sooner? Would some of my family still be alive? Something happened in the woods today. Something I am still trying my hardest to understand.

Should I tell them everything that happened? Are there some secrets from the weekend that we need to keep between us? In the past twenty-four hours, only half of us made it out alive. I look down at my watch to check the time. The cracked screen offers me no answer. Turning the phone over in my hand, I wish I had checked the time because now all I see is a black screen. The phone died shortly after I powered it on and called for help. It had enough battery to make the call, including several failed attempts. When I called, I was hoping whoever was on the line could hear what I was saying. I couldn't be sure they would, but they found us.

The lights are bright, the sirens loud, and all I want to do is cover my ears as I see them approach. Panic sets in as they get closer. I know they are coming to help. I still haven't decided how much I am going to tell them. As they approach, two words sum up everything…..

Something Happened.

CHAPTER 1

JAYSON

The phone dings as I step out of the shower. No one really texts me these days, and with the trip ahead, it must be someone in the family. I look at the screen, realizing the text is from everyone. It's a series of texts within our group chat. Going through them one by one, I'm reading what everyone has said. Too annoyed and now anxious, I don't know if this is something I want to do, but for me to move on, I need to go.

I don't reply to any of the messages because I need to finish getting ready or I will be even further behind schedule. I quickly make my way to the bedroom, passing several family photos on the wall, all from the trips we've taken over the years.

Entering the bedroom, I put on the clothes I laid out the night before, posing in front of the mirror. Being vain is just a part of me, but I am also trying to work through some self-confidence issues and continue to check myself out.

I'm wearing my favorite tight blue shorts with seven-inch seams. Ale calls them slut shorts. I would disagree, a few more inches off and they could be. You can see the tattoos on my thighs. I have been obsessed with Alice in Wonderland since childhood and have two tattoos of the illustrations from the original book on both thighs, The Mad Hatter on my right and Alice on my left. She is on her knees with a tray held out in front of her in the style of a pin-up girl. On top of the trays are the bottles and cookies that read 'eat me, drink me'. "Isn't that risky? Are you really going to walk around like that?" my mom said after I got them. She was originally against tattoos, but when she got one herself at forty-one, I figured I could start getting them too. Once I started, I never stopped. She would say, "You're covered in them", but I only have about twenty with two on my legs and the rest on my torso and arms. There is a desire to get more; standing at five foot nine, there is ample legroom. I just don't know what to get. Turning around in the mirror, I check out my ass, which is one of my best features.

I'm wearing a white tank top that is cut deep both in the neck and the arms, where you can see more of my tattoos. Working out has helped me stay in shape and I would consider myself mildly attractive, but my self-confidence fights those thoughts all the time. Six-pack abs or bulging muscles have never been important to me, as I am not your stereotypical queer. I never wanted them and I'm ok with the fifteen extra pounds I carry from what would be an ideal weight by medical standards.

I share my mother's eyes, all except for the color that everyone talks about. "It's a shame no one has your eyes, they are stunning," and I agree. Her eyes are a deep blue while mine are light brown. Mine borderline on an almost hazel-like color, which is as close as I will get to hers. We both share defined cheekbones, think Cher in the '70s. My mother's features end at the top of my head as I have my father's hairline. My hairstyle is short in order to hide my premature balding, preserving what little youth I am holding on to. I lean toward the mirror, zeroing in on my nose. *Should I get a nose ring?* I laugh because I had one in high school. Me and Ale got them together at the mall. That's a silly idea to think about again, but not one I completely dismiss.

I'm heading towards the kitchen when my phone rings. I stop and consider if I should let it go to voicemail, but whoever it is on the other end might just call again, especially if it is someone in my family. We are all anticipating this weekend but for different reasons, so I decide to answer, pressing accept and placing the call on speaker so I can continue with what I was doing.

"You're coming, aren't you? You know how much these mean to me," Mom says with a hint of guilt. She knows how to lay it on, but that is what moms do, right?

"Yes, I will be there…. Don't I always come?" We hang up the phone after some back and forth and I go back to what I was doing. I appreciate my mom, but I also hate when she makes me feel guilty. I don't have a complicated relationship with my mom, but sometimes I feel sorry for her. She's had to deal with us our entire lives, and we are not the easiest bunch to get along with. Each of her kids is unique, and my father is a piece of work.

My parents met each other when they were young, working at a restaurant in Chicago where they both grew up. Dad bussed tables while mom bossed him around. When she talked about those times when she used to work and make her own money, there was a sense of pride and identity. Things quickly shifted once my sister Cat was born and mom quit her job.

Cat started as the family's golden child; she could do no wrong in my parents' eyes. All the attention was on her. Then

I came along and that changed for my mom, but not so much for my dad. He was fine with one kid. He wanted my mom to move forward with an abortion, which she fought him on and won. I found this out a lot later in life through an argument with my youngest sister, Gina. Looking back on that secret, I am grateful that Gina had told me. The feeling of being left out by my father made sense and I knew it wasn't all in my head.

My mom calls me every time we decide to get-together just to make sure I am going to be there. Most of her calls feel like the one I just had, a little of excitement and a little of guilt. It's not like these family gatherings are voluntary. They are mandatory according to her, despite her pleas of "I wish you could join us". If you miss one, you'll never escape her wrath for missing it. She knows the relationship I have with the family. I love them, but I do not always like them—most of the time, I don't even know if what I feel for them is even love. We have a troubled past, causing us to fight and argue and some of them don't accept me for who I am: Gay. That was hard for my father to come to terms with, and I know it's something he's still struggling with. This year, though, I am not going on this trip alone. I decided I am bringing along my best friend Ale who will help me get through it, just like she always does.

This isn't her first trip with the family either, so she knows how this might end. It's been some time though since she's come along. In fact, I don't know why she ever stopped, because I never stopped asking. One day she just stopped coming, but she jumped at the chance for this one. It surprised me because the last trip we went on was to Mexico, a place she had never been but always talked about wanting to visit. So why would she want to spend a weekend in the woods?

Ale is great—she is likable, and with her around, I think

my family will be on their best behavior. Why? Because that is how my family works. They never want to appear dysfunctional. My parents have created a facade where everything looks perfect from the outside. A picture-perfect family like the ones you see in frames at the store. A mother, father, and four perfect little kids. They don't see the yelling, screaming, and fighting. They don't see how awful things have gotten in the past.

Ale understands this dynamic. It is what she wanted her family to be like. Her family is the opposite of that picture-frame family my parents push us to be. Ale's father was an alcoholic, her mother addicted to booze and pills. Some of which were illegal, some prescription. When I first met Ale, she told me about her family. She described them and I imagined that picture-perfect family. They seem so normal. She told me that both of her parents worked and she talked about spending a lot of time together. I didn't suspect that she had those issues in her family. Over time, the truth came out, and I never asked her why she lied to me. It must be hard having parents as addicts. These are things I never had to worry about in my family. My family had other issues.

My father drank, and when he did, it was heavy. He would drink and crank the music so loud it kept us up all night. Luckily, he wasn't physically abusive, unlike Ale's father. His abuse was different, he was verbally and emotionally abusive. You could spend a few minutes with him and end up thinking horrible thoughts about yourself. There were times I walked away from him questioning my moral character, including my existence. The thought of ending my life was something I dealt with during High School and college with a singular attempt a short time after I came out to my family. An attempt that I am grateful was unsuccessful, as I have grown to appreciate life and myself a little more than before. I am still a work in progress, an unfinished piece of work.

My dad was a storyteller, but not the before bed type. His stories were manipulative and full of lies, but most of the time, you ended up believing them. One day we were at a store, shopping for random things, and he wanted a TV, so we got it. When he got home, he told a story where he argued with the staff, demanding discounts because he was a premier shopper. He had an inflated ego which came out a lot in public and was often embarrassing. In his story, there were many dramatic moments, confrontation, tossing money on the counter, and in the end, getting his premier discount. A whopping fifty percent off in his story. The story of course, was a complete fabrication. Even I, who had been there and witnessed the actual events, still somehow believed him. He didn't get his discount, and he was extremely nice to the staff, but in good old-fashioned Dad storytelling, it went a completely different way. We entertained his stories, and I am honestly not sure why.

These lies didn't stop with strangers. No, they were worse when they involved us. He would pit us against each other growing up. Either academically or with sports, or with our love and affection towards him. He was a narcissist, and if they ever had a picture of someone in the dictionary under the definition, it would be his. I wonder if maybe I should submit one to Wikipedia? It doesn't matter much now as we don't have to tolerate his lies or his emotional abuse anymore. Being adults mostly and living our own lives, we just need to tolerate him on holidays and during these trips.

Maybe we put up with it because we felt we had to, he was our father and he provided for us. We had a roof over our heads and clothes on our backs. Something my mom would always remind us of. We're not battered and bruised; we're only broken.

I sadly don't have many memories of us doing things together. In fact, I don't have many memories of me and him at all, which sometimes brings me down. The few things we did like shopping, taking long car rides, and going house hunting on the weekends were more so for him than anything. Years later, I found out the houses we were looking at were the houses of the women he was seeing behind my mom's back. Our shopping trips were his chance to show off his money. Those didn't always end up with us having fun either.

He used to make us play this game where he would give us two or three minutes in a store to run around and grab as much stuff as we wanted and could hold. Since DVDs and CDs were still popular and my go-to, he knew how to get me. Looking back, I don't think it was about fun, but a control thing. He would keep the time knowing that we would lose track of it and run out. Only to be left standing with bundles of stuff that he would make us put back with shame. He would laugh and say, "You should have gone faster." It was cruel, even damaging. I have issues with shopping now and I always wonder if that has any connection to those experiences.

My phone rings again, and it's my brother Victor this time.

"Are you going this weekend because we need to talk about what happened last time."

"I told you I do not want to talk about it again," I say. "What's done is done and what's said can't be unsaid." Disconnecting the call before I even say goodbye, the anger in me was intense. Was it the best response? No, but my brother will never own up to the things he's said. I love my brother, don't get me wrong, but he is so much like my father. He always makes you think that you're the problem when he talks to you. He is usually on the quiet side, but when he speaks up, he reminds me so much of our dad.

The argument was silly and started over a game of Scattergories. We had similar words and neither of us wanted to back down. This led to the back and forth, which escalated on to something bigger. We ended up arguing about which one of us stole the remote from who when we were five and seven years old. It ended up with one of us going to the hospital for a busted lip.

Another time, we had been watching TV before bed, our usual routine. My mom stopped us and told us to wash up. We were at that age where my mom pushed for good hygiene. She handed me the washrag, and I washed my face. My brother snatched it from me, and I snatched it back, starting a game of tug of war for who would have the cleanest face. My mom yelled, "Stop it and let it go!" Of course, I did what she said, and my brother flew across the room, smacking his face against the wooden edge of the couch.

"Jayson, what did you do?" she screamed, rushing over to my brother.

"I listened, I let it go."

"You know that's not what I meant." She was panicking as blood trailed down my brother's lip, spilling onto the ground. "You are seven years old, Jayson; you should not be fighting with your little brother." At that moment I honestly thought I had killed him.

My dad came rushing into the room, scooping Victor into his arms. I remember that stare, one of hatred and disgust. He never stopped looking at me that way.

"He is going to die, and it's all your fault."

I believed him and cried while they headed to the hospital.

Seven years old or not, I did not start it, but I finished it. I didn't get into much trouble afterward, maybe because of the sheer panic of the situation. When they got home from the emergency room, I was already in bed. I waited to see if they would come into my room. I heard them tuck my brother in and retreat to their room. The next day, everything was normal and we never talked about what happened. That was typical in our household though, we never talked. The only memory of that night are the ones we each have and the scar on Victor's lip.

Victor and I have a hard relationship. You would think that because we are two years apart, we would be closer. We sometimes dressed identically growing up, giving off the impression we were twins. Something we would play up around people. There were times I enjoyed my brother's company, and there were times I hated it.

Victor wanted to go everywhere with me. When I would say no, he would manipulate a situation and once even stole money from my parents, blaming it on me. The punishment was harsh. I couldn't see my friends and I couldn't take part in an after-school program I had been looking forward to. I say it was harsh because staying at home was the punishment, not missing out on activities and spending time with friends. Being at home meant I had to be around people who I felt hated me and ignored me. Victor avoided me that week. He had friends come over and spent a lot of time with our father. I don't know why he did that. I questioned if it was because he wanted to make me jealous or prove he got away with it.

My pocket buzzed; it was a text from my brother.

Hanging up on me is mature Jayson. I guess we can talk about it while we're camping in the woods for three days. It is going to be GLORIOUS.

Oh, it is because I am finally going to do what I should have done three years ago. I almost sent him a reply but stopped myself. I don't want to get into it right now.

CHAPTER 2

JAYSON

The texts between my brother and I would normally cause me to spiral. I'd go over everything we'd have said and worry that I did something wrong to push his buttons. This time I didn't do that, I had too much on my mind. In under an hour, I gathered my things into my bag and started my drive to Ale's house. It's a scenic ten-minute drive that takes me past some of our favorite places growing up. There is the park where we each had our first kiss, the burger joint we met at after prom, and our favorite record store.

Checking to make sure I have everything, I grabbed the two portable chargers that were charging for the trip. I wanted to make sure I could disconnect from my family and connect to the outside world when needed. Several games are downloaded on to my phone that don't need internet access just in case the signal is spotty. I need to stay busy and distracted. My therapist suggested these games as a coping mechanism for when I am stressed. They don't always work, but they don't hurt either.

I grabbed my Kindle and three paperbacks off the book-shelf. There is more than enough on my Kindle, but there is something I love about holding a physical book in my hand that makes me happy. I don't know if it is the smell of a book or the nostalgia of picking through a book until you get the right one, but I have an extensive library at home of physical books. If you need a thousand books to be considered a library, then I am over halfway there.

"I am on my way," I tell Ale as I slam the trunk shut. "Thank you again, it means the world to me you're coming. I hope you're ready. You know how my family can be."

"Jayson, all families have drama, but there is something about yours that I do not understand. I am always here for you, babes. Plus, I have gone on vacation with you before so it will be fine, trust me."

She hangs up the phone rather quickly, but that isn't out of the ordinary for her. When she is behind schedule, she is behind schedule. I just hope she'll be ready when I get there.

We've been friends since high school, and now after ten years and recently turning twenty-five, I feel like we are in it until the end. Nothing could end this friendship. Well, maybe one thing, and that could happen this weekend if my family isn't on their best behavior. Ale has a high tolerance, but something hasn't been right with her and my family for some time. Especially with my father. I am not sure if he told her something. He often goes behind our backs and confronts people if he has a problem with them. I've noticed recently she has been looking at him differently, and it makes me a little uncomfortable.

Ale was already outside waiting for me when I arrived. It took me twenty minutes to get to her. She was tapping her foot like an impatient mother, cigarette in one hand, a bag slung over her shoulder and a large duffel bag in the other. Sitting at the base of her feet are another two small bags. Why does someone need so much for a trip out in the woods, especially since it's for the weekend?

She's dressed in jean shorts that are too short for my comfort level and a black tank top. Her sunglasses are over her eyes as if she's trying to hide behind them. They're large and give her a sense of mystery. She places them on her head as soon as I pull up.

Ale gets in the car, reaching into my small bag thrown in the back seat almost immediately to where I stash the Xanax. She takes one out and hands it to me, then pops one into her mouth. "It helps me calm down before shit goes down. Where is this place again?" She says playfully, putting an emphasis on the shit part making it sound like she pronounced it with a z.

"I don't know. My sister Cat picked it out. It's someplace new, more secluded. Did you bring those extra battery things I had sent to your house from the ZON?"

"Yup, all charged up. Are we going to have service while we are up there? What if we don't? What if something happens?"

"Nothing is going to happen." I smirk, "Maybe some yelling about something stupid and then packing up and leaving." Last time it was my sister Gina, the year before, my mom threatened to leave. Four years ago, I made it only two hours into the trip and left. Luckily that time we were in Florida, and I headed to the Keys to the Island House Key West Club, clothing optional, I had a weekend of fun.

"Well, everyone knows where we'll be because I told them I'd be going camping with you and I'll check in when we get there," she said with a smile on her face.

She loves to make our other friends jealous. We have a small group of close friends, and everyone knows how close we are. Conjoined twins you'd say, joined at the hip. I know it bothers them because some have come out directly and told me.

Ale is difficult to get along with sometimes, and this creates a lot of tension in the group. David wanted to come along but backed out when he found out Ale was coming. I asked him first and Ale kind of barged in on the plans. She does that a lot and invites herself into everything. I didn't mind because I wanted her to come, but I also wanted to spend more time with David as we've been developing a bit of a flirtatious relationship lately, or should I say, again.

I met David during my freshman year of college and introduced him to Ale. He didn't like her and said his first impression was that she was too clingy with me, like she was jealous. I must admit that I agree with that. Ale and I have had this discussion before. We both know that we're a bit codependent with one another and have had a conversation about whether we should take some time away from our friendship or at least make more time for other people. We always decide against it.

I don't always know what David and I are. Sometimes I think we are turning into something; other times, I think we are growing apart. Sometimes it's sexual, sometimes we're clearly just friends. All I know is that Ale doesn't like David that much because I think she thinks he's a threat. Someone to take me away from her. Like she owns me or something but she's just afraid of being alone but so am I. It's why I don't challenge her enough in our friendship.

"We need to stop for gas, and I need to grab something to munch on." Ale rolls her eyes as we pull into the gas station. I know what she is thinking. Why didn't I get this all done before I picked her up?

While at the gas station, I grab beef jerky, Smarties, bags of chips, and several sodas. The Smarties are nostalgic; they are so Ale and I can pretend they are drugs and pill pop all weekend like we did in high school. This was before we experimented with drugs. It sounds silly now, and honestly, it was. I still don't know why we thought that was cool, and why I want to reminisce about that time in our life.

Recognizing the clerk at the store as someone I hooked up with a few summers back, puts me off. I read his nametag to make sure it's him, Enrique. I've had no serious relationships and have only dated here and there. The clerk smiled at me but didn't seem to recognize me. He scans my items and places them in a bag. I swipe my card, and he hands me the receipt. I thank him, using his name, "Thanks, Enrique." He looks confused but then looks down at his shirt. I chuckle and walk away. It must not have been a good hook-up if he didn't recognize me. I see him adjust his name tag as he stares at me walking away, maybe he recognizes me now.

As I walk out of the store, I pass a girl who looks like she'd been through something. Her hair was in a mess, and she appeared confused and shaking. As I pass through the door, I hear her say something, "I'm Jenny, I need—" The door closes before I could hear the rest. Thinking about my friendship with Ale, I wonder if this girl had someone in her life. Someone who she could go to. If she did, would whatever she had just walked away from have happened to her? My thoughts immediately wander to something dark, and I immediately think kidnapped, this girl could have just escaped from her abductor. If that was the case, I would see this Jenny person on the news at some point. One thing is for sure, something happened. The door opens again as a group of around my age walk in and I hear Jenny explaining something about thirteen hours and I shudder at the thought that maybe my dark thoughts were right.

When I reach Ale, she gives me this look and nods back towards the door, "Do you want to skip camping and follow them."

"As tempting as that looks, I think we need to get going."
I do consider what we could get into if we decided to skip
this trip and find a way into that group of hot guys; it might
just be more fun and a way to get over David ditching me.
When I look back, I can see one of them staring back giving
me a wink. I smile and toss the bag at Ale suggesting we
move before I really change my mind.

She opens the bag immediately inspecting what is inside
and pulls out the Smarties. Ale and I both dated people with
drug problems in our early twenties and sometimes I wonder
if Ale has one herself. That is why I am not sure the Smarties
are the best idea.

Ale is always in need of money and will never tell me
why. I know she uses Xanax to help her sleep and take the
edge off. I also know she does not have a prescription for it.
Sometimes I give her money and some of my pills because
she's my best friend, and that is what best friends do. *Don't
they?*

I have a prescription for Xanax because of my anxiety. I
get anxious around people, and since moving out of my family's home after high school, the anxiety has only gotten
worse. It's especially bad when I know I am going to be
around my family. I started getting Xanax when I was sixteen.
I saw the school counselor, and she referred me to a
psychiatrist.

The psychiatrist was my first crush and my first inappropriate relationship with someone older. They flirted with me,
and I knew how to flirt back just enough to get what I
wanted, but not enough to cross that line. When I say it was
inappropriate, I don't mean that anything sexual happened.
Not under my clothes at least. We just used each other. I
stroked his ego and would graze past him a little too close,
and he gave me pills in return. We both knew the game that
was being played. I don't see him anymore and I get them

now from another doctor. She wouldn't be interested in those tactics, and neither would I.

We've been on the road a few minutes now since leaving the gas station. I see Ale grab a book out of her bag. I can't believe she is reading it again. *How many times has she read it, four or five?* I brought one of my favorite books with me too.

She's looking at her phone a lot, like she is waiting for someone to call her. I want to ask, but when I go to turn the dial on the radio, she pulls her hands closer to herself and flips her phone over. Something is up with her, and I want to know what it is.

CHAPTER 3

ALE

I really don't know why I am going on this trip with Jayson. Well, a part of me does. It's something I have been wanting to do for the last three years, ever since the night at the restaurant. He's my best friend for crying out loud. I should have stuck up for him and done more, but I didn't. Letting that opportunity slip by, it's been in the back of my mind ever since.

I have many regrets in my life and that night is one of the biggest. I also regret my habit of using Jayson. Even when we are mad at each other, I still use him. Sometimes I wonder if he notices, but it doesn't matter because this weekend I am here for him, and I'll finally stick up for him. I just hope I grabbed everything I needed. I am also hoping I am not the reason this goes bad. Sometimes Jayson gets a little mad when I forget things or do things in a way that he wouldn't. He's a little OCD but says it's his anxiety, and I think he's right. I also think he has a little of his father in him. Who wouldn't? We are our parents' children after all. Look at the habits I have developed, which I can thank mom and dad for.

I know how messed up I am, and I should get help. In fact, there was a plan to check in somewhere but changing my plans to focus on my friend felt like the best thing for me. It's called being avoidant and I do it well.

It didn't take long to get myself ready. I had bought everything I thought I would need—there was even a box of beef jerky, my go-to snack, our go-to snack. It's what we bonded over that first day at school ten years ago. The smell of jerky in the air—dried meat and spices. It does something to you.

We were sitting in the grass just a few feet apart. Jayson was always alone. He didn't have friends, and neither did I. I saw him there every day that week sitting alone, just as alone as I was when I heard him tear open his spicy stick. I know the sound it makes because I eat them every day. The sound of deliciousness as the plastic tears so easily down the side, revealing a stick with a little meat juice glistening in the sun. My mouth waters every time I think about it.

"Shit," I heard him say. I looked over, and I saw that the tear in the wrapper wasn't all the way down like it should be, the way we both like it to be. I laughed, and he shot me an embarrassed look.

"Sorry, it's annoying when these don't tear right," he said.

I held up my stick and smiled, "I know what you mean." I slid across the grass, and we sat with each other for the rest of the lunch hour talking. Mainly about our favorite brands of beef jerky, music, No Doubt, and how much we hated school.

Popularity was never my thing, and it wasn't for Jayson either. He was a scrawny little kid but has grown into his looks; it's too bad we don't play for the same team. We never sat alone again for lunch or anytime ever again from that point on. Two peas in a pod, peanut butter and jelly, Will and Grace.

He told me about his family, and how he wasn't born in the area. They moved here when he was ten. He's from the big city my family would say, Chicago, and living out in the suburbs was what his family wanted because it had better schools. They wanted to get their children away from the city and all its dangers. Since Jayson's father's business was doing extremely well, they could afford it.

I don't get the Naperville hype. It's nice there, but I don't live there myself—my aunt does, and we use her address. I told Jayson I lived there when we first met. I didn't want him to know where I really lived. It's not like where I am from is bad; it's just not great. Every Sunday night I was driven to Naperville by my mom, and I stayed the week with my aunt. Living with my aunt was better than living at home, and I did that until I could drive myself. That's when my parents also stopped letting me stay the week with my aunt.

Mom drove me versus my dad because it was easier to drive on crack and pills than it was to drive drunk. Plus, it was easier to avoid his verbal abuse, so I didn't mind. The more I stayed away from home, the more I could avoid the other forms of abuse. Mom was aware he hit me because he hit her too.

It's only when he's drunk. He doesn't really mean it. She had always said it like she was trying to excuse him. Why do battered women stay in relationships? It was something that I had questioned growing up, but I've managed to learn as I've gotten older. What I don't understand is why a mother would stay in a home knowing her kid was being abused; it's something I am still working through.

I don't remember the first time he hit me, but I remember the last. It was my senior year, just before I moved out. Me and Jayson were working late at the mall. I had to wait for Jayson to close his store, and he usually got out later than I did. Jayson worked at Hot Topic during his goth phase. I think he still has some of that side deep down but hides it to make his family happy. His rebellious stage, they called it and it didn't last long and neither did his employment at Hot Topic.

It was always my idea to go to Taco Bell and eat in the parking lot, knowing it was already late, and Dad most likely wanted Mom to go to the store for another beer run. I think I subconsciously waited because I knew if my mom started using, she wouldn't want to go, and he would just hit the hard liquor at home and pass out. Sometimes I wasn't that lucky. As soon as I got home, the arguing would start.

I remember the last time he yelled at me.

"You little tramp, why are you home so late?" I was trying to ignore him, but he jumped off the couch stumbling towards me. "I told you to be home right after work," he continued to yell. I flinched when he stumbled towards me because I didn't know what was about to happen. He took that flinch as me gearing up to hit him. Before I could do anything, he pushed me up against the wall, my head smacked hard against the spot where the wood trimming and wall met. It felt like my head was about to split open. I got dizzy and felt a sharp pain in the back of my head and liquid warmth down my neck.

It was easy to push him off me because he was a drunken mess. He stumbled backwards and fell over the chair, crashing into the liquor cabinet. As he hit it, something clicked in his head. It was like he didn't realize what just happened. He bent down, opened the door to where the vodka was and grabbed a bottle. I left and headed to Jayson's house, stunned and in pain. The drive to Jayson's was a tough one. I stopped at the park. There were many memories shared here. Now it would have one more. I pulled over and sat on the swings for about twenty minutes going over every option I had. Would I go back, or would I start over? I didn't have the means to start over, but I had Jayson. I thought about what it would be like if I took my life, but that thought ended quickly as I reached into my pocket and found the wrapper to our favorite snack.

Jayson didn't ask many questions when I told him. He didn't bat an eye when I told him I needed a place to stay. I always stayed at his place when shit went down. His parents didn't seem to mind. I would hear the occasional, "She's from over there. What is that going to look like," from his father, which I knew meant he didn't really like me, but he did like to look at me. It made me feel dirty, but Jayson was my best friend and things didn't get awkward with his dad until much later.

Today when Jayson texted he was leaving, I knew the drive was ten minutes, so I waited fifteen, and then went outside. Waiting another five minutes, I felt I was becoming impatient. I just want to get this started so I can get it over with. Looking down at my phone I wonder if I should send a text. I don't want to start the trip off on the wrong foot, but I need this to be over.

CHAPTER 4

I planned all of this after dinner that night. I just needed to wait for the perfect time. When is the perfect time to kill someone? Make sure it's done right, no survivors. You also need to make sure you don't get caught, and that is the hardest part. Do you frame someone else? You need to make sure that it's air-tight and that the authorities are clueless so that you would never become a suspect. These are questions I've had over the last three years and I can't spend the rest of my life in jail. I wouldn't survive a night in jail, let alone prison.

I wish sometimes that my father ended up in prison for something, then this wouldn't have to happen and I could go on and mind my own business. There are things he could have gone to prison for, but that would cause even more problems.

I need to curb these thoughts, or I won't go through with it. There is a hunger in me, so I tear open the snack in front of me, smelling the meat and looking at the glistening of the grease across the stick. It's smoky with a hint of spice; it's a smell that not everyone loves, but I do.

Everything is in the bag, all the supplies I bought over the last few weeks are where they need to be and carefully packed. I go back to that night at dinner, coming out should have been the best experience. Family should be supportive but they weren't in fact, that's when the name-calling started.

"I don't want a faggot for a son."

"What is everyone going to say?"

"I love you but..."

It was embarrassing. I couldn't hear everything over all the yelling and talking over each other. It was supposed to be a family dinner.

The entire restaurant was now staring. Making comments, getting up, calling over their servers and whispering. There was a glass that was knocked over and that's when I had had enough, and I got up and walked away.

I went home and thought about things for hours. I decided I would do something about it. It's been about three years since then, and finally, the chance is here.

As I am driving, I go through a mental checklist. I know I grabbed my favorite book. I checked the stove and all the lights, and I made sure the kitchen was in order. We appeared to be in good shape. There didn't seem to be anything that I missed. It was three years of planning. Did I grab those things from under the sink? If I forgot them, I would have to make do. I need to make one quick stop and I hope no one is home.

I turn on the radio to FM 103.3, nineties music. No Doubt is on —I laugh and start singing.

CHAPTER 5

VICTOR

I can't stand when Jayson and I fight. I know I shouldn't have sent that last message, so I hope it doesn't cause him to turn back around. He's never done it before, but there is a first time for everything. I really want to do what I should have done that night at dinner three years ago and stand up to my father to show Jayson I care. I know he doesn't believe it, but I do. Even when I act like I don't, which is often, I care. He can be an annoying shit, but what brother isn't?

I walk over to the sink to do the last of the dishes. My place is beautiful. I look around and realize how grateful I am for what I have, but I am also worried that I might lose it all. Dad helped me buy this house; he gave me the money for the remodel, the down payment, and helped furnish it.

I stare into the window just above the kitchen sink and notice my reflection. In front of me is a tired man who hasn't been sleeping well. The person in the reflection looks a lot like Jayson—he's shorter and has more hair but that will change.

He's slimmer because he enjoys the gym, but he's exhausted and worn out.

There are a few things still on the counter, and I see them behind me in the reflection. I turn around to grab them so I can get things cleaned up and head out the door. When I turn around and look at myself again, I don't know if I like the person staring back at me. Who have I become? I don't want to spend my morning self-analyzing, so I try to finish getting the place cleaned up.

Mom helped me design the kitchen. She loves to cook, and the kitchen is her safe space. The island, almost identical to the one at my parents', was different; I had them build a double sink. It was a difference from my parents' house despite modeling my entire home after theirs. They have one of those deep sinks back at home. Mom liked to soak dishes overnight. I remember the pile of dishes every morning before she would start. The dirty water and smell of last night's dinner decomposing, with a slight lemon scent.

Below my sink are a few things I need to grab for the trip that I can't forget. Reaching underneath I brushed past the supplies to clean the counters, wipe down the stove, and spray the windows. Past that are the few things I don't want to forget to bring with me. Finally, my hand reaches for a brillo pad. There are some dishes and a pan I need to scrub, and the pan has been sitting on the stove for a day and it's going to need something tougher than the scrub brush. I clean when I get nervous, something I got from my mom. It's why the house was always clean growing up. I also want to make sure everything is spotless because when I get back I'll have too much energy to worry about the house.

I take my anger and frustrations about our family and this upcoming trip out on the plate I am holding. Scrubbing the plate feels like I am scrubbing away the past and I can feel my fingers tensing more and more. My fingers slide over the textured edges and along the floral design on the plate, the plate slips a few times. I don't want to break it because I don't want to clean it up. Yet, it isn't long before the plate is crashing into the sink, breaking into several pieces.

Each piece represents a family member. There is one for my dad—the smallest piece, I think to myself—my mom just slightly larger. Then the biggest piece I see reminds me of Jayson.

Staring at the broken pieces in the sink I am taken aback. It's like watching a scene play out. I stare blankly into the porcelain void of a box in front of me, wishing I could close it and seal up.

"What did you do?"

"It slipped; it wasn't his fault," Mom says.

"Then why is he standing near the sink?"

"I didn't want mom to get cut," Jayson said with a tremble to his voice.

"I swear you are useless." Dad walks away without a fight this time.

I knew Dad didn't believe it, but he must have been too tired to argue or challenge them. Jayson hurried up and cleaned the broken dish. Mom immediately tossed it and covered it up in the trash, it was Dad's mug, the mug Jayson had bought him. I am sure Jayson broke it on purpose. He and Dad had gotten into an argument earlier. Jayson wasn't even supposed to be doing the dishes. It was Cat's turn, but she'd gone out with her friends after dinner to study.

I am not sure Dad even noticed his mug was missing after that, or maybe he was just grateful he didn't need to use it anymore since Jayson bought it. Mom would serve him coffee in it every day and I would see him look at it as he stubbornly drank from it. He would never have grabbed it on his own.

Even though Dad treated Jayson like shit, Jayson still tried to connect with him. He tried to do everything right.

Later that evening I tried to talk to Jayson, but he acted like nothing happened, and that he was OK. I wanted to ask him if he had done it on purpose.

"How did you break dad's mug?"

"I didn't break it, Mom did."

I know mom wouldn't have done this. Not on purpose or by accident, she was too careful with things. "Jayson, you know mom didn't break it. Why won't you tell me why you did it? I know you and Dad were fighting earlier." I wanted him to tell me the truth.

Jayson ignored me and sang, pretending he was listening to his headphones, but I could see the radio wasn't even on. Jayson could be so annoying at times and this was one of them.

"You know you always do this. I am just trying to talk to you." This interrupts his singing.

"Well, I don't want to talk to you, at least not about why *Mom* broke the mug."

"Mom didn't break the mug, you did, and you're annoying the shit out of me."

"You are annoying the shit out of me. Now get out of my room, I need to study."

"Yeah, you study, bring home the grades, Jayson. Make Dad proud." I knew exactly what I was doing when I made that statement.

Staring at the broken plate in the sink, I notice that the water has a slightly pink tint. I only snap out of it when I feel a slight sting on my skin. Did the comment I made all those years ago sting like my cut stings? Does it hurt and cause any pain for Jayson still?

I used to be jealous of Jayson, but that was because they

liked to brag about him when he wasn't around. Thinking about how my dad treated Jayson though, I feel sorry for him. He talked about Jayson, but has never really shown him he cares, not like my Mom does.

If Jayson got good grades, he would tell us how proud he was of him, but never in front of Jayson. It was like he used Jayson's success and accomplishments to rub in our faces that we weren't as good as him. He would tell neighbors, friends, and family members all about the good things Jayson was doing and stare at us with a look of disgust. It made us feel like we needed to compete with our brother. This way Dad had another child to brag about. To this day I compare myself to Jayson and the big brother I should be like, the brother that my father doesn't love. That's a bit of a confusing concept, no wonder I see a therapist twice a week.

Dad wasn't the nicest to any of us really, but he was especially mean to Jayson. From early on I noticed small things. Walking into the room and ghosting Jayson. Bumping into him like he didn't see him there. Asking everyone how their day was at dinner except Jayson. Sometimes dad would forget to invite Jayson to come along with us places.

One morning we all went to breakfast. I thought Jayson didn't want to go. He skipped things around this time. While at breakfast Dad's phone rang, he picked up, "You weren't up! You don't get to come. I am not responsible for waking you up. How old are you?" I could tell that Jayson then asked if we could bring him back something. "You didn't come, so you don't get food." That was hard to hear, so I ordered a little extra food and brought it home and put it in the fridge. It sat there causing me pain because I didn't know if he was avoiding me on purpose or was just upset.

We didn't see much of Jayson growing up as he kept to himself and hanging out with Ale in high school might have

<figure>33</figure>

saved him. He was always involved in activities to get out of the house, acting, art, music, reading. He always had a book in his hand and that is what got me into reading, to be honest. Seeing him always immersed in his books, I wondered what was so fun about it.

That first trip to the bookstore, I got it. Jayson found me in the fantasy section; he was always in horror and thriller. I picked up a book and examined the front and back. I remember thinking I would start with this one when Jayson took it from me, put it back, walked me over to horror and handed me something different. He said I needed to read this one. It was one of Jayson's favorite authors and Jayson wanted me to pick up one of the newer releases from the author. I bought it after browsing through the store and we headed home. When we arrived back at the house, the mood of the day had shifted.

Dad didn't like that Jayson and I spent the day together. I am not sure if he hated the fact that we got along or that Jayson had influenced me to pick up his hobby. Dad immediately ripped the book out of my hands and tossed it. It fell behind the couch where it stayed until Jayson retrieved it later and hand delivered it to my bedroom.

The details of what Dad said after he snatched it are fuzzy. I stood there stunned and felt the room around me fade. Dad stood in front of me, his words muffled only a ringing in my ears as the sounds around me faded into the background. I don't think he was even yelling at me, but he was yelling.

Jayson was giving back what my dad was throwing at him, the yelling distorted and bouncing off the walls around me. I couldn't understand what was being said as I stood shocked, almost frozen. When I snapped out of whatever trance I had been in, Dad was walking away, and Jayson was already out of the room. Mom was standing in the doorway upset with a single tear rolling down the side of her face. She stayed out of the argument but stayed in the room. I went to my room and waited for things to cool down. I didn't want to grab my book or talk to Jayson just yet.

I remember the knock on the door. Jayson always knocked, he never walked into someone's room or invaded someone's space. He was respectful despite the way our father would come into our rooms without warning.

"Hey, Vic." Jayson says after knocking and slowly entering.

"I'm sorry dad went nuts earlier,"

"I know, I don't get him sometimes."

"Sometimes he's ok and sometimes he's..."

"Victor, it's me. He hates me, he always has. This has nothing to do with you or the book or anything. Dad saw we had a good time together, and he wanted to mess that up for you. He always wants to mess things up. It's because he isn't happy unless everyone around him is unhappy."

"I don't think that."

"Victor, trust me, if I was gone and something ever happened to me, he wouldn't care. He wouldn't even notice. His life would just move on."

Hearing Jayson talk like that was heartbreaking. I cared, my dad may not have but I know mom did. She talked about Jayson all the time along with the rest of her kids. She was one of those moms who loved to bring up her children and it was cute because who really wants to hear about what someone's kids ate for lunch or how one of us aced or failed, in my case, another test, no one. Mom just wanted to talk about us because it distracted her from my father and her own past. She liked to distract herself from her marriage, and her kids were the best way to do that. She would find an excuse to bring us up even if it didn't make sense but I guess for her it did.

I don't think there was ever a time that I could remember

where dad and Jayson seemed happy to be around each other. It was always awkward silences and conversations or a screaming match. If I had to put money on it, I would— Jayson could kill my father and walk away with a smile. I know I said my brother was respectful and all that, but this is the one thing that I could see him doing and not have any remorse and I wonder if I could do that or if I should.

I read the book we got from the bookstore that evening. Sometimes I forget the title of it and other events from that night and many other nights. That book turned out to be one of my favorite books that I still read every now and then. It's mine and Jayson's favorite author and maybe our favorite book. My therapist said that people who dissociate have memory problems. But I don't see how I could forget the name of the book that meant a lot to me and reminds me so much of my brother. Maybe I am just trying to forget about them because I have to. Especially after this trip.

I am planning something special for this one. It might be the last time we are all together and that is ok. I am tired of these trips. No one really has any fun anymore and mom just wants her group picture. We can still do that for her and not go on these trips, there is a thing called Photoshop that might be able to make up for it. We only do this for her as she deserves it for putting up with my father for all these years.

There is a nervousness running through me. The car ride isn't that long and music is how I wind down so I turn up the radio, cranking it as loud as I can tolerate. I am immediately taken aback. *Don't Speak*. It makes me laugh. Who doesn't enjoy a good No Doubt song? They were one of Jayson's many musical obsessions growing up. It's something I loved about Jayson; when he got into something, he really got into it.

Gina is heading up alone, and mom and Cat are riding

together, I think about texting them and asking them a few questions. Staring at my phone I wonder if I should just wing it or try to get hold of them. My nerves are on edge just thinking about the weekend.

Something just doesn't sit right with me about it.

CHAPTER 6

JAYSON

Ale and I reach for the radio, turning it on at the same time, we both look at each other as *Don't Speak* plays through the speakers and we both start singing along. The music brings me back to times when things were just easier. I see Ale texting someone and I lean over to get a glimpse. Before I get the chance to see it, she turns her phone over. This is the second time she has concealed her phone from me. This is not what we do. I consider asking her what's going on when she jumps in first.

"You know, Jayson, I was thinking about your coming out dinner."

"Don't remind me." I roll my eyes not only because I don't want to talk about it, but maybe she will get the hint that I am not in the mood. It doesn't work.

"OK, I won't bring it up, but I never forgot what happened."

She is about to launch herself into a tangent that I am not in the mood for, so I cut her off.

"I never forgot either. How could I forget?" It was the worst day of my life. I thought there would be some awkwardness, but I didn't expect to be embarrassed and shamed publicly, I never wanted to forgive them for that night.

Gazing out the window, I think about the times before coming out and those times after. Processing how I thought there was going to be a big shift, big self-revelations. There wasn't; things stayed the same, but that made everything feel even more painful. I expected life would get better, and in some respects it did. Eventually I moved because of my family. I focused on school and my chosen family, Ale and David.

I remember thinking after that night when nothing changed something was wrong with me. Realizing only sometime later that there was something wrong, it just was with my family. I realized that the way they treated me was unusual and the way we interacted as a family was toxic.

I needed to step outside of my family, outside of that toxic environment in order to see how bad things were. I have many regrets and I have a lot of resentment. Not towards my family, but towards myself because I stayed for too long with them. It wore me down and continues to wear me down. I blame myself for not stepping away or making changes sooner, that is what I resent the most. Yet how much of it is really my fault? I struggle with that every day. Resentment leads to revenge for me and this weekend is a little about revenge.

We're approaching the highway and this next stretch appears to be over 30 minutes long according to the GPS. We slowly merge onto the expressway and there isn't much traffic. It is a two-lane highway in one direction and two lanes in the other. Beautiful vegetation separates the two directions and I pay attention because this is sometimes where police hide to catch those who try to speed their way down the highway. I've driven in this area before, so I know where to look for those hidden police cruisers.

We were out drinking once and had gotten pulled over; it was down this same stretch of road. Between the illegal drugs and the prescription pills Ale was on, we could have gone to jail, and I would not survive a night in jail if we had been arrested. She handled everything that night, and for that, I guess I owe her.

When I saw the lights flashing behind me, I panicked. We had been out drinking and had just dropped off David, we were using this stretch to sober up before going home. In my drunken state, I forgot the cops like to hide and catch people like me. Drunk and in a hurry. No care in the world. Music blasting and the windows down.

The cop who pulled us over was attractive. I innocently played the victim. When he asked me to step out of the car, Ale jumped out pleading and crying for mercy. She went from someone afraid of going to jail to a seductress the second she stepped in front of him. She had a way with men that could make them do exactly what she wanted. What she wanted was for us to get home and not end up in jail and in the drunk tank. We got out of getting a ticket that night and avoided a night in jail, and Ale agreed to go on a few dates with the cop. He lost interest after realizing that Ale had a substance problem.

The fear I felt that night though, how mad I was at Ale for having so many drugs on her, stirred something inside me. How could someone who cares about you so much risk putting you in danger? I still loved Ale and wanted to still spend all my time with her, but I wondered how much she cared and how much it didn't bother her that she would want to risk us getting in trouble.

There is something I never told her about that night. The

cop she was seeing, he started texting me after they stopped seeing one another. He said he was checking on me. I didn't understand at first, but when he asked me out, I met him a few times. I knew what he was after. We didn't date, we only hooked up, but I never told Ale. I don't think she would be upset or anything; she didn't really like him. She had a thing about rejection though, so that would have bothered her. I didn't want to stir that up, so I kept it to myself. I wonder if I will see his car sitting there and if so, would he pull us over? We pass up the spot and I see no one is there.

There isn't forest on this stretch of the drive. It's the Midwest, so it's mainly cornfields. That eerie sense of children running out of the fields with corn hooks scares me to this day. I always picture them in my mind when I drive past an area like this. It's early in the season, so the stalks are low and it looks like you can see for miles. As I glance towards one of the open fields, I can see what reminds me of a wave, flowing through the field and it reminds me of waves on the ocean.

Gina mentioned a cruise this year as the family vacation. That was an immediate NO from me. When I had got the call from Gina, as she was handling most of the plans this year, my initial thoughts went to throwing my dad overboard and nudging Victor or Cat off the edge as they reached for him.

There were thoughts of murdering my family on a boat that were interrupted by Gina, "Jayson, are you there? I said I don't know if I can afford a cruise, but it would be fun."

"Yes, I heard you. If you can't afford it, then we need to do something else and I am not sure I can afford it either." That was a lie but being stuck with them for over a week on a boat just didn't sound like fun.

"Do you think dad would just pay for everyone?" she asked.

"No. When has he paid for me to do anything?"

"Yeah, but you can afford it." The assumptions she made that I could afford it, irritated me.

This was something that constantly came up. Dad would pay for everyone but me when we did things. His excuse was, "You have money and the rest of them don't. You can take care of yourself." At first this was something that made me feel proud. I thought, Wow, Dad thought something positive about me. No, it was simply because he didn't want to deal with or pay for me. Another harmful moment in our relationship and another painful memory in my life. I could afford it but I would have to make a few slight adjustments and I didn't want to make any more adjustments for them.

Ale is still talking about something as we pass a farm with cows and horses in a field. I have always wanted to live on a farm. Just me and possibly Ale visiting or living there too. Picturing David and I having drinks on the front porch with dogs running around makes me smile. I am not sure what part or role David will play in my life, I just know he will be there, at least I hope he is. I forget I am driving, when Ale's singing brings me back. She's about to say something and I assume I know what it is.

"Look, I don't want to think about that day. I just want to get through this weekend." I turn the music up and we forget the conversation we just had and pretend to sing, although I don't know the lyrics to whatever is playing.

Ale had called me the night of the blowup dinner, but we didn't speak long. Apologizing for what happened, I told her it wasn't necessary; she did nothing wrong.

"I could have said something, I could have yelled at your father." I could tell by her tone she had a lot of guilt after that night. Guilt I think she still holds on to.

"Ale, there is nothing that could have changed what happened."

I sometimes feel like Ale makes that entire night about her

when she does this. It is part of my story, not hers. I don't know really what she's feeling inside because she isn't one to always talk about things. I immediately thought about what I wanted out of that evening.

Taking the time to role play in my head proved an ineffective way to prepare for the conversation. A part of me didn't plan for it to go wrong because if I did, I would have never done it.

I've known I was gay since high school and there was never the question of "Am I?" I just knew. There wasn't the shared feeling the other boys had about girls and locker room discussions were awkward. Staying quiet felt safe so I kept to myself, changed quickly, and got out. I didn't have the same thoughts about boys yet either, but something was different. To say I was a late bloomer is an understatement. I didn't experiment until college, and I came out at twenty-two when I thought I was ready to have a boyfriend.

That is how I met David and I invited him along, but his relationship with Ale needs work. My feelings for him are strong, and if I'm being honest, I might love David. He's who I want to be with but there is just so much history to work through.

David had been in a few of my psychology classes as that was both of our majors. It was our undergrad degree, so all of the boring introductory classes and all the heavy material. We sat next to each other a few times and struck up casual conversations. We would talk about getting together to study and I could feel the sexual tension between us. In the library with our bodies close and the heat radiating off each other, I was always left wanting more of him.

We ended up casually dating and hooking up. Nothing steady enough to say that we were boyfriends, although we argued like it. The jealousy was real, and it was annoying at the same time. I never understood why we fight so much if we are just friends.

Our first kiss was something special. We were at my place because we got together to study and watch Drag Race, one of our favorite shows. It was an impersonation night on the show and we couldn't stop laughing the entire time. After the show we were cleaning up and debating on what to do next. We couldn't decide if we wanted to go out for some drinks or stay in and watch a movie. I didn't want to just call it a night because I enjoyed his company so much.

We kept brushing against each other in my small kitchenette. There wasn't much space. Along one side was the sink, refrigerator, and a counter, the other side the stove, trash can, and more counters with no space for a table or anything. Cleaning things up meant David had to walk past me several times, no, brush past me as I did the dishes.

After I finished the last dish, I turned around to grab the dish towel, drying my hands, coming face to face with David. Our bodies, not even inches apart, the heat radiating off each other. It was maybe a few seconds before our mouths were on top of each other. I never felt so much heat in my life and after that we stayed in the rest of the night.

Ale showed excitement when I told her that David and I had hooked up that night. I don't think she realized he would stay in my life. In my casual dating era myself, I didn't know what was going to happen. I didn't know what we were doing or what I even wanted.

Ale interrupts my thoughts about David by asking about my brother. Although he is younger than us, I think she has the hots for him. He isn't younger where it would be inappropriate, but he's still my brother. That yields drama for two reasons, and they are Ale and Victor. Ale is not in a stable position to be dating anyone, let alone someone in my family or someone I know. Victor is unreliable and I am not sure how much he will be around after this weekend. He's been distant lately, and if this weekend goes wrong, which I am sure it will, he won't be around at all to date Ale.

Victor talks to my mom and Cat often, and I wonder if he's checked in with them. I couldn't be the only one he called today about our trip. Cat and Mom live close to each other and are most likely together or driving up together. I grab my phone and consider sending a group text when I see Ale grab hers again. I try again to look at what she's doing and fail. This secret she's got must be big for her to be hiding so much.

CHAPTER 7

MOM

"I want a divorce." Saying it out loud, despite being the only one in the room and completely alone in the house feels liberating. I decided a long time ago, I just never thought I would go through with it. It's why I am driving with Cat and not with my husband. Even if I wanted to drive together, he would've had meetings scheduled or excuses to avoid being in the car with me. I don't think we've spent more than an hour in the same room with each other, and it's been like that for years.

The drive will take five to six hours depending on traffic and how many times we stop. My bladder is not what it used to be, so I am sure we will stop at least twice before we make it to our destination. Cat is impatient and can sometimes get moody when things don't go her way and because of that it was hard to get her to agree to come with me. She had wanted to drive up alone and said she had a lot to do, saying that it was an inconvenience. All I heard was that I was the inconvenience.

"Cat and I have some running around to do before heading up," that was how I explained it to my husband, and it's not a complete lie. I needed to get some stuff, but I'll be doing that alone. Spending the morning with my daughter when I am going to spend the weekend with her doesn't make the most sense. I couldn't order everything online, so I told my husband we needed some last-minute items for the trip and I'd be in a rush to leave so he should head up on his own. He knows about my avoidance of shopping in person, as my anxiety has gotten worse over the years. What started out as waiting for low traffic hours in stores has turned into me primarily shopping online and having even our groceries delivered or I have started doing drive up pickups where I don't have to even get out of my car anymore. The store employees recognize me as I make two trips a week, as that is my only connection these days to people outside of my house and family. He adds more stuff to the list for me to grab and I think, *Will there be enough time?* I need to head to the bank one more time before we head out.

My anxiety is already starting to take over as I think about everything. *Did I turn off the stove and the lights?* My memory is so bad, so I walk around and check everything for a third time. *Did I put the milk away?* Glancing at the counter, I realize I didn't even drink milk today. It has to be my anxiety. I feel scattered. I take care of everything around the house, so it gets overwhelming. *Did I do this? Did I do that?* I can't keep up anymore. I stop pacing and questioning myself out loud when I hear something move about the house.

"Is someone there?" There was a noise coming from the next room, stopping what I was doing I peer over the kitchen counter and gaze into the hallway, my palms resting on the counter, I try to lift myself to gain just a little more distance to see if anyone is there. It was the sound of floorboards creaking, I am sure of that. Despite being alone, I know what I heard. Every house has its creaks. We've needed repairs for some time now, and I am not sure if it's just that the house is still settling or someone else is here with me.

Walking past the threshold that separates the kitchen to the hallway, I slowly peek my head around. If someone was there, it would be so easy to slice my head off in one quick movement. My thoughts always go to a dark and morbid place and to no surprise there is no one there. The foreign sound is just that, a sound and everything looks fine.

I pass the hall mirror on my way back to what I was doing, stop, and look at myself. I've put on some weight since we got married. No longer being the small slender woman I once was, I also stopped dying my blonde hair and what sat underneath that blonde was a dishwater blonde, but now it has all turned gray. The gray color looks nice on me and I wear it with pride, but I still miss the blonde as it reminds me of my youth.

Being overweight by around fifty pounds and standing at five foot two, my height doesn't hide my extra weight. As I lean in close to inspect the bags under my eyes, I stare into my eyes that still hold that blue color I was born with. My pale white skin needs some sun, maybe this weekend I can get a little color. That is, if I stay long enough to get some sun. I notice the scuff on the wall and stop criticizing myself.

It's still a mystery where the scuff mark came from; no one has ever admitted to it. I noticed it about two years ago. No one confessed to bumping into the wall, but my husband said he would fix it but that was over a year ago. My husband does nothing so what is my husband good for if he doesn't help around the house? It's a partnership and you would hope you can be reliant on one another, but I cannot rely on him. My kids are useless as well. Except for Jayson, he was always willing to lend a helping hand. When things needed to get fixed, he would volunteer his time to get them done.

There was this time Jayson was in the bathroom fixing the sink when I woke up one morning. He wasn't handy in that way so I am not even sure how he fixed it. The new faucets arrived and sat there for almost a year. Jayson had been using that bathroom for years despite having had a few in the house. At this point he was the only one using the first-floor bathroom towards the rear of the house. The faucets had broken, and my husband was supposed to replace them. You could turn the handles all the way and only a drip came through which is why we fought about hiring someone. My husband said it was an easy fix and that he would do it but it was because he was always so cheap with spending money that he never called for anyone to come out. The only time he enjoyed spending money was when someone else was able to see it and usually that someone was anyone outside of our immediate family, it's the way a narcissist works.

"I can do it myself," he grunted every time I brought it up.

"Then get to it or I can call someone." I was so angry I wanted to hit him. "How long do you expect us to have one less functioning bathroom?"

"You're useless. You should do it yourself if you want it done so bad." My husband was yelling, his hot breath on my face. I wanted to take a nip out of that ugly nose of his, bite it off and watch blood gush out of a vast hole in his face. It didn't happen; I held back everything else I would have liked to have said. Backing up I continued to clean the kitchen with him yelling in the background as he was never able talk to me in a normal tone or with an ounce of respect that I deserved.

Jayson walked in during the argument and stood off to the side. He seemed to appear anytime my husband was yelling at me. He stood there like he was guarding something, standing erect, tall, and expressionless. I wonder what went through his head during that argument. Did he also want to do awful things to his father? Did he want to bite his nose off, or knock him on his ass. The argument ended, and we all went back to our respective places in the house. Me cleaning, my husband somewhere doing who knows what, and Jayson retreating to his bedroom.

I woke the next morning to the sound of muffled banging. Jayson was up and fixing the sink, working quietly as he was not trying to wake anyone up, especially his father. Waking him up when he could still sleep would cause more problems than a broken sink. Jayson did what he could as quietly and as quickly as he could. He didn't want his father to know it was him, didn't want credit for it, just wanted me to be happy and partly because he also wanted a functioning bathroom. My husband didn't ask who had fixed the sink, he just went about his business and casually used the bathroom and never brought it up.

Gathering my belongings, I notice the time. It's important that I get on the road soon because I need to pick up Cat. If she decides to stick around after I tell my husband and everyone else that I am leaving him, she can ride home with him. We need to make a stop before heading to the campground for my husband's request, he likes a particular brand of beef jerky and gets cranky when he can't snack on it. I enjoy them too but only occasionally. My husband's request felt more like a demand that I make sure I pick some up. This will be the last time I follow any of his demands, I am no longer willing to simply do as I am told anymore.

As I head to the front door, I notice that it's not locked and not even pushed closed. There is a small space where the door still needs to connect with the doorframe for the door to click shut. How long has the door been open? Did I do it? I was in a rush when bringing things in from the garage earlier but I thought I pushed it shut. In fact, I know I pushed it shut and now I am questioning again if I am losing my mind.

I decide to do one last walk around, checking the litter

box, the cat feeder and wonder if the cat sitter will get my last-minute email asking if she can still stop by for an hour a day. We trust her and she adores our cat. We rarely leave her alone because she's such a needy little girl, but we are only going for the weekend and the cat will be in expert hands. It should be fine and I'll be home in a day or two at most. Best-case scenario, my husband leaves and I can stay the weekend with the kids. My plan isn't to stay very long; in fact, I am hoping to get in and out, but if I have to, I'll be heading to the second apartment. It being a short distance from our home means I can always swing back there to check on her. Checking my email for the third time since I emailed her, I see she finally replied. My heart beats a mile a minute; I don't want to worry about the cat. It's a simple reply of, *sure thing*.

Walking up the stairs to the bedroom, I see our wall is full of portraits of the kids and a few of our family photos, with my favorite being from Christmas eight years ago. The only time we didn't end up fighting was when taking the pictures. I stop and stare at the only picture of me and my husband on the wall from our wedding day. I have good and bad memories from that day but this picture is one of the good ones representing what I hoped would have been the start of our happily ever after. I can feel myself starting to tear up and notice that I am about to touch the picture but instead I wipe away the tear that started to fall from my eye.

I reach the top of the stairs and stare at the abandoned bedrooms my kids once occupied. The rooms are now converted into guest rooms and usually stay vacant. The kids sleep there from time to time when they need to, but it isn't the same. I walk towards our room—the room my husband and I shared but haven't for a very long time. Now he's always at the second apartment because he says it's closer to his office. He gives the excuse; he isn't a morning person, and he wants to get up and start work soon after.

He's there right now and I haven't seen him for a few days. He calls and checks in and sends texts throughout the day. I think about the apartment and what he does there as I haven't been there for years. I am not sure I even remember what it looks like anymore especially since the remodel which had caused a big argument.

"I need space and a quiet place to work."

"Then go to the office. I don't understand why we need a second apartment. You could rent an office space." I never understood why he wanted to flaunt his money the way he does. It makes me sick.

"I just need a quiet place away from everyone and everything."

"Away from your family, away from me, your wife."

"I can't talk to you when you're like this. We're getting it and that's that."

Was he cheating? He must be cheating; I've caught him in the past, and I see the way he looks at other women. The way he flirts with them in public right in front of me, it's embarrassing. Sitting at a restaurant while your husband flirts and sometimes degrades you is the worst feeling. He's done it in front of the kids, and I regret not setting a better example for them, but I won't have to deal with it much longer.

Entering our bedroom, I take a deep breathe in taking in the room for what might be the last time. Years of a life together, years of also being alone. I reconsider my decisions when I realize this isn't our bedroom, it's my room and was never really ours. We shared brief moments of life together, but I cannot remember the last time I felt like we were a unit, a pair, a couple. Something jolts me from these thoughts as another sound is coming from inside the house.

"Is someone there?" Saying this for the second time, I wonder if someone is here with me. I keep hearing noises. Could someone else be in the house? I reach for my phone and look around, noticing a few things out of place. I am very particular in the way I place my things. Scanning the room, I look for evidence that someone else was here. Something feels off, and my grip on the phone tightens.

Seeing the bottom drawer open, panic rises over me. The will is inside; I put it in there after I was looking over it the other day and was in a rush and tossed it in when my husband almost caught me. I knew he would have questions about why I had it out and my intentions were to move it back, but I lost track of time.

Needing to be prepared, I had been reviewing it to protect myself because I want to know what I will walk away from. My friend had asked me to scan it over to her since her husband is a lawyer. He advised me not to leave without taking what would rightfully be mine especially since we've been married for so long. I had a hand in helping build his company. While he was away at work, I took care of the house and kids and I even signed for his loans. He couldn't have done it without me and yet I stand here with a fifty percent chance of getting nothing.

I've been a house-wife since we got married then a stay at home mom, getting pregnant shortly after, a decision I don't regret. Growing up, I had always wanted to be a mother and I think I did a good job. My mother wasn't great at raising her children so when I had kids, I wanted to do the opposite. Not wanting my family to experience what I had gone through had been a priority for me.

I turn when I hear another sound in the room next to me, it's coming from the guest rooms. I spin around and rush out the bedroom door pushing open the doors I see the windows open and Raven, our cat, is on the windowsill peering down.

"Get down from there or you'll fall," I scream. The screen appears to be open and if she jumps I may never be able to run down the steps and out the door fast enough to catch her.

She's startled and I rush towards her which causes her to jump off the ledge and onto the bed and scurries out of the room in a haze of blackness. No one has been in this room for weeks but I know the window was closed. Someone was in the house, and was lurking and shifting through my things. I don't know if I should call my husband, the cops, or just get out of the house.

I want this weekend to be over with and I want to be done with everything. My husband is somewhat of a con man and has done some shady things in the past, so it could have been someone looking for something that has nothing to do with me. I remember the stack of money in the drawer with the will and I panic once again.

Rushing out of the room I stub my toe on the edge of the bed. It hurts like hell and feels warm and I'm sure that I am bleeding. My shoe feels like it might be filling with blood, so I kick them off and check. There is no blood, but it throbs, and I know it's going to bruise within the hour. I continue heading out of the room, sliding my foot back into my shoe, wincing at the pain.

I turn the door handle to my room in such a hurry that my finger twists in on the handle and I bite back a yelp. Why am I being so careless and clumsy? I try and shake off the pain as I reach the drawers and move around the clothing looking for the money. My plan had been to come back home and grab it. I didn't want to carry around stacks of money—fifty thousand dollars to be exact—and I sure would not keep it in a bank or our safe. I've been hoarding this money for years.

"Damn it." Slamming the door I fall to my knees and begin to cry. At this moment everything feels like it is going to be over. I can feel my chest rising and falling in rapid succession feeling like the room around me is changing shape. Everything around me feels like it's moving further and further away from me. My hand goes out to reach for the drawer again, but it feels like it is now out of reach because the money is gone.

My phone rings, snapping me back into reality but I reject the call and try to focus on what is in front of me. Not knowing what to do now, I wonder if I could still divorce my husband.

I was very careful when I withdrew the money and I never took out more than what would cause suspicion. A little here and there at the grocery store as cash back, buying generic and saving some of the grocery money. I even started doing my own nails and hair and saving that money too. My husband liked to show me off, so I needed to keep up my appearances.

This is not how I wanted the weekend to start. I can't call my husband and I can't report the money missing. I'll have to deal with it later; my plan needs some reworking.

My phone rings again, and it's Cat. I'm sure she was the one who called just a minute ago. Now that I've had a few moments to gather my thoughts and calm down, I pick up. She immediately goes into some sort of rant.

"Mom, I'm not home yet. I had to run a quick errand. I forgot to tell you I was at the house the other day and I think I might have left the window in the guest room open."

"Why were you in the guest room?" I find her confession a bit odd seeing as I just discovered the money missing and I suspect she can hear my confused tone when I asked her just now.

Hesitant she answers, "I couldn't find Raven and when I was in there, I heard a noise. Someone was outside, and I opened the window and screen to look down. No one was there. I was in a rush so I left but I cannot remember for the life of me if I shut the window and I don't want us gone all weekend and you coming home, and Raven being gone."

"Did you go into my room?" There is a long silence on the other end of the line. "Cat, did you go into my bedroom?"

In a lowered breath I hear the response I was dreading, "I know, mom, I saw the will, and I found the money. You're leaving dad, right?"

"Well, the money is gone, so now I'm not so sure." I don't know how to really respond. Could Cat have taken the money? Did she really come to the house the other day? Was someone in the house earlier or am I forgetting things like locking the doors?

"What do you mean the money is gone?" She responds with a rather quick and pressed tone.

"It's gone, Cat, and I swear someone was in the house. But now that you're saying you left the window open, I am not sure anymore." I don't want to think Cat took the money, but she has always been bad with money and was just asking for ten thousand and didn't say why.

"Are you going to report it missing?"

"I can't. No one knows I had it." I'm shaking because I really do not know what I am going to do. "Cat, I am on my way. Please, Cat, say nothing. I need some time to figure all this out."

I go back to the guest room and close the window, making sure it's locked. I grab my purse and a second stack of money I had hiding underneath the dresser in the guest room. This is another stack of fifty thousand. I was stupid to hide the money in my drawer so openly, but I wasn't stupid enough to leave it all in one place. I am glad my friend has the additional stack of fifty thousand at her house. $150,000 is a lot of cash and will keep me set until I can figure out how to make money. I know in a divorce I can get more.

I grab the bags at the front door and pat Raven on the head, hoping I will get to see her again; I meow at her, and she meows back. Locking up I head towards the car, feeling eyes on me. I see a car that looks a lot like Cat's pull out of a parking spot. It's a blue Camry. It took off as soon as I looked in my rearview mirror. I felt like someone was watching me, studying me. That's why I had looked behind me. I put my car in gear and head off considering if I should make a U-turn and follow the car. I don't think Cat would take the money, but you never really know someone. Even your own kids.

CHAPTER 8

It was risky being there and I wasn't sure if anyone would be home when I arrived. The house is never empty, rather it's typically filled with the noise of some anxious person busying around. I wanted to get in and get out as quickly and quietly as possible, undetected and unseen. If someone was home, I wanted to make sure I slipped in because it was fun to lurk and watch them knowing they had no idea I was there. You know the expression "to be a fly on the wall", that's how it felt being there when I shouldn't, and today someone was home.

I couldn't tell where in the house they were, so I opened the door slowly, afraid that someone would be on the other end staring me down. There was no one on the other side so I shut the door not closing it all the way to avoid any unwanted sounds. I didn't want the sound of the latch or door clicking shut, to alert someone of my presence, of my unwelcome intrusion, just in case.

I decided at the last minute to come here; this trip wasn't planned. I don't know what I was looking for or why I came. Was it one last time? Was it because I'm bonded to them?

Slipping through the living room, still trying to not make any noise, I could hear someone in the kitchen. It was bold of me to try and get a peek at who it was. Tiptoeing through the hallway was risky. It wasn't until I was halfway into the kitchen when the floor decided to creak followed by someone's voice calling out.

I hid behind the wall outside the hallway that leads into the open floor plan of the living room and dining room, a vast room for a family who rarely uses it. I've seen some quiet dinners here while most were loud and often chaotic. Holding my breath, I hope they wouldn't come this way. I still couldn't tell who it was. Too afraid and startled to notice who the voice had come from; I headed upstairs to the bedroom as soon as they went back into the kitchen.

I went through the jewelry boxes on the dresser, in the closet, and considered going through the chest at the end of the bed. Holding items close as if I was forming a connection or trying to find some memories. I wouldn't see anyone anymore after this weekend because this was the weekend I decided, this would be the weekend something happened.

I pulled open the dresser drawers and found their will inside one of them and in the same drawer I discovered a large sum of cash.

I heard someone call out again, their voice muffled in the distance. Since I had time to hide, I immediately grabbed what I could from the drawer and headed into the guest room. The amount in my hands was unknown but there were stacks of money, easily thousands, possibly tens of thousands. The window was open, and I contemplated jumping out but hid under the bed. The cat was curiously looking out the window. When they came into the guest room, I feared I'd be caught but they weren't in there long. They ran out stubbing their toe screaming in pain causing me to jump. I recognized who it was when I heard them cry out in pain. I know how much that hurt because I'd stubbed my toe in that same spot before.

Making my way out of the bedroom, I snuck downstairs and out the front door. I pulled the door shut this time and jumped right into my car. Panicked and labored breathing, I sat in the front seat for a few seconds considering if I should count the money but decided not to. I didn't want to draw any unnecessary attention to myself because I needed to get out of there.

Knowing I should get going and now having more than everything I needed, I watched them come out of the house glancing in my direction. I couldn't tell if they saw me or if they recognized me. I am not the only one on this block or in this neighborhood with this car. It's a common car, just another blue Camry.

CHAPTER 9

CAT

Mom was on her way over to me, and I needed to get home soon. Everyone says that I am impatient, and I get that from my mom, but she is the worst one out of all of us. She couldn't get there before me, so I ran through several stop signs and a red light just to beat her. When I turned onto my street, I breathed in a sigh of relief because she wasn't there.

Pulling my car into my parking spot, I put everything in my bag including the money. It wasn't the first time I took money from them. A little here and there hurt no one. At most, I would take a hundred or two just for groceries or small bills. I know where my dad kept his money, and he never counted it so I suspect he never knew. If he did, he didn't tell me, I had needed some money for gas and I was hoping to find a little in there. Finding more than I needed, I had just reacted and grabbed everything in front of me. I only looked in that drawer because it was slightly open, otherwise I would have just gone to where my dad hides his.

It would be a matter of time before I had to confess, but

maybe I could explain my way out of it. I needed to get ready because mom would be here any minute. Looking at the money sitting in my bag, I am ashamed of myself. The money is really needed and I've been struggling more than I let my parents or anyone else know. I saw the will was in the drawer, but the money had distracted me the most. Grabbing what I could, I decided maybe I could come back another time and look to see if things inside the will had changed. I've seen it before so I know who and what's in it. At that moment I just wanted out.

Dad stopped trusting me with money after the last time I asked. He had been keeping track, and I was surprised when he rattled off the total. Twenty thousand and I had little to show for it. I always intended to pay them back, but things got out of hand. There was a lot of debt, and I didn't know how to get out of it. I started doing freelance consulting work when I got laid off. Too many late nights partying with co-workers. Kissing the manager's son when I was dating his daughter might have been what got me fired. I didn't know he was watching us on the dance floor.

I didn't even know he saw. It wasn't until the morning I got fired when my friend pulled me to the side. She worked in HR and gave me the heads up. I had my desk packed and ready before the end of the day and they always wait until the end of the day. Why would they fire you in the morning? They needed to get a day's worth of pay out of you before they ruined your life.

I had been given three months' severance which was typical in the industry but usually when you voluntarily decide to leave. It's considered a smooth transition out while you look, but what is smooth about being unemployed? The only reason why I got it was because of my relationships at work, which was a good thing because the next phase of my life wasn't going to turn out so well.

I didn't get the benefit of working with the appointed work coaches due to the circumstances and I was on my own. The severance I got I stretched to five months, but I started asking for money almost six months ago.

The relationship I was in also ended when my job ended. It turns out an unemployed millennial is not as attractive as you would think, and I never saw her again. Her brother tried to reach out to me and wanted to apologize and asked if he could talk to his father for me. I almost agreed but realized that I wasn't happy anyway, both at the job and in the relationship. I took my severance and moved on hoping that things would be ok.

I haven't found a new job and instead just do freelance work. Things are slowing down, and my connections are running out so I need to figure something out. The economy has been shit and because it had been so long since I last worked, other consulting firms would question my reasons for leaving my last employer.

If things couldn't get any worse for me, Dad recently started asking for his money. After seeing the pile in their bedroom drawer, I knew it wasn't his and the call with mom might have confirmed it. I'm not surprised she's decided to leave, but that is a lot of cash and I am sure he doesn't know about it. I wonder how she was able to save that much and how long she had been putting it away.

I had a busy morning and made several stops, with some of them being unplanned. I used some of the money but tried to keep it to a minimum. It was easier to pay in cash. It felt good to pay in cash instead of charging when I knew I couldn't pay the credit card bill anytime soon. I felt responsible. I felt like maybe this could help get me out of debt and I promised myself as I paid the cashier at the last store that this would be the last time I let things get this out of hand.

Needing stuff from inside the house I grabbed the duffel

bag. Staring at the money for what seemed like an hour, which was maybe mere seconds, I brought it in so I could toss the things I bought inside it. I didn't have time to really sort anything, so I tossed the shopping bags inside the duffel bag and head towards the door.

"Shit!" I yell out as I notice I left my door open again, something I have a bad habit of doing. "I swear one day someone is going to rob me."

It's not like I have anything worth taking. I have been selling what I could because my plan was to talk to my family this weekend and head off somewhere overseas. It is cheaper and I could get some remote work and live off grid—I could try to find myself again.

It was becoming harder and harder to survive these days, and with the rising gas and grocery prices, everyone I knew was drowning in some sort of debt. I could work half of what I do now and still be fine somewhere else.

I know everyone will disagree with my decision, especially my mother. She wants us to stay close despite everything. I mean, it's weird because she wants out now too. Now that I have some money, I could move my plan along. The supplies I needed are going to make this weekend easier, but no matter what, it is still going to be hard. I love my family. I love them a little too much, but I also need to get away and be free of them.

I don't know why Gina chose to go camping or even why she chose the place she chose. It lacks amenities or even people because it's an older state park, one I had thought was closed. I don't know why she still wants to do this either. If I just stopped responding to the group texts from mom, maybe she would have gotten the hint. None of us want to do this anymore.

My phone vibrates again alerting me to another message in the group chat, this one's from Gina. Opening up the group chat named "Camp Trip, Survival of the Fittest" I cringe at my sister's humor. I don't understand the name or why there is a picture of a clip from *Friday the 13th*. She's a horror buff, so whatever. I read the text with the most annoyance I have ever had. I exhale and read it aloud in my Gina voice.

> I hope everyone is ready. I have a lot of fun stuff planned and I hope you all make it out in one piece. lol, jk, Let's reconnect and have fun. I love you all. - G

She's been joking for weeks that we won't survive the weekend. It's been so long since we spent time outdoors like this. I honestly cannot remember the last time we were camping as a family. I sometimes will have vague memories that pop up but nothing significant stands out. Each one is at a different age, so I know that we have been camping as a family more than once.

I walk over to my living-room table and open the tabletop where my photo albums are stored. I flip through the album I know has pictures of us when we used to go camping; there is one of my mom lying on a picnic table. I laugh because Dad is in the background holding the grill tongs, I have a memory of him saying we're eating butt steak. I laugh at this and wipe away a tear because we've had good times before. I am flooded with emotion and feel the tears slide down my cheek. Feeling the wetness connects me back to myself. Despite the good times, there are so many bad times. You don't always realize how toxic a relationship is until it's too late.

I'm not the only one struggling financially, my Dad is too. Gina told me the business isn't doing well and he might lose it. She was doing his books and discovered that he was hiding money from the government. They are auditing him, and they could lose everything.

I guess this weekend might just be the last weekend for us. Or at least it will be for some of us. According to Gina, we won't make it through the weekend. My phone buzzes yet again.

> It will be a weekend of fun. A weekend of sorrow. A weekend of whatever you want it to be. - G

That last message was a bit strange and I don't understand any of it. Is she trying to freak us out, or play with us even before we get there?

CHAPTER 10

GINA

Messing with my family is one of the easiest things I can do, and I take pride in how I can make them uneasy with a simple text. I know my sister Cat is the most annoyed by my behavior and I've always been able to get under her skin. It is one of my talents and I take pride in that.

My love of horror movies goes great with my sense of humor and the messages I left were to screw with them. The last message I sent I was trying to be cryptic because I wanted to put them in a state of unrest and vulnerability. It's all part of the plan, and everything was planned out in order to accomplish one thing. It just needs to go according to plan or all my work would have been for nothing.

I created a bit of a game out of the weekend, with hints and clues throughout the trip leading up to the very end. That's if everyone makes it to that point. I got the idea from several movies, taking a bit from this one and a bit from that one, creating my own game. We either come together as a family or we don't. It's simple. I am not even going to tell them what's going on because they will find out when they wake up tomorrow morning.

I am not an evil person; in fact, quite the opposite and I am tired of how things have been going between everyone. Everyone has played some part in something, causing us to drift apart. We all had something happen to us and we all reacted in ways that broke our family down, one incident at a time.

Having just a few hours before I need to get on the road and there before anyone else, I hurry to get ready. I wanted some time before everyone arrives to really work through my feelings, but I am at least an hour behind schedule. Maybe I should change my mind? I can't, we need this to happen this weekend. We need to figure things out or we won't be a family anymore.

I hurry to gather everything. I was at work yesterday when the last few boxes arrived from my online shopping and was too anxious and busy to open them and sort through everything. Now today I am opening them up, tearing through the bags and tossing things aside. Once I am done, I start to put everything in their separate bags. There is a bag for everyone except Ale because she doesn't need to be a part of this. I would rather Jayson bring David because I like him. He's good for my brother, he'd be good for anyone and I hope that one day Jayson wakes up and sees that.

Jayson never said that he and David were together, but when you see them, you know there's something between them. We've all hung out a few times, and I've seen firsthand how they look at each other—getting lost within themselves. Jayson and I tend to get along the best out of everyone in the family. He's my favorite sibling and the one who would have my back in a family argument which is why this makes me feel guilty.

I still can't believe what happened a few years ago at

dinner when Jayson officially came out to the family. I had already known because we talked about it and had confided in one another. I told him about the things going on in my life and who I was and wasn't into. If the gay gene was a thing, we all most likely have it. All of us identify as queer in some respect except for Victor, he doesn't share much about anything with anyone. He's been like that since we were kids. I don't have any memories of him opening up to anyone, but then again none of us really do.

I was shocked when dad reacted the way that he did. I could see everyone at the restaurant staring including the guy at the table across the room who looked especially disturbed. I remember the look on his face and him shaking his head. He gathered himself as if he was directly affected by it. Maybe his parents had the same reaction, maybe he was gay or maybe he was affected by something else another feeling of internal shame going on inside him. As I glanced around the restaurant, I saw more heads turn. Faces scrunched and noses turned to the ceiling.

A guy walked up to talk to the wait staff. He looked uncomfortable, and I couldn't tell if he was disturbed by my father's outburst or by my brother's lifestyle. Whatever it was, I know Jayson wanted out, and I wanted to follow. We didn't talk for weeks after, and I waited for a clue that things were ok. When I finally called Jayson, he did everything he could to dodge talking about what had happened. I could tell he needed more space from everything, so I backed off and gave it to him.

I finish packing the bags and I check them to make sure I haven't forgotten something important. Trying hard to wipe the memories that just resurfaced, I wipe away a single tear. It rolls down my cheek and lands on the hand-written notes I place into the last bag, Jayson's bag. I always cry when I think about that day and when I think about how hurt Jayson was.

He's my older brother, he was my protector and someone I looked up too. Even though he is five years older than me, I wanted to protect him that day and I had failed. Now I want to show everyone and help rewrite that evening.

Wanting to feel clean, I head to bathroom and slip off my pants. Standing in front of the mirror with my camisole and underwear still on, I look at myself hating the way my body looks. Growing up had been hard, comments had always been made about weight in our household. If someone gained a pound, it was brought up and it was the same if someone lost a pound. No one in the family was fit and healthy, we all are slightly overweight but still healthy. The family just tended to nit-pick and call things out. Jayson suffered an eating disorder in high school and I suspect we all did because I battled it during high school myself.

Opening the cabinet and shifting through the insides I look for my medications. They weren't packed because I needed them last night. My anxiety and sleep has been off, and I don't want to forget them as they might be needed this weekend. I closed the medicine cabinet, jumping, because something passed between the crack of the open bathroom door and the hallway leading to my backdoor.

Quietly I listen, turning around and holding on to the handle of the bathroom door. I open it just a little stopping when I hear a creak. My heart starts to pound as I am not sure where the sound came from. With one hand on the door, I reach for my pants and my cell phone. It buzzes causing me to jump again and release the door handle. The door opens a little more and I hear another creak.

It was just the bathroom door I heard the first time, and now I find myself laughing off the fear. My heart starts to settle and my mind begins to calm down. Maybe what I saw is just my Oscillopsia. I was recently diagnosed with it, and it explains why I see shadows or things move when they don't.

I am still getting used to the diagnosis and understanding that my vision will now always be affected.

Continuing to get undressed, I get in the shower. My little heart attack I just had now has me on edge and I am falling further behind. I'm in the shower when this time I hear a sound coming from inside the house. Was that the sound of a door closing? Someone came in, I'm sure of it. Quickly rinsing off, I grab the towel, draping it over myself and quickly walk to my room with my phone in hand and 911 ready to be called.

I am looking from room to room. It's a small place, so it doesn't take me long to check everything before I shut the bedroom door. I hear a car start and I look outside and see a familiar car pull away. Was Cat just here?

We all have keys to each other's houses so it wouldn't surprise me. Everyone's except for Jayson's. He's private and I don't even think everyone knows where he lives. I quickly get dressed and shoot off a text to my sister asking if she was here. One word with a few dots.

NO...

I am sure she was here so I don't even bother to text back. I decide that I will deal with her later. I finish gathering everything and leave to load up the car. It takes just three trips to load everything. It would have taken two if I hadn't kept forgetting things. The last trip I made I grabbed my cash and portable chargers because I wasn't coming home right away. I had plans for after the weekend. I had made these considering I would need more time to myself after a big weekend. My therapist suggested time for myself and she said that she didn't think the time with my family would be enough.

I chose this place because I didn't think any of us had

been there before and I wanted something close but different than the last decade of trips we went on. There needed to be something special about this trip and since we used to go camping this seemed to align perfectly. It was a nice drive, but no one needed to fly or be inconvenienced. It was secluded, and it wasn't "glamping". We had to rough it out. Yes, the place had outhouses and stuff, but it was within 30 minutes of other known campgrounds, so that meant no one would really be there. It was a state park, but from my research, this time of year it was empty. That was in part due to the nearby campgrounds that had all the amenities. If anyone else was around, I didn't have to worry because it was large enough, and I had been out here a few weeks ago to scout out an area. I put danger signs up so others would stay clear of the area. It would only help the game.

I fumble with my car charger and get myself connected. I check my rearview mirror. "Damn that car is popular." I squint because it looks like Cat's car, but I know it can't be. We have the same car. We got it the same day. A gift from our dad.

She is driving with mom, and they should be meeting up later. With the way she gets ready, she isn't lurking around my house. I put the keys into the ignition and started up the car.

I turn on the radio and catch the last of whatever song is currently playing. I recognize it because who wouldn't? It's the final chorus of No Doubt's *Don't Speak*, another memory. I turn up the volume and start singing the last few bars as I head off.

CHAPTER 11

DAD

Spending time with my family was not on my list of things to do this weekend; I had a lot of other things to take care of. Work has been stressful, and a vacation is needed, but what is more needed is me leaving the state, possibly even the country. The business isn't doing well and the loans are piling up and I am not sure I see a way out. The only thing going for me in this situation is my wife's name is on every-thing for the business. Her credit was better than mine when I started things off and I needed her, but now I need to figure out how to get us out of this.

I'm pulling up her number when my phone rings. It's Ale, and I immediately rejected the call. I gave her enough money already. That sneaky bitch is out to ruin me. The good thing is she is going this weekend and I can deal with her then. I don't know why my son is even friends with her. He's too good for her.

When Ale entered my son's life, I knew she would be trouble. I knew this was going to be a friendship that would get in the way somehow. I just didn't know how bad at the time. I guess that's why I kept Ale close as well. It's better to keep your enemies close, especially when your son wasn't going to let this one go so easily.

I regret the way I've treated him because he's a good kid. Lost his way with the whole being gay thing, but still a good kid and great to his mother. He's done more for her than I have our entire marriage. At least after this weekend things will be better.

I ask the maid if everything is ready for me. Since my wife isn't here at the office to help me, I had hired a maid to come once a week. Cleaning wasn't my thing, and I didn't want to keep up with the place on my own. I asked her to come an additional day this week because I needed to tie up some loose ends and was lazy and didn't want to pack for myself. We had a brief affair after she started working for me, and I kept her on when it ended. She had a deadbeat boyfriend and got pregnant shortly after she started, and I couldn't see her out on the street struggling with a newborn and a kid from a previous relationship.

She wasn't a stranger to me though. It was about eighteen years ago, and we had met at a bar hitting it off. We ended up sleeping together and that continued for a few months. We ended things of course as we were both married and started to develop feelings for each other. A few years after we ended things, I found out she was divorced, and had a son. Her husband left her for someone younger. About six years ago she came to me asking for help, struggling with her first son, I decided to hire her as a part time maid. The affair started hot and heavy but was over quickly. She was dating someone at the time we started sleeping together and ended up pregnant. Affairs should be one and done, but this one turned out to be a bit more ongoing. She knows I will never leave my wife, house, and kids, but I also won't toss her out onto the street with her kids.

I stopped by the house earlier, discovering that someone was home. I crept in and out hoping no one had heard me. There wasn't time to deal with my wife and any lingering questions, but I found something hidden. I guess I am not the only one looking for a way out. My family is a mess and I wonder how much of it is my fault.

I've never thought about how my actions would affect my family. I never considered all the pain and hurt that I might be causing them. I know I am not normal and the things I do are a bit narcissistic. I've had to do these things to survive. It is how I made it to where I am today. It is how I can run a successful business. It *was* how—until recently.

Everything is crumbling around me. My marriage, my relationship with my kids. I am running out of money, and Ale had information that she shouldn't. She worked during the summer for me. We got a little too close. She knows too much.

I don't know what came over me. Especially when I knew she was trouble and had already been asking me for money. She has a way with men. I've heard about this.

I am pacing back and forth when the maid comes in to ask if I needed anything else.

"Your bags are at the front of the door. I am going to head out. It's our son's graduation." She looks at me with a stone-cold stare. If she was medusa, I'd be frozen. I know those words have more meaning than I want them too. I take care of our six-year-old financially both by employing her and by paying for his schooling.

Waving her off without as much of a reaction has me on fire. It is what Ale knows and what could destroy everything. I grab my belongings and leave minutes after she does. I get in the car and turn on the radio.

"Who listens to this shit?"

It's that damn No Doubt song—I can't stand it. I don't know if it's because it reminds me of my son or if it is just an annoying song. Before long I am pulling out and humming the words. I catch myself singing a few lines under my breath.

CHAPTER 12

24 HOURS PRIOR

How many ways can you commit a murder and how many ways can you cover one up? I've asked myself this question before and with opportunities to do it in the past, I could have done it, one by one or all at once. It would have been easy. These vacations were common for them despite how much they didn't get along. Who gets together every year nowadays? A family who loves one another I would assume, but that wasn't them.

A question I continue to consider, who would be killed first? A father or the siblings? I guess it would depend on the way you would do it and therefore I made a list.

I've spent many sleepless nights going over the reasons. When did I really decide though to go through with it? I know the thought came to me the night after that dinner. I was awake in bed for hours. Going through everything I had gone through and seen that night. It's what one does when they can't sleep. Insomnia can cause you to stir and contemplate all your life's choices or all the choices you still might want to make.

Making it look like an accident could be easy. I could have waited until everyone was at the house and set the place on fire but that would have been too painful. Not for them but for me. Not being able to stick around and watch would upset me. It would also be too risky to get caught, and I wanted to watch my work. Not all of them deserve it, but I want to see them suffer. That was the other problem. Who deserves to suffer and who makes that call? It's something that I'm still not sure of, and time is running out. The plan is set, and I hope easy enough to get done because times up for them, I've made that determination, but I still wonder, do I spare any of them? Will there be a survivor or two and who? The one who needs to be rescued and saved? I'm not sure if I am including myself in this equation.

With so much to do tomorrow, I need to get some rest. The sleeping pills I took are kicking in and soon I will be asleep. Reaching over to grab my glass of water I knock over the bottle of Xanax, picking it up, I am not sure I'll need these much longer. For now, they offer me comfort so I keep them and decide to take them with me.

My glass of water is placed on top of the list. I still don't know why I wrote the list out, a list of ways to kill someone. Crumpling the paper, I need to get rid of any evidence and any trace of this getting back to me. Pausing one more time to review the list, I ball it up and toss it in the trash. I'll be taking it out tomorrow, right before the trash men take it.

CHAPTER 13

JAYSON

We are coasting along now enjoying the drive, which is almost six hours, give or take. This all depends on how many times we stop along the way. Long drives are a way to decompress, and I love them. David and I used to jump in the car when we were bored and pick a highway and drive. We once ended up in Springfield, just over four hours from Chicago, just past the witching hour, making it an eerie experience. After getting lost we ended up turning into a cornfield and quickly followed by a local cop. It was a terrifying experience and one we hate to look back on because it could have ended in a different experience than it did.

When we were pulled over, I thought, that's it, this is where either the children come out and slaughter us or we're taken further into the field and murdered by this cop. Nothing like that happened; in fact, the opposite did. The cop was family, and since it was a small town and he was most likely the only gay person in town, we chatted for a bit. He asked a lot of questions about the city and the gay scene since that's where we were going to school. He gave us a *warning,* and we were on our way.

David was friendly and charming, and this had a lot to do with us not getting in trouble. He also caught on quickly that the cop was gay. I don't have what they call gaydar, but he had caught on to it rather quickly. David's been such an important part of my life; I wish he was here. I didn't buy the excuse he gave for not coming this weekend and I eventually want to talk to him about it.

Ale stopped asking questions or bringing up things that were hot buttons. My family is something I do not want to talk about anymore. We can talk about them later. Right now, I want to enjoy the rest of the drive and mentally prepare for what's coming. This weekend is about me and doing what's right for me.

Someone was home when I stopped by the house earlier. I wanted to slip inside and look around and was hoping no one was there. Discovering more than I was bargaining for. I need to let it go for the weekend and focus on what I need to do to end this with them. Knowing my boundaries and my limits, I think I've had enough.

Turning to Ale, I think about all the things we have gone through. All the things I might want to walk away from too. Not quite decided yet about our relationship. It does mean a lot to me, but I also know it's toxic. How do you know when it's time to let something go? Is it when it's served its purpose and how do you really know that then? What are the signs? I know I have been pushed to the limits with my family, but with Ale I am not sure.

Changing the dial on the radio and looking for something else to distract my mind I cut off Ale midway through her song. I just needed to clear my head and refocus. Not even knowing what she was singing, I just needed it to stop. I've been in my head too much already.

"What's wrong, Jayson? I know something is up. I can feel it."

"Nothing, I'm just really distracted right now."

"I can tell, you've swerved several times and I can tell you're deep in thought."

"Do you know what you want out of life, Ale? Do you know what your purpose is? What makes you happy?"

"Yes, babe, money and sex."

"I'm being serious here."

"Is this about David? Jayson, you need to decide about him, this thing you're doing. I don't know what it is, so I am pretty sure you don't either. Is he coming? Are you going to ditch me?"

"That's the thing, I told him about it and invited him. He told me he couldn't. He had something else to do."

"I'm sorry, babes."

"Yeah, me too."

I'm thrown off with this exchange. She seemed interested and almost concerned about this. Does she want me and David to be a thing? There are times I think she likes him, and there are times I know she hates him. I need to know which it is. She's important to me and so is he.

Deep in thought, I catch myself and my vehicle swerves, but I correct it quickly. If you didn't know I was distracted, you would think I was driving drunk. I need to stay focused and get us there in one piece. Ale says nothing about my driving, which means she is distracted too. I still don't know who she is texting.

We're now five and a half hours into the drive, and we are both getting tired. I want to get there, get things set up, and just go to bed. We stop again to stretch our legs, grab cigarettes, and fill up again on gas since we'll have to make the trip back. As I pumped the gas and Ale went inside to pay, I think about everything again from the guys earlier to my family.

Going back and forth between them, David, my dad, my mom, Ale, my siblings, it's like I'm having flashes in my head. Like I am pushing one of those viewfinders over and over, searching for something. Each of those images, a snapshot of the different relationships I have in my life. When the images start to slow it's like I panic, and I am rapidly pushing the button again and then the gas pump clicks and I am pulled out of it.

When I look up, Ale is standing there and has several bags of junk food in her hand and smiles. "In case we run out." We are going to gain some weight this weekend if I don't put a stop to her madness. I glance into the bags as she comes around the side of the car where I am pumping gas. I peer in and spot a box of beef jerky.

"I think we have enough." I open the car door and open my bag to show her my stash.

"Never too much jerky." She tosses the bags in the car and gets in through the back seat and climbs over to the passenger side. I don't understand why she makes things so complicated, but I laugh and shut the door.

"Alright, let's get this over with." I climb into the driver's side and start up the car. It isn't long before my mood shifts, and I am quiet again. It is strange how I can go from chipper to down so quickly when I think about my family.

"I am tired," I finally get the words out. I want to include Ale. I want her to know completely what she is getting herself into. With 30 minutes left of the drive I can fill her in.

"I can drive."

"I can't do this anymore. I can't go on any more of these stupid vacations. This is it, this is the last one, Ale. I give up, I can't keep trying when I get nothing in return. I need time away from them. I should have done this a long time ago, but I need some serious distance from them."

"Way to go, Jayson! Do you need me to start up the wood chipper?"

I laugh at this; I am so glad she is breaking the mood up a bit. We joke about the wood chipper all the time. It's how we planned to get rid of a body, even though it's just a joke, something we came up with a long time ago.

"No wood chipper this time, but I wanted you to know that this weekend can go south very quickly, and I didn't want you to be surprised. I didn't want you to be blindsided."

"I am all in, wood chipper or not. It's time you set some of them straight. Starting with your father. I can't wait to see the look on his face"

I decide not to go into any more details as we just talk shit about them for the next 30 minutes of the drive. My mood shifted, and I am feeling a lot better now. I think this is what the problem was with the entire drive. I needed to include Ale because I needed her on my side. Sometimes I doubt our friendship and I don't know why, our friendship is solid.

Ale punches me in the arm and giggles. "Do you remember prom?"

"Are you in my head? I was just thinking about that."

She dives into the story of sneaking off to kiss our math teacher. I knew what she was up to when I saw her walk up to him and they left together. I knew she wasn't leaving me for the night. She had been with him a few times by the time prom happened. She was already 18, and he was a fresh teacher out of school. Still inappropriate because of the dynamics between a teacher and student, but if you saw what he looked like, you would approve.

We laugh and share more stories. She's bonded to me and to my family. I know she feels it as she says this.

"You know, I don't know why, Jayson, but I feel bonded to your family. By the way, I stopped by your house."

"When did you stop by my parents' house?" I am confused by this statement. Why would Ale stop by? I wanted to ask even more questions when I noticed the GPS recalculating. I need to focus on driving, but I am interested and distracted by so many things at the moment.

"I think you were supposed to turn back there."

I slow down and veer off to the left so I can cross over at one of the turnabout areas. I see one coming up so I know we can get back on track. Usually, I would be pissed, but I am confused, happy, and worried because so much has just happened in the last few minutes.

We're five minutes away now and I've dropped her comment as she blasts the Backstreet Boys on the radio. With less than five minutes left of the drive, I decide it isn't worth bringing up again. She's close to my mom. Maybe it had something to do with checking in on her. She always favored my mom over my dad. For obvious reasons.

As we approach the area, I am shocked at how it looks. It went from open roads and cornfields to the dense forest quickly. I see a map and realize this isn't really a campground —it's a national park. I don't see any cars in the area. This place seems off the map. Maybe I was too distracted to really pay attention to when this change in scenery took place.

Gina gave us the address yesterday, waiting until the last minute because she said she wanted us to be surprised. I thought it was because we were going to go to the place we went to as kids, but as soon as she sent the address, I knew it wasn't the same place. I googled it and found some stuff, but I really wasn't paying much attention. I was busy and figured I would play along with her surprise.

Gina has been acting strange lately. We were close once and used to hang out often, even going out dancing a few times. Despite being younger and being her big brother, we have a lot in common and have never had any real arguments. I don't think there has ever been a time I've been upset with her. It's one of the few relationships in my family that I've preserved.

She tried to talk to me after my dinner a few years ago, but not wanting to talk, I withdrew. Then so much time passed that I simply wanted to erase what I could of that night from my memory.

As we get closer, I see a familiar car. I turn to look at Ale and her face has confusion written all over it. When she notices I see her, the expression shifts. I look back to the car and I see the door open and who steps out. I immediately feel my heart sink.

CHAPTER 14

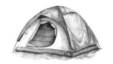

JAYSON

Getting out of the car, I feel a bit shaky but continue to walk towards a familiar face.

"What are you doing here?" I don't know whether to be mad or happy as I stare at David waiting for an answer. He smiles and extends his arms out for a hug since Ale is standing next to me, he scoops us both up. Ale doesn't say anything, she just gives an awkward giggle and I can't tell if it's is forced so I mimic her response.

"I thought about it, and I thought this would be fun. I knew Ale was coming, and I figured we could all kind of bond." David says this with confidence and authenticity. He was never one to lie.

David wants to spend time with Ale? In complete shock at this point I think, something isn't adding up. Excitement and confusion engulf me, and Ale doesn't seem to be upset by this. Maybe she's coming around to the idea that David and I can one day be a thing and she is finally ready for me and her to branch out and really start dating, like seriously start dating because it's not like we won't continue to be friends. That will never change, but in order for us to find someone, we need to start spending a little less time with each other.

"I think it's a great idea. David, I know I might come off as a this big bitch and all but Jayson is like my best friend and if I am going to share him with someone, I am ok with it being you."

I take a few steps back and my hands immediately go to my neck, gasping, "Well, Ale." David, too, has a shocked look on his face. Both because of what Ale is saying and because it sounds genuine. I am not sure what is happening right now, but I like it. I love it, in fact.

"I brought my own tent and stuff. I just need help to get everything set up." David is opening his trunk and looking at his bag and tent thrown haphazardly in his trunk. It's a mess and needs to be cleaned up which is a bit like our relationship or whatever it is that we are or aren't.

"I can sleep in the tent by myself if you guys want to crash together." Ale is being too nice now. Offering up to sleep alone, in the woods. I don't know whether or not to really believe that this is happening. Did I crash somewhere on the interstate, and this is the afterlife? "I have some reading to do and could use the alone time tonight."

"It's ok, Ale, I can sleep alone. I am, in a way, crashing the party."

"Why don't we get set up and figure that out later," I say in case this turns into something it doesn't need too. "We could also just sleep in the tent together too. I brought the family-size one for space, so it sleeps like 3-4 people." They both look at each other and shrug at the same time.

"Slumber party!" David and Ale laugh and she helps him get his stuff out, leaving his tent in the trunk.

We start to unpack and in the process, I almost forget the other car parked in the area. It's a blue Camry; Cat and Gina both drive one so I am not sure who would be here. I am assuming Gina because mom is coming up with Cat, and I am assuming they would ride together in mom's car. I guess we will find out once we get to the site.

I used to have the same car as it was one of the few things my father bought me. I heard my mom fighting with him about it. He had already bought Victor one and then Gina and Cat were going to get theirs in a few weeks. Mom was yelling at him telling him how unfair it was that he had not thought about buying me one.

A month after my sisters got theirs, I came home and there was one for me. Mom gave me the keys and dad didn't come home that weekend. I was glad he stayed at the other apartment because I had the opportunity to enjoy the gift even if it wasn't given to me out of love. When I had enough money saved, I traded it in and bought myself something else. I wanted to give it back, but I knew my mom had to go through a lot to get him to buy it.

When I asked if it was ok to trade it in, Dad said, "Do what you want with it. It's yours."

I traded it in and just recently paid the new car off. It helped as a big down payment for what I drive now—my red Toyota Rav4. Ale and I always dreamed of owning a car like this. We don't know what drew us to it, but we wanted it. She had one of her own but hers had been used when we got them. She had opted for black car, as black as her soul she would joke which always made me laugh.

"Hey, Jayson, how do we know exactly where we're setting up?" Ale has a puzzled look on her face as she stands with her hands on her hips. "Did your sister tell you or draw you some sort of map? This place is bigger than I thought it would be and there isn't a check-in desk or anything. Is this even like a real legit place? Why did she choose this place? I thought it would be more like glamping or something fun like you guys usually did." She fired off her comments, quickly annoyed and it was hard for me to figure out which to answer first, mainly because I didn't know.

"Honestly, I have no clue. She did give us some directions." Gina's making this out to be some sort of game. I pull out my phone and look for the text because it seemed she'd laid out in detail how to get to where she wants us to set up. I show Ale and David and they both look at me confused. The directions aren't as simple as I thought they were. I'm good at directions, but this has instructions like *turn right, walk 5 mins, turn left, walk 3*. How fast should we walk? Were these estimates or did she come out here and figure this out herself? If she did come out here, that is dedication, and strange. Also, if she did map this out herself, was she carrying stuff and would our dragging all our stuff change the time it took? Would five minutes really be six or seven? I realize she also described some landmarks.

I try to send Ale and David a text of the directions just so everyone has them, but the text doesn't go through. "We have a problem; I can't send you a text."

Ale pulls out her phone, "Are you kidding me right now? Jayson!" She starts dialing someone's number. "No service either and I have no bars, do you have anything? Shit, I didn't download my playlists. What if something happens? Jayson, we are ten minutes from the main road driving." She is panicking now, and it also comes out as a whine.

"I'm sorry, I didn't realize." I don't know what else to say, Ale is clearly upset, and David doesn't look so happy either.

"It's going to be ok." David sounds like he's trying to calm both me and Ale down after noticing the concerned look on my face. He seemed to go from upset to reassuring rather quickly. "Look, nothing is going to happen. It's not like we have bears in the Midwest. Any other animal we can easily scare off. I don't think we need to worry."

"He's right. It's a little inconvenient, but it's going to be ok. And, look, I downloaded some music, and we have the backup battery packs to keep our phones charged, and who knows, service may come in and out. Aren't we planning to bond?" He nudges her trying to shift the mood.

"I swear I am going to slap your sister, Jayson." Ale is pissed but I can tell she is already starting to calm down a bit. David did a good job defusing whatever was about to happen.

"Your sister is strange. If it wasn't your family we were here to spend time with, I would think we were on our way to get murdered." David laughs and nudges me with his shoulder. This isn't what I expected him to say after just calming us down. I look over at Ale wondering what this will do to her.

"I wouldn't put it past his family," Ale says with a blank stare. She looks a little worried, scared in fact. Her mood is shifting again. I've never seen or heard her sound afraid around my family. Yes, they were a weird bunch and yes, they were toxic as shit, but dangerous?

"Let's just find the area and get settled." I'm sure some-one's here already or will be soon. It's a bit awkward as we gather up our belongings, but I brought a wagon to put our stuff in as we take the thirty-minute trek to where Gina said to set up camp.

I feel someone's eyes on me as I am loading up the last of our things. I shut the door and turn around with a look. It's beautiful and eerie out here. My head wavers back and forth looking to see if I see someone. I don't know why, but I do not feel like we are alone. David stands next to me and takes a deep breath and exhales.

"I am so happy I came; we should talk too."

I look at him, and he is smiling. I am not concerned at all. I think this is a good thing. Ale comes up on the other side of me, and we are now all standing together, the three of us, looking out and staring into the forest. Ale shudders and I think she feels the eyes too. David says nothing but I feel him get a little closer.

"Are we waiting for someone?" I sense fear in his tone.

"No, I just wanted to take this all in." I turn around and they follow.

Once we had got off the interstate and turned into the wooded area, it had been another ten-minute drive to this destination. It had been a scenic drive, but I did take in how secluded and creepy it was. This would be where one could dump bodies, and no one would find them. It seemed Gina really wanted this to be *off the map*. She succeeded in adding the creep factor too; nothing about this area screamed fun and safe.

We enter the clearing just fifty feet from where the cars are parked. It's an open area, one of two that Gina mentions in her directions. There is no question that this is it. Just to be sure I jog over to the other area to look. As I approach, I hear a rustling backpack. I question if I got it wrong. Seeing one of my sisters' cars, I wonder if maybe it's them. I peek into the open area, and I see the brush move as if someone walked into it. But it isn't dense, and if someone had been there, I would still be able to see them. I give it a minute before I hear Ale call out.

"Is it that one?"

I hurry back shaking my head and must have a puzzled look on my face as both ask at the same time.

"What happened?"

"Nothing, I thought I heard something and then I saw the trees over there move like someone walked through but no one was there." Ale is about to grab her stuff when David stops her.

"We're not doing this, and this just started, I am really looking forward to spending time with you." David glares into my eyes and smiles and then turns to Ale. "You too, I think we all need this."

David doesn't know all my plans for this weekend. He doesn't know that I want to talk to my family and how this will be the last trip I plan to take with them. I consider telling him now, in this exact moment, when Ale shakes her head. I wonder if she is hearing my thoughts or something because I just smile and grab my bags. "Let's go, these directions are whack but we'll figure it out. Walk six minutes until you see a sign right?"

"Does she say what the sign says?" Ale asks as she lights a cigarette.

"Hey, be careful, you don't want to set the place on fire." David laughs. "What did ole Smokey The Bear say? Only *you* can prevent forest fires."

"Ole Smokey doesn't have my anxiety." Ale laughs and David laughs back.

It seems that everyone is starting to get along. We take the six minutes up the path, and we find the sign.

"The fun starts here?" I read the sign aloud. "Gina was here." I knew she had to have been here.

Ale and David both look at each other. "That's dedication. How many of these trips do you guys take?" David asks.

"We've been going on them since we were kids. When we were younger, we didn't have much money, so we went camping. As we got older and Dad became successful, we took better trips, bigger trips."

"So why this trip, why back to your roots? So, to speak."

"Honestly, I have no clue." I have been questioning this since Gina mentioned it. I mean we had fun when we were younger, but I figured if we were going to walk down memory lane it would be where we used to go camping. This out here doesn't make sense to me.

We all turn around because we hear rustling again. We all look at each other. It's getting louder and closer and I am not sure if I should run or stay put.

"Hey, guys." It's Victor, he must have pulled up right after we walked in. He doesn't have much, which explains why he was able to catch up so fast. Ale runs over to give him a hug and I look over at David rolling my eyes as he's squinting his eyebrows. He has no idea I think Ale and Victor may have the hots for each other, so I'll have to explain this later and why I think it's such a bad idea.

"How long have you been here?" I want to question him because maybe he is who I saw in the woods on the other side. Maybe he was the one who went in the wrong clearing and came back this way.

"Oh, I pulled up and saw you guys walk in. I was going to beep, but I saw all the stuff you had and figured I would just catch up plus I had to take a piss." He looks over at Ale. "And not in front of the lady." Stopping for a second, he looks and nods up at the sign, "Who put the sign up?"

"Gina," both I and Ale say in unison—at least we suspect it.

"Well, it looks like we follow the sign and the little arrow under it and walk another…" he looks down at his phone. "Shit, no service." He realizes it now—we have no connection to anyone. "It's another seven minutes." He didn't seem to be worried about it.

He starts walking, grabbing a bag from Ale and doesn't offer me or David any help. I think David gets my eye roll from earlier because he's now rolling his.

We go on and continue to follow the directions. Another right for a few minutes. Another left. Watch out for the poison ivy, she warns in the directions. We finally make it to a large open area. It's empty though.

"I thought I saw one of the witches' cars out there."

"So did I." I look around trying to find any trace of their belongings and come up short.

"Are we in the right spot?" Ale asks and lights another cigarette.

"I don't think we made any mistakes." I noticed a sign on one of the trees, and I read it out loud, "Sometimes the past has its good memories, sometimes it has its bad memories. This weekend we will figure it all out. At least some of us will. BTW you're in the right spot," signed with a smiley face.

CHAPTER 15

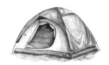

VICTOR

Sitting there puzzled, I'm not sure what to do. I want to leave already, no, I need to leave. This is not a safe space for me I realize as I look around. The area itself seems dangerous and being around my family is toxic. I don't feel safe around myself at times and not being able to control how I sometimes go into these dissociative episodes scares me. I don't like what Gina has in store for us as well. It doesn't make me feel comfortable.

This all seems like it is going to be some sort of game, and I don't do well with games. I stare blankly at the sign as Jayson reads it. I feel like I am disconnecting from my body, but this isn't the time or the place to disassociate. I have not even told everyone I was diagnosed with Depersonalization Disorder. I immediately start to breathe in deeply and trace the insides of my hands. It's a trick my therapist taught me that I can do subtly to calm myself down.

I meet with my therapist weekly, sometimes twice a week because I think that once a week isn't going to be enough for all I must unpack. The things I have learned have been useful, like finger tracing, so I find myself doing it a lot. The feel of my fingers running alongside each other connects me back to myself and starts to ground me. The sensation it brings travels through my body, and I feel a spark. It feels like I just jumpstarted my motor. I am disconnected from being disconnected.

It works, and I start to get my things together. I quickly set up and walk over to help them out. The sooner everything is ready, the sooner we can just relax. It's still early so everyone else should be getting here within the next two hours or so. I look at my watch and try to time how long it would take for everyone to arrive. I mentally calculate the distances and the times, as if I'm studying for a math quiz. I'm too anxious to really figure it out so I just tell myself it should be two hours. I'm ruminating now—something my therapist tells me isn't healthy—so I think of another way to break that spell. Putting it in the filing cabinet to deal with later is another trick my therapist taught me. It's a metaphor for telling myself it's there but I can deal with it later. I can take out the file and review it, but I can't deal with it now, so it goes in the cabinet.

I didn't expect to see David here, but I am happy for my brother. I think David is a good match for him. They seem to make each other happy. I don't know what they are to each other because he is in and out of his life so much, and I've never asked either. I should ask, I should take the time to get to know my brother more and his partner or best friend or whatever they decide they want to be. It would make me a better brother just to talk to him more.

After everything is up and ready, we sit around what looks like the fire pit area. It doesn't look like it's been used in a while. There aren't any traces of wood or ashes. You can tell it's the fire pit area because the earth dips and there is black dirt. Something burned here at one point. I think about what that could be. Was there a family here? Were they roasting marshmallows? Were they telling stories? Were they fighting and arguing?

My thoughts turn dark. Did someone burn in this pit? Did some psycho killer come through and murder a family and then burn their bodies, packing up the ash as they left so there wouldn't be a trace of who and what existed in this spot? I shake my head as if I am trying to remove these thoughts when I hear a voice.

"When do you think everyone will get here?" Ale stands up, she stretches as she says this, and her shirt rides up. I see a flat-toned stomach and a small tattoo which I've never seen before so I assume it must be new. I know what Ale looks like because I've seen all of her before. She's been to our house enough and practically lived there when she left home. She's seen all of me too and I wonder if she has the same thoughts I have. She's only two years older than me, so it's not a big deal, I can't possibly still be seen as Jayson's little brother.

"I don't know, but I am starving. Gina told me to bring the stuff to cook with and I had to order stuff on the Zon. She said she and mom will grab food on the way." Jayson reaches into his bag and pulls out some beef jerky and hands them out.

"I brought some too." I get up so I can go to my tent and get them, but David passes me his and reaches for another out of Jayson's hand. I notice the pause that takes place when their hands touch. It's cute seeing them like this. I am sure they've hooked up before, as I have heard Ale and him talk about it. I just don't know if they have ever actually dated or is this some odd cat-and-mouse chase. Maybe I can help them this weekend in between everything else I need to do. Wouldn't that be something good? Something to show that I am a good brother.

Sitting back down, I stare at the ground and a million

images start to flash in my mind. Happy memories, sad memories, violent memories. I hear in a weird voice that isn't my own say, "Sometimes the past has its good memories, sometimes it has its bad memories. This weekend we will figure it all out. At least some of us will." I feel like I have heard this before. It sounds too familiar.

"Victor, want another one?" I am hit in the face with a spicy stick. It breaks the dissociative trance I was just about to enter.

"Sorry, I spaced out," I say as I pick up the beef jerky off the ground. I start to unwrap it, thinking I need to focus and somehow remain calm.

"You looked really deep in thought, bro," Ale says as she sits next to me. I want to be open with them. It's been hard hiding the things I've been experiencing lately. I've had to take time off work, and I've had to start seeing two different therapists. One for talk therapy and one for something called EMDR which I still don't understand, but it's starting to help.

"Hey, is everything all right? Want to take a walk? You didn't seem like you were just spacing out. You looked like you checked out completely." Ale seems concerned, and I wonder if she knows.

"No, it's ok. I have a lot on my mind with work and everything." What's funny is I am currently off work, again.

I don't have these episodes only when I'm around my family, I'm having them all the time now and I don't even know when that started. All I know is I've become more aware of them as I've got older. Looking back, I think I've always had them. I have memories of people snapping their fingers in front of me or nudging me, asking if I've heard them. My therapist says she thinks that something traumatic happened to me in my past, but I don't think that's it.

My family is a bit nuts, but I cannot think of anything that would have been so traumatic that could have started this.

My therapist explains the concept of escapism and complex PTSD. I am not sure if it's that, but I can say that it's a possibility. I know I have anxiety along with the rest of my family. From what I understand, we all have a prescription of some sort and most of us are on medications for anxiety. I've seen the pills we all carry around and pop like candy. There's a bit of shame in taking them in front of them as my family can be judgmental. Except, why should it matter if we're all taking them? Family judgment can be so complicated at times.

Giving them the excuse, I need to pee, I stand up, walking away from Ale because I feel she's about to get personal. I don't want to get personal with her, not in that way. I feel the wrappers from our snack in my pocket. I am looking for a place to get rid of them. I have one more in my pocket and decide to eat it.

"You have a weak bladder."

I remember why she says this now. I told them I had just gone the other way to take a piss before meeting up with them. I don't need to use the bathroom again; I just need to get away, to breathe. I am about five minutes away from where we set up camp when I hear a sound.

The sound is coming from just beyond some bushes. I walk over and see something in between some branches but I can't make out what it is. Is it an animal? Is it a person? I have no idea who it is or what is going on, but I am spooked, and I decide it's time to turn back around.

As I am turning around, I hear a voice and I can't decipher if it's in my head or if it's coming from somewhere else.

"Sometimes the past has its good memories, sometimes it has its bad memories. This weekend we will figure it all out. At least some of us will."

CHAPTER 16

I need to regain focus but so much is going on. It took me longer than expected to set up my tent because of the distractions going on around me. I could hear them talking, they were being so loud I wanted to go over there and make them stop. Their voices were driving me to start the weekend sooner than I had originally planned. I dig through my bag looking for something to snack on because right now I need something to calm my nerves and the last thing I want is to take another Xanax.

I am standing here taking everything in as I tear open the spicy stick. I hear the surrounding birds, the wind rustling through the trees and bushes. Nature has always been a safe space for me. Growing up I remember spending a lot of time in the woods. My siblings and I spent many days playing hide and seek. As memories flood my mind, my stomach has other plans. The ache in my belly tells me I need to eat something. Lifting the dried piece of meat, I stop just short of my nose and inhale taking in the scent. Not holding back, I eat it in a few quick bites. Crumbling the plastic wrapper, I turn when I hear something off in the distance. I look around to see if anyone is nearby. Wanting a few moments to myself

I realize I am not alone anymore. I just needed a few moments to myself and collect my thoughts.

"Sometimes the past has its good memories, sometimes it has its bad memories. This weekend we will figure it all out. At least some of us will."

I am not sure if I say this out loud or if someone else says it, but I am sure I just heard it. I can't get it out of my head. I take off, dropping the wrapper.

CHAPTER 17

JAYSON

I'm the first one back from our bathroom break that Victor just started. When he got up, we all just decided to take the opportunity to relieve ourselves. I wanted to go with David but decided that it was best if we all found our own spots to take care of business.

Ale comes back just a few seconds after me and out of breath. "I saw a snake." She shivers as she says this.

"It's not the wild west, so I am sure it was a garter snake." I'm laughing at her because she always goes to the worst-case scenario. "I am sure that there are no poisonous snakes in the wild, wild Midwest."

"Who saw a snake?" David says a little too excited. "We could eat it." There is too much enthusiasm in his voice.

"I am not a cannibal," Ale says.

"It's not cannibalism if it's not human."

"Same difference," Ale snaps back at me.

"I only said that we could, I didn't say I wanted to," he

says in slowed syllables indicating that this is a joke and he was only stating a fact.

Victor comes back in a hurry, like he was trying to get away from something. What did he see?

"Hey, is everything ok?" I ask him because he looks pale; he doesn't look like the tanned boy he should look like. He looks like he spent the entire summer in a basement. Something feels wrong.

"Yeah, I just heard, or I thought I saw…never mind. It might have been in my head. I think I am not cut out for this." He says this as if he is trying to get several thoughts out at once—he is a jumbled mess. He starts to head for his tent, and I stop him.

"Don't do this, don't leave." I really don't want to be here myself, but I don't want everyone coming here thinking that I have done something to make him leave.

I notice his breathing is off and he's starting to have a panic attack. I look over to Ale and then David and they nod seeing it too.

They approach us, and I put my hand up to stop them. I don't want them to make it worse, even though I know they only want to help me help Victor.

I turn him around back to where we were all sitting. I snap my hand at Ale or David and make the motion of taking a drink of something.

I sit Victor down and start to ask him, "What's going on? I noticed you were off earlier. You spaced out a few times. It's ok. You can talk to me." His lip quivers and he's about to say something when David hands him the water bottle. The moment is interrupted. Victor seems to be calming down, and now I don't think he's going to answer my question. That's if he even heard the question.

He twists off the bottle cap and takes a drink of water. As he tilts back his head, I can see his Adam's apple bob up and down. He takes a few more drinks—gulps I see. The bottle is half empty when he pulls it away from his mouth. A dribble of liquid spills down his chin and onto his shirt.

"I am ok, I just freaked out. I think I heard something or saw something. Or maybe it was just me ummmm maybe I spooked myself". Victor looks calm but with just a hint of confusion.

"What do you mean maybe it was you?" Ale says this with a puzzled look on her face. "Do you like to talk to yourself or like something like that?"

"Ale, shut up." I don't know what she is implying, but now is not the time to call my brother names or insinuate he hears things and talks to himself.

She steps back as she realizes what she's implied. I don't think she meant any harm by it. It was a mistake and a question at the same time because even I want to know the answer to it. I noticed growing up Victor always seemed to space out, he was always in another place in his head. I heard my mother talking to my father about it one time in their bedroom. They were talking about taking him to talk to someone because they worried that something serious was going on with him. They never said they caught him talking to himself, but I got the sense that is what they meant. I never saw him do that. I saw him look confused, like he lost time. Like he was somewhere else, detached from his body.

I look him in the eyes and see if I can see him in there. Is he here? He pushes me back and laughs.

"That's uncomfortable," he says with a smirk. "You know how to really bring on the creeps." He puckers his lips and mocks a kiss. We all start to laugh, and the awkward tension is broken.

Everyone sits back around the firepit. We're quiet. I don't know if I want to start the conversation or if I should wait for someone else. I feel like we need to refocus. I think to myself,

Why did I come here? I gaze over at David and know that he is not the reason. He wasn't even supposed to be here. I look toward Ale, and she isn't the reason either and then I look over at Victor. He's part of the reason and I'm not sure I want to do this anymore, nor am I sure that I want to blow the family apart, maybe not this weekend.

Maybe I can start by setting better boundaries. I've already started to have my own life so I don't need to blow everything up. I can have relationships with whoever I want when I want them. If that means not having one with my father, then that is how that will be. I don't need to force anything that doesn't feel good to me or doesn't add any value to my life.

I look around and see several people who add value to my life and smile. David catches me, causing my smile to grow wider. That's a relationship I need to work on if I want to see where it can go. I don't know if I love David, but I can start to love him. But, can he love me? Can he love someone who is broken?

Victor breaks the silence, "So I was thinking maybe we can tell ghost stories tonight. Maybe we can try to scare the shit out of Gina for setting this whole thing up. She likes to be scared, doesn't she? Maybe we can get her because I am sure she was planning on getting us this weekend. If this place doesn't scream massacre, I don't know what does." Victors looking around taking in the surrounding area with his palms raised and his shoulders shrugged, both a question and a statement.

I shudder when I hear him say the word 'massacre'. "She's going to kill us?"

"I don't mean that. I mean this place was picked for a reason and I think that reason is to scare the shit out of us. You know how she is." Victor is now smirking and has an evil look on his face, but I am loving this idea.

Growing up, Gina loved Halloween and loved to play pranks and scare us. Maybe this was our turn to turn the tables around and scare her. We all turn at the same time. We all heard it. It was a loud noise. We couldn't miss it.

"What was that?" Ale looks terrified. "Did you hear someone yell?"

"I totally did." David looks at me and then around at everyone else.

"Someone else must be here. The other parked car—" I am interrupted before I can finish my sentence.

"Looked like your sisters' car." Ale says this in an annoyed tone. "Maybe Vic is right, maybe we should turn the tables on her. Scare her. I bet she is here already watching us. Laughing at us."

"Ok, so how do we want to do this?" I am now anxious with excitement. This sounds like a good plan after all. I think we can do this. I think I want to do this. I don't think this changes my plan, but it complicates it.

We start to brainstorm different ideas, different stories we can tell. We start to wonder if we should do it tomorrow and plant the seed tonight. Tell some ghost stories that will spook everyone out.

Ale brings up the story of Resurrection Mary. It's too common—everyone from the Midwest, especially Chicago, knows about it. It wouldn't be spooky. We think of some of the Mexican folklore stories our families told us growing up. La Llorona. It doesn't apply to us here while we're camping. David brings up Bloody Mary.

"Do you see a mirror anywhere? That isn't going to work." After I said it, I immediately thought I was too quick and too negative. David doesn't look bothered by my statement, but I don't want him thinking I think his ideas are bad.

"Let's just tell some spooky stories. Let's set the mood tonight with that. Tonight we can come up with a story that involves the woods or something. That way we can have everyone on edge, and then tomorrow we can lay the scariest story that will have them shaking, and then we can get Gina when everyone goes to sleep."

I am about to tell them about faking a kidnapping and dragging her out of her tent when we're interrupted. More of my family are arriving. I can hear Cat and my mom in the distance. They sound confused, and I think they think they are lost. I wonder how long I should let them struggle, but David decides to interrupt that.

"We're over here!"

CHAPTER 18

MOM

"I told you we should have come together. I almost missed the turn following you, you were driving too fast!" I don't want to argue with my daughter, but when I got to her place, she was in a hurry, and something was wrong. I've seen what she looks like when she is guilty of something—it's always written all over her face. You learn these things being a mother, especially those looks on your own kids' faces.

"You drive like an old lady. Can you just slow down? I want to talk to you. Now who is going too fast? You could have tried this on the road." My daughter seems angry and avoidant. More reason to think she is guilty of something. I can think of 5,000 reasons she would be guilty, but I don't want to be accusatory. I don't want to put her or myself in that position right now, before we are with everyone else.

I am about to say something when she rolls her eyes. Wanting to slap my daughter, I hold back. The way she talks to me sometimes not only hurts, but it pisses me off. Her eye rolling is one of my biggest pet peeves. It's what makes me want to slap her across the face, a face that reminds me so much of her father. She especially reminds me of him at times like this. When she gets like this, there is no reasoning or trying to get her to see things any other way. She is stubborn —we all are stubborn in the family.

My arms are full, and I am constantly switching my bags back and forth from arm to arm. It's not just the weight of things, but the number of things we have. We have way too many things to carry. I think about why I packed all of this. Are we really going to need all this? Did my anxiety cause me to over-pack?

I wish we would have left everything in the car and sent the boys back to get it. My boys can be helpful when I need them to be. As I have gotten older, they have matured and help more. They can be a gentleman, as I think *I raised some fine children.* That thought stops when I see my daughter. She's good, but right now I still want to slap her. What's that saying, "I love you, but I don't like you." It's what I am feeling right now.

I see my son's car and a few others, recognizing the Camry. The other car in the small lot, I am not sure who it belongs to. Maybe there are other people staying the weekend here as it's a public park after all. Secluded and eerie, but maybe that's because I spent the week watching horror movies alone. I loved the Friday the 13th series. Probably not a series I should have watched before a camping trip. What if there are more campers? That means I'll have an audience this weekend. There will be a show for them when I tell my husband I'm leaving him.

I spent a long time getting up the nerve to leave my husband. I've had darker thoughts in the past. Thoughts that I never shared with anyone. How I would kill him and make it look like an accident.

People who knew my husband would surely understand.

I might even get a few thank you baskets out of it, a few casseroles or pies, and who doesn't love a good pie? The sympathy phone calls would be nice too. I could take them while eating one of those pies that should help me mourn his loss. I wouldn't mind hearing more from my family or friends, so that would be a benefit. But these are not thoughts I would share with anyone. I keep them locked inside my head. I am still convinced that if he died, those who knew him wouldn't care as much. My husband's an asshole and everyone is aware he had cheated.

When I was pregnant with Cat, I caught my husband cheating on me. I had seen the emails on his laptop. This was when he was still coming home to work. He was in the other room working and decided to take a break. He came into the room and demanded that we make love. It was after he was in the shower that I heard the "swoosh"—the sound the computer makes when an email comes through. I still don't really understand technology.

Curious, I headed over to his laptop. It wasn't password protected and he must have had a long delay for the screen saver to come up because I saw the title of the email. I clicked it and saw the attached pictures and a short email. The details of the email were gross. Begging my husband to do things to her we've never done. Does my husband really like those things?

I didn't tell him I came across the email or that I looked around and found more. They came from different email addresses, so this wasn't the only one. The pattern showed email exchanges back and forth for several weeks to a month or so, and then they stopped. I assumed they used him for money.

We're not doing so well financially and that was in a combination with what I have been taking from him and what he's been losing from poor business deals and spending his money on other women. I am not one to call another woman a bad name, but everyone knows my husband, and everyone knows he isn't single. So, what do you call a woman who knowingly sleeps with your husband?

Deleting the email that came through when I was snooping, I thought someone was blackmailing my husband. But who? They had sent him threatening emails. It's what gave me the idea that I could kill him myself and get away with it. I'm sure I wasn't the only one who wanted him dead. My husband's reputation has caused him to have many enemies throughout his life and career.

Thinking about different ways I could do it, I thought about how I could get away with it and make it look like an accident. I had watched enough crime shows and episodes of that show where women finally reach their end and snap. I thought about my kids. How much would this hurt them? How hard would this be on them?

He got out of the shower, and I was back in the room getting my things together to shower after him. Wanting to wash his filth off me had me in a rush. I didn't like sex with my husband, and I hadn't for a long time, but I stayed with him because of the kids. I couldn't provide for them without his help. He wasn't a good husband, but he provided. I knew things would be a lot harder for me and the kids if I would have left. So, I stayed and dealt with it. Not a day went by where I didn't want to kill that bastard. I still did. Maybe I would. Maybe this weekend.

"Cat, I need you not to tell anyone about what we talked about."

"We didn't really get to talk, and don't worry, I won't say anything. It's about time you got away from dad. I am surprised you haven't killed him yet. The way he treated you and the way he treats Jayson and the other…"

I cut her off before she could say another word because I

don't want to hear her mention the other women. It's something I don't want to be reminded of, and something I don't want to talk about with my kids. "Where is the campsite? Didn't your sister send you a text or something? I feel like we should have found it already." I pull out my phone but drop it because I am juggling way too much.

Cat is already looking around and finds the marker described in the text. She nods her head, and we silently head in that direction. Conversation over.

We're a bit lost again; that didn't take long. I sense something though. Like someone is watching us. We stop again to look at the texts and we both turn at the same time. We both heard it too, off about twenty feet away. It sounded like the rustling of plastic. Not a bag but something like a wrapper. My stomach growls and I realize I forgot to eat, something I forget to do a lot these days.

"Did you hear that?"

"Yeah, I heard that. We're close, so it's Jayson or one of the others." She pauses, then starts back up, "Or there's an ax murderer out here." Cat says this with a smirk as she puts down her things and slowly creeps in the direction of the sound. My heart begins to race. We've only been here ten minutes and I am already feeling like I need to go. I don't think I'll enjoy camping anymore, not like when our family first started out. Those were the best camping trips I ever had.

Cat is ten feet away from the area where we heard the sound. She turns around to shush me even though I am not saying anything. She must be nervous, because her pace has slowed. I can't imagine anything happening to her and I regret my thoughts of slapping her.

She's now seven feet away and getting closer. My heart is beating a million times a minute. I don't know why, but I am terrified right now. It's the middle of the day, but that doesn't mean someone, or something, won't pop out of those bushes and tear her apart. Ripping her limb from limb until she is nothing but body parts—pieces of my daughter. She's a few feet away now.

I don't see her anymore, as she's gone in a blink. Panicking, I drop my things onto the ground. I'm fumbling for my phone and trying to press the buttons. What's my password? How could I forget my password? I need to call someone. I need to get help.

Feeling a wave come over me, everything around me fades to black. The combination of the panic and not eating must really be getting to me. I am still fumbling with my phone, and I feel the sweat beads develop around my hairline and down the back of my neck.

"No one is there." Cat pops up. She must have bent down. My heart stops and restarts at a slower pace. She didn't disappear, but the thirty seconds she was bent down, she had picked something up off the ground. How could thirty seconds feel like a lifetime? She's holding up a wrapper as she walks closer. I notice it's for beef jerky, my family's favorite brand. We both say Gina's name while rolling our eyes and arch one eyebrow up, our signature family trait.

"She must have been hiding here. It looks like her game is already starting."

"Game? What do you mean, game?" I am not sure if I am in on this weekend's plans. Is this a game for my kids? Is spending time with each other so horrible that they need to come up with something extra to make it enjoyable? I remember when there was a time we enjoyed each other. This doesn't feel good or sit right with me. I want to storm off, get back in the car, and drive home.

"You know what I mean, you know how she is. She is always trying to scare us or teach us a lesson of some sort. What kind of game do you think I was talking about?" Cat puts her hand on my arm. She must sense that I am upset and the kids hate when I get upset. As much as we annoy each other—because families do that—they care about me and each other. We are very protective of each other. Well, most of us.

I grab hold of her hand and smile. We both grab our things and start heading back in the direction we think the site is. It isn't long before we hear someone shout, "We're over here!"

CHAPTER 19

JAYSON

I get up first thinking my brother is going to join me, but he stays seated. Whatever is going on with him, it is clearly still happening, and he won't talk to me or anyone else about it. David sees me looking at my brother and gets up. Maybe while David and I are helping mom and Cat, Ale can work her way into getting him to talk.

I see the way they flirt and stare at each other. He's only two years younger than me but a year and a half younger than Ale. Whatever happens at this point, happens I guess. I shudder the thought away because I know Ale and I know my brother. I love them both, but it wouldn't be a match made in heaven.

David and I start heading towards them. As we leave the campsite, David pauses and grabs my hand. It's a gentle touch and we both stop. We're far enough away from the rest of the group where they can't hear or really see us. David smiles and it's the same smile he has when he wants to tell me something cute.

"I was afraid when I saw you get out of the car. I couldn't tell if you were happy to see me." He pauses, fidgeting as I can tell he is nervous. Despite being friends for a long time and occasionally hooking up, I still get nervous around him. I take him all in, from head to toe he is stunning. I want him right now, more than I have ever wanted him before. There is something about him right now that is driving me wild in all the right ways.

"I am glad you decided to come but I'll be honest. I was scared at first when I saw you, and angry, but that changed. Something about being around you changes me David." Taking a step back, I'm hoping he can tell I am both admiring him and giving him space to say something in return.

While I wait for a response, I take in how gorgeous he is, the way his cheekbones stick out. His tanned complexion and dark hair. He'd look good with long hair, pulled back in a bun, but I love his short hair. Not many people our age can still rock a faux hawk and get away with it like he does. He has the darkest brown eyes I've ever seen. Some would see his eyes and think they were empty, but I find mystery behind them. My eyes don't give off that same feeling. He's taller than me by a few inches, and is built in a way I find mesmerizing and dominating. He's toned and thick in areas I want to reach out and grab.

We stand there for another minute in silence, and I fight the urge to want to kiss him. It's not like we haven't kissed before, but this moment feels different. It feels intimate in a way that I think we both need and as I lean in; I get that feeling again of being watched. I haven't stopped feeling this way all day. In fact, something has felt off all week. I look behind me and watch David look towards my sister and my mother and I can tell he feels it too.

"Let's go help them. I'm getting hungry." Putting my hand to my stomach, trying to ease my mind and change the mood, I continue, "I hope Gina and my dad come soon because he's in charge of bringing the grill and this food won't cook itself." I'm not sure if I am upset that the moment has passed. I just hope we get another chance because I would have loved to feel David's lips against mine.

"Oh shit, I forgot! I have a small grill in my car. My cousin left it in my car a few weeks ago, and he still hasn't come back for it. If you want, we can grab it and start cooking now." David is always looking out for everyone, but I think we can wait. I tell him this so we can just get back to everyone else. If too much time passes, we may go back and interrupt something between Ale and Victor.

As we approach, I notice how much stuff they have with them. I wish they would have just come and got us and told us to go get everything instead of trying to get here with a disorganized mess in their hands. Mom is struggling with everything, and Cat looks annoyed. Something clearly happened between them, but I can't tell what it is. It isn't anger I see, it's something else and now I want to find out.

We head over to see if they need any help. As we get closer, I could tell how excited my mom was. She has always loved David; she can talk to him for hours. When I first brought him over, I was nervous. She was the one person who mattered when it came to accepting David. She first met him before I came out. Mothers always know though, so she welcomed him with open arms.

She gives him a hug and does that old person thing. Grabbing him by both his shoulders and stepping back. "My, how you've grown. I don't mean taller—you've always been tall— but you clearly have been working out. You should take Jayson with you. He needs a little muscle on him." She winks at me because she is being cheeky, and I am ok with it.

"Mom, I am carrying the weight of the world on my shoulders. Any given day I should have the muscles of a

Greek god." I say this lightheartedly, and she gets that. I start to grab some stuff from Cat so she can get herself together.

"We're still waiting on Gina and your husband."

"Gina isn't here?" My sister says in a tone I find confusing. She looks over at my mom and she also has a look on her face.

"On our way, we heard someone in the bushes, and then found a wrapper for those beef jerky things you all eat. We assumed it was Gina." Mom doesn't look as cheerful anymore.

"Maybe they blew over? We ate some a bit ago after we set up. We didn't know when you would arrive, and we wanted to get some food in us," I told my mom, hoping this would ease her mind. There must be more people around here. We can't be the only ones here, which is probably what I've been sensing. I am interrupted by my mom as she is trying to get us back to the campsite.

"Maybe. Let's just get back and get everything set up."

By the time we get back, Ale and Victor are just sitting there and they are quiet. I am glad we have interrupted nothing, because I am not in the mood to walk in on them or anyone in my family.

Victor gets up to give my mom a hug and, seeing her, seems to have calmed him because his mood suddenly appeared lighter. There is a presence my mom gives off that is, in fact, calming. It's why we gravitated towards her more than my dad. It doesn't help that he's distant himself and narcissistic, and sometimes I wish he wasn't part of the family.

I do hate the way I think about him because my thoughts can get too dark. My hope is something changes this weekend because I know that what I am feeling, other people in my family are feeling it too. We all can't go on hating each other or being uncomfortable around one another. I would love to have a relationship with him and with everyone, but that is not possible.

After we set up my mom and Cat's tent, we sit around the campfire. There is no wood, so I volunteer to go look for some. I stand up, once again hoping that someone will volunteer to go with me. I am hoping it's David. Ale stands up and wipes off her jeans when I tell her she doesn't have to go.

"Oh, I wasn't volunteering, I was just stretching."

She sits back down and smiles and looks towards David. He gets up when he sees her stare at him.

"You can wait here; I'll just grab something to get things started. I would rather have it going before it gets dark."

"I can help. Two hands are better than one."

"I have two hands."

"I meant four." He puts up both of his hands, showing them to me. He walks over to me, grabs my hand, and we walk off together. I hear someone make a kissing noise behind me. I am surprised when I turn around and it's my mother.

"I needed another minute alone with you, Jayson. I need you to know that after this weekend if we aren't a thing, I can't do this. We can't just be friends anymore. I know we tried the whole dating thing in the past and it didn't work, and I don't know if you were even trying. I wasn't sure if I was ready, but I am now. I want us…"

I don't want to hear him explain anything else, so I lean in and kiss him. I need him to shut up because everything he is saying is something I want to hear him say. He kisses me back, slipping his tongue into my mouth, and I match his. The speed is intense, and I am getting excited. We pull each other close, so close that I can feel him. I am enjoying this, and it doesn't feel like any of the times we kissed before. This feels completely different. It feels new and exciting. Maybe we are both ready now. I am not sure what we were before, but I know moving forward we are going to be something.

I pull away and smile.

"Are you going to say anything?"

"You said it for both of us." After an awkward giggle, I stare at him and lean in to kiss him quickly on the lips and pull back. "Let's go get the wood. I am second guessing the idea of me, you, and Ale sleeping in one tent."

David punches my arm and has a clever comeback, "Well, she can always sleep with your brother."

Rolling my eyes, I smile. "That might need to happen." Now all I want is to be alone with David. Right here, right now, later tonight. Now that I know how he feels and where we stand, this weekend is becoming a bit more confusing for me.

We're walking around looking for wood to bring back with us when we stumble upon someone's campsite. It was hidden behind some bushes. It's not even in an area where there is a fire pit or anything. It isn't even in enough space for comfort.

I see a green tent that sleeps one. It's one of those military-looking tents. A perfect triangle-shaped tent. Literally enough for one person to crawl in. No space to lounge about. I don't see any bags or anything. They must be inside the tent. I reach out to stop David because he looks like he is about to open it.

"What are you doing?"

"I want to see if anyone is inside."

"You can't just go inside someone's tent."

"I won't go inside. I will just knock on it."

"It's not a door."

"You know what I mean."

He walks up to it and taps on the outside and the tent flaps open, revealing the inside. He pushes the flap further to the side and I see a rolled-up sleeper and another bag tucked in the corner. From where I'm standing, it's a small maroon bag, one of those drawstring types. This is someone's stuff, and we are just poking around which makes me feel uncomfortable.

"Let's go before they get back."

"We're not doing anything. Maybe they're young and hip, who knows, hot and want to hang out." David is always trying to change the mood, but I don't find amusement in him right now.

"I don't know David, they didn't bring much. Look, I don't like this. It seems really off, and why is it so hidden? I just want to head back." I'm eager to get out of here and David senses this and nods, walking back towards me.

"Just grab that wood over there and head back." He takes control, which I find calming.

We gather up the wood we had already collected, plus a few more pieces, and make our way back. The walk back is quick, which we complete in silence. I don't like what we just stumbled upon. Something about it seemed peculiar. No food, no other belongings, and clearly there was only room for one person. I feel uneasy as I continue to think about it and hope that I am just overthinking it.

As we get back, we hear more voices. It's Dad and Gina and in the last fifteen, both have arrived. My initial thought is I hope they didn't forget the food. I don't hear any arguing, so that's a good sign. It's sad to have those thoughts that, "Oh no, someone's fighting," like you expect something shitty happening or going on.

As we enter the campsite, Dad is the first to look at me. He isn't smiling, but he isn't angry. There is an expressionless look about him as he looks at David, his eyes moving back and forth between the two of us. I don't care if the sight of David makes him uncomfortable, and suddenly that expressionless face morphs into a smile. I don't understand this at all. Dad never smiles, and he never smiles at the sight of David or anyone that I bring around. Before I know it, David walks up to my dad and is giving him a hug. Am I in the Twilight Zone?

There's an eerie feeling with the scene in front of me. Instead of enjoying things I can't help but sense that something is off. Not just with David and my dad but with this entire weekend. Turning around and scanning the area I feel that there are eyes on me. I can't figure out who or what is watching me but the feeling of dread washes over me.

CHAPTER 20

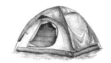

DAD

The drive isn't long and gives me enough time to go through the things I need to consider. I have decisions to make and a mental list of things that need to be done this weekend. A list of things that I have been putting off for different reasons. Avoidance—it's what I do best.

First, I want to finally tell my wife. I want to tell her about my affair and our kid. I don't want to hold this secret any longer as it's not fair to anyone involved, especially my wife. She's been through enough and with the last message from Ale, she is close to telling Jayson. Although I want to repair my relationship with him, that will be impossible if she gets to him first. Repairing the relationship with him is the second thing I need to do.

I regret everything that happened the night he came out to us. I hadn't suspected it, so when he came out, I felt betrayed. I felt like everything I worked toward, including my legacy and name, was going to be ruined. That's not the case and I've had time to think about it and learn. What my family doesn't know is the brief stint of therapy I had a few months after it all happened. I only went because I was hoping that I could fix myself, but I am old and stubborn and feel that I am beyond help. I did walk away with the information I needed to process my son's sexuality. I was just having a hard time with it. I still am. That's why this is so important to me, and I don't want my relationship with my son to end over my ignorance. There is still love for my son. I know I've treated him like shit over the years and there is no excuse for the way I've acted, but I need to repair things before it is too late.

I get a message from Ale on the drive over.

See you soon…Daddy.

My blood starts to boil as it seems like she is mocking the situation. I grip the wheel tight and under my breath; I scream out, *BITCH!* I am sick and tired of her and her games. She's going to tell Jayson this weekend, I know it. She is going to blow everything up and I am going to need to get rid of her once and for all. The third thing on my list.

I picture my hands wrapped around her throat. Squeezing until there is no air left. Watching as her eyes fade from green to black. Feeling her body go limp in my arms. These are dark thoughts, but I can't seem to think of anything else right now. I notice I'm excited, and it disturbs me that something so dark and twisted can do this to me. I loosen my hands on the steering wheel to adjust myself. I breathe in and think about Ale again but not in the same way.

Ale's presence is enjoyable, after all she's beautiful. Her body, slim and toned. I've watched her many times when we've been on vacation. We've taken her with us on some of our more extravagant vacations, so I've seen her in a bikini, and that's the thought I have as I continue to adjust myself. This isn't the time nor the place.

Needing a distraction, I turn on the radio. I need to think about how I am going to tell my wife about the affair and my child. The child my family doesn't know about, the child I have ignored. I open Ale's message and the dots on the phone light up. She is about to send another message as I see the dots on the screen showing that someone is actively typing. I type one of my own, then stop when the dots disappear and nothing comes through.

How does she even know? The affair happened before she worked the summer at my office. The kid was already born and I'm assuming the maid had told her. They'd gotten close, taking to one another a lot quicker than I thought they would. Ale tends to lure people in, it's a manipulative trait she possesses.

The fourth thing on my list is coming clean to my family about the state of the business. I need to tell them because it affects us all. I still pay for a lot of my children's things, and I want them to know that there will be significant changes moving forward. My kids are adults, but I still provide for them. I know I am a shitty father, but this is the least I can do. It's the lesson I learned from my parents. Take care of your family—just not emotionally.

The GPS alerts me that I am close. I recognize this from the last time I was here. It hasn't changed much. I think there are more trees, and it feels a lot denser than before. That could be because it's peak summer, though. When I was here last time, it was in the fall and the leaves had already begun to fall. When you looked through the trees, you could see a lot. Now with everything in full bloom, it looks like a dense forest. An unusual scene when you're from the city and this is the Midwest.

Pulling up next to the cars that are there, I see that everyone's here. I get out and I am getting things out of the trunk of my car when I hear another car approaching. Another Camry. I turn and look at the cars in the lot and it doesn't make sense. Did someone invite someone else? Is there an unknown person camping in this area too?

I came here before because of how secluded and off the map this area was. From what I know of this place, it isn't visited by many people.

The Camry parks across from the rest of the cars. I am assuming I don't know who the person is. When the door opens, I recognize my daughter. Someone else is here. This other Camry isn't one of the ones I'd bought for my kids.

She doesn't say much as I walk over to greet her. She never does. Gina is the type that waits for you to talk to her first. She likes to observe the situation and then decide how and when she wants to interact with you.

"How beautiful is this area you picked!"

"Yeah, I did some online searching and found it. I wanted something different but that reminded me of when we were little."

"You were such a young baby; I am so surprised you remember." I smile, those were the good times, the easier times in our family. I was a better husband back then. I wasn't perfect but I was a better father. It wasn't that money changed me, but the way that I had to get money that changed me.

"Dad, this weekend needs to go well. Our family is holding on by thread. I can feel something about to happen."

I was right—she was observant. She must sense that I have something going on. It leads me to my fifth thing I need to do or think about. I haven't made the decision yet. I was going to make a decision on our last night here. I wanted to feel my family out. Was there redemption?

We gather our belongings, and I am about to suggest we make a few trips when she pulls out of her trunk an old *Radio Flyer*. The one I bought the kids when they were younger. I smile and she smiles back. I turn away because I feel the allergies kicking in. I hear her laugh when I turn around.

"Dad."

Without turning around, I answer back, "Yes."

"Can you help me load this up." She doesn't seem annoyed, but I think she knows I am not going to turn back around just yet.

When I finally pull myself together, I turn around to see her zipping up her large duffle bag. She slings it on her shoulder as I walk towards her and help load things up.

"I got it." She holds the duffle bag tight against her and I want to ask what's in there.

"Ok, let's head this way. I don't need to look at the directions on my phone."

We head straight for the campsite. I know this place, as I've been here before. Now I am even more confused as to why my daughter picked it. It infuriates me when she plays these games. She knows so much about everyone. Somehow, she has been able to be on everyone's good side and bad side simultaneously. She's good like that. I just wonder how much she knows.

This weekend would be the perfect opportunity to deal with Ale, despite wanting to just avoid her altogether. She's been blackmailing me for some time now. It started with a few hundred bucks here and there. I didn't question why she needed it; I knew she had a rough life, but I suspect she may have been into drugs. It's now a few thousand dollars every time she reaches out. With a few thousand in cash, I hope to get rid of her one way or another.

While we walked, there was small talk with my daughter, nothing too intense. I don't want to overwhelm her or cause any discomfort. I need to gauge whether she knows I've been here before, but I get no signs she knows. She's good at hiding things though, so I don't close off that thought.

We approach and I can hear the family, so I let Gina walk

ahead of me. She picked this place, and her taking lead won't give away that I have been here before.

As we enter the area, I see my family, but my son isn't there.

"Is Jayson here?"

"He went with his...he went with David to get some wood so we can start the fire." My wife stops mid-sentence and corrects herself. Was she about to say his boyfriend?

"Oh, David came along."

"Yes, he met me and Jayson up here. He was here when we pulled up."

The voice sends me into a cringe, as I know exactly who just spoke. My heartbeat races and I turn to see her—Ale. I wish she would find another family. I walk over to where she is to greet her, whispering in her ear, "We'll talk later." I look around and take in everything. It brings me to the fifth thing I have been thinking of.

I've been thinking about ending my own life for a while. It will free me and my family from everything. The financial burden would be over, and everyone would be left with something. I wouldn't have to deal with telling them the financial state of the family's affairs. It would bring the list down to nothing. This one simple act would erase everything else I was thinking of doing this weekend.

A part of me wanted to be dramatic and do it this weekend. I'd planned it. I brought my gun with me. I wouldn't do it in front of everyone. I would do it while they were asleep. I don't want to traumatize them that much. I don't want to do that to them at all, but I do want to free them from myself. Free them from all the pain I have caused them.

I look over and see my son and David. David comes straight over to me like he's known me forever and gives me a hug. I return the gesture. Have I just made the decision to the fifth thing on my list?

CHAPTER 21

GINA

The drive was quick, and since I had done it already, I knew where to go. I still had my GPS on for comfort. I tried to enjoy the drive, but I had a sense of impending doom. I drove in a daze, watching the landscape pass. I almost missed some of the cutest roadside animals and some not-so-cute animals dead on the side of the road. Driving distractedly, I almost missed a turn or two, I even went the wrong way for a short period of time as my GPS kept re-calibrating. As much as I tried to focus on something good or positive, my mind was brought back to years and years of family drama. How will this weekend play out? Will we all get along? Can I get away with everything? Can I save my family? Or will I destroy everything?

Playing the fixer is my role which I enjoy. I don't like it when we fight, and I don't like to see anyone upset. I like to make a game out of things, which is why I prepared the bags that I am going to pass out later. They are filled with things meant to bring everyone together.

The GPS alerts me as I turn. I am glad I recognize the area, as the signal is bad out here. No signal means the less we are distracted and the more we can focus on each other. I turn into the drive and notice how beautiful everything looks. It's not long before I am turning into the area where several cars are parked.

Dad's already there when I pull up. It didn't take long for us to get our things together. His face when I pulled out the *Radio Flyer* was priceless. I got it earlier in the week. I had stopped at the house to grab it, even rummaging through some of our old toys as I was searching for it. I knew where mom kept it. She kept everything. She had a hard time getting rid of anything, but it was even harder to get rid of our things.

As I loaded up the Radio Flyer, I could see that my dad remembered it, the look on his face full of memories. He was getting choked up. I could see the tears building in his eyes as I watched them turn to glass. Not wanting to lug everything over to where the campsite was and make two trips, I asked him to help me load it up. This was a distraction from the emotions I saw taking over him. After we were ready and he had gathered himself together, we headed towards where everyone was. It didn't take long to find them.

Mom was there with Victor, Cat, and Ale. They all were doing something different when we walked in on them. Apparently, Jayson and David were grabbing some wood for the fire. It was getting late, and we needed to get things set up. I was starving and I am sure everyone else was too. Knowing my family, they were too nervous to worry about food, so everyone most likely ate little to almost nothing. Most likely surviving off beef jerky.

Ale was there not doing anything really, which I found annoyance in. I had been told about her coming ahead of time, so this wasn't a surprise, but I still don't know how I feel about her. I am not her biggest fan, but she hasn't done anything wrong to me. It's clear that my dad isn't a fan either. I saw the way that he went up to greet her. Why her? Why did he go up to her first? Mom was standing there and watched this interaction play out. Victor noticed it too, yet no one questioned it. There is something there between them, and I hope it isn't anything inappropriate. It is the last thing this family needs. Ale has a way with men that we are all aware of. People talk and they love to talk about her.

Things get even weirder as I turn when I hear both Jayson and David return. David is hugging and shaking my dad's hand, and they are talking. Jayson sees this too, and I can tell he has some questions of his own. Why is this happening? What is going on? How do we stop this?

Dad always has motives, so I feel like there is a motive here. Dad wants something, but I just cannot figure out what it is. The walk over to the campsite was weird. I noticed how he took the lead and then halfway through slowed down and we switched places, leading him to the campsite. I notice these things because I like to think of myself as an observer having spent a lifetime watching everyone around me including my family.

As we always did it was a lot of small talk. He asked about work, and I asked him about the office. The conversation didn't last long so we moved on and he told me about his favorite tv shows. He talked about the maid, and I only listened. We all knew that there might have been something going on with her and I just wanted to ignore that topic and so I stayed quiet as he talked about the things, she did for him. I answered any question he threw my way because nothing he asked came off as too personal. The conversation felt disconnected, but it usually felt this way. You would think we were friends and not father and daughter. Everyone had weird relationships in our family.

The bag I packed is heavy and I toss it to the ground. There isn't anything breakable in it. Just everything I need for the weekend. The bags I made for everyone are in the duffle bag on my shoulder. I am going to pass them out tonight when everyone's sleeping.

There are some fun things inside there. It isn't all scary, as I am sure they will think when they wake up to find them. I'm debating if I'll be here when they wake up as I haven't figured that part out yet. Looking around, I scout out a place to set up my tent. Once I spot the perfect location away from everyone, I ask for help.

"So, who is going to set up my tent?"

David is the first to offer to help. Leave it to David to be the first to speak up. He is overly caring and pretty handy. I look over at Jayson and smile, giving him a wink.

Jayson and David's on-again-off-again relationship is no secret to me. I want them to be more, and when Jayson smiles back, I think that something has happened. I caught it earlier when mom almost slipped and called David Jayson's boyfriend, so I think it's clear. They are finally together; my other guess is that we are all just waiting for it to happen.

Everything is going well so far, as we got everything set up in a pretty quick time. We fired up the grill and made some burgers. I can see the exhaustion on everyone's faces, and I feel it too. It's early evening and I want to take a nap, but I am sure that this nap would turn into me sleeping the whole night. I decided to ask Ale to come on a quick walk with me. I want to ask her what that was about earlier—the exchange between her and my father.

"I need to use the powder room. Ale, will you come with me?"

"You're speaking my language. But there is no powder room here. We just have to keep an eye out for snakes and bears." She gets up with no hesitation, her mouth twisted into a grin, and goes into her bag, grabbing something. I don't see what it is as she's concealed it tightly in her grip, placing her hands quickly in her pocket.

"There are no bears or snakes." I know this because I was here already. At least no poisonous snakes, just those garden snakes—and Ale.

I don't wait to bring it up, and when we are far enough away from the family, I come right out and ask her, not tiptoeing around it.

"What did my father say to you?" I pause because I don't want her to lie. "I know he told you something and I want to know what it is."

"In due time, all will find out G." I hate it when she calls me that.

"Look, I have plans for this weekend." I am about to keep going when she stops me.

"We all have plans for this weekend, G. I think you need to let everyone else do what they came here to do because it is important. Don't get in the way or you'll lose everyone. I am sure you don't want that to happen. Something tells me you are trying to fix them. They need to work on themselves. You can't do that for them." She's on to something. I can't repair my family. They need to figure things out on their own and do something quick because we can't go on like this. The longer this goes on, the more resentment we will have for one another.

"I wasn't trying to fix them, but I wanted them to see we can still make this work. Make our family work. I know we aren't as fucked up as other families. I mean, look at your family." I regret it as soon as it comes out of my mouth. Ale was not trying to be a bitch. She was trying to give me good, sound advice, and here I am insulting her.

"Ale, you're also a part of this family and we enjoy having

you around. At least, most of us do. That is why I want to know if you are screwing my dad."

"G, that's gross! No, I am not screwing your dad!" She looks mortified, disgusted. "But he is screwing someone or has been, and he needs to stop. I am not going to get involved, so that is all I am going to say, but something tells me he is going to come clean this weekend."

It's at this point we hear someone laugh. It was brief and harrowing, and scared us. A sound you hear in your dreams, a nightmarish laugh that raises the hair on the back of your neck. It was loud and then muffled, like someone tried covering it up. Someone's hand clasping against a wicked mouth, keeping the sound of laughter trapped within. With mixed thoughts, I think to myself that this is funny because my father would never come clean about anything, and now I want to laugh too. He is not the type of person who would admit to anything, nor would he try to apologize. My next thought sends shivers down my spine. *Someone else is out here. Someone else is nearby and watching.*

Ale and I look at each other, unsure of what to do next. Raising my finger to my lips, I point toward where we think the laugh came from. I take several steps forward and look around, not wanting to think that someone followed us. It could be Jayson or Victor, but I don't know why either of them would. I hear something within the bushes and take more steps forward. The sound of breathing is shallow and deep. Someone is trying to hide that they are beyond the bushes.

I wave Ale over to me because I don't want to go alone. Reaching out for her hand and feeling nothing as she refuses to grab it makes me furious. If she thinks I am going at this alone, she's wrong. Looking at her she shakes her head. I do not understand why she won't come close. It's just getting dark, so there is still daylight left. I shake my hand; she finally takes a few steps towards me and I feel the warmth of her fingers slip through my fingers. She's not holding it, rather her fingers, loosely intertwined with my four fingers, are almost childlike. Her grip almost slips and I grab a hold of her, dragging her closer. I can feel her pulse beating through her hands. She is sweaty and scared.

We hear movement and I see a blur dart deeper into the woods. Someone was there and now they are gone. We jump back because we know what we saw—it wasn't something; it was a person. Someone else is here, and with the camp in the other direction, we look at each other and start to run. The sooner we get back, the sooner we can see if it was someone from our group. The person running was too fast to be mom or dad, so that leaves four other possibilities.

CHAPTER 22

It was funny listening to what they were talking about, comedic in a way. I tried to cover my mouth to silence my giggles. Was it a mistake to get this close? Gina wouldn't try to explore where the sound came from, would she? Trying my best to muffle the sound of my laughter, I notice she glances over.

I take off running because the last thing I want is to get caught. She was feet away from me, so close I was sure she could smell the fear coming off me. I was afraid of getting caught and of not being able to finish what was started. I didn't come all this way to leave, only to have to plan all over again.

Should I be running the other way? A bit turned around and not sure exactly how to get back, I notice it's getting darker, which means if I get lost, I'll have to wait until morning. There wasn't an exact plan on which day it would happen. It was fun watching everyone, taking everything in and I could start tonight or tomorrow, there was no rush. There was enjoyment in the wait, a rush of adrenaline in the anticipation. I noticed that as soon as everyone arrived, they seemed different. They almost seemed to get along which was awkward, but interesting. It isn't long before I am *turned back around, and in the clear so I head towards my tent to consider what to do next.*

CHAPTER 23

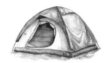

JAYSON

Needing a few minutes away, I make way towards my tent, but this time by myself. No one noticed me slip back in, which makes me think that no one saw me leave either. It was easy since everyone was getting food ready. There are times I wonder if we are busy or don't care enough about anyone else to notice when someone goes missing. I look around and I don't see Ale and my sister. All I see are my parents and siblings and David. I tried to get back before them in case they asked any questions. I am surprised I made it back before they returned themselves for a second. I had got turned around but found my way back and now need to figure out what I was going to do.

David is just walking around trying to do something on his phone and appears frustrated. He is swiping up on his phone and has that look. It's both anger and frustration—or gas, the thought causing a low chuckle to form. Before I know it, David catches me and smirks, noticing my little chuckle. He knows I just told myself some inside joke. I'm trying to get myself in a better mood but go back to conflicting thoughts. My original plan for the weekend seems to shift. Now I want a better life for myself and for David since we decided we're giving this a real shot. If he wasn't serious, he would not have met me out here. How will this weekend end? There is still a lot of mystery going on in the family that I sense with every one of us.

It's only been a minute when Gina and Ale come running. We all stop what we're doing and look over at them. Their breaths are heavy, hands on their knees, doubled over. I can see their chests rising and falling rapidly and they have beads of sweat around their hairline. I have never seen my sister or Ale look like this, with terror splashed across their faces and fear in their eyes. Ale is the first to point behind them. She is waving her finger and pointing, but it's Gina who speaks first.

"Someone was out there, someone was hiding and watching us." I can see how panicked she is as she is trying to get the words out. Looking over at my dad for a response, she seems to direct all her attention at him. It makes me wonder if she really thinks he cares or will do anything about it. He is not the savior she wants him to be. Not right now, not in this moment.

"Someone was watching you do what?" He seems a little angry at first.

"We weren't doing anything. We were standing there talking, and we heard someone, we heard someone laugh." The way she responds shows her annoyance with him already. How quickly things have shifted. She isn't looking for a savior; she's looking to prove to him she saw someone.

"You heard someone laugh?" My dad's confused, but keeps grinning as he goes back and forth with Gina.

"A laugh is a laugh; I don't understand what you're

saying. This place could be full of people." Cat jumps in and adds nothing to the conversation.

I cut them both off because if that was true, then why were there only our cars parked out there in the lot. We were the first to arrive and we assumed the car we saw was one of my sister's, but maybe it wasn't. Since no one else was here, whoever's car that was belonged to someone outside of our family. It's a weird coincidence that the cars matched, but I only realize it now. Ale seems spooked and she doesn't spook that easily.

"I felt someone was watching us earlier. There was a car here that I assumed was one of your cars, but since everyone came after us, someone else is here." Everyone is staring at me now. Is there something on my face? Do I not look convincing?

Dad walks towards Gina and places his hand on her shoulder. "It's going to be fine. I don't understand what all the panic is about. Didn't you pick this place? What could go wrong? Maybe someone walked up on you, saw something, got embarrassed and walked away. Were you two using the bathroom or...?"

"No, we were talking. We hadn't even had the chance to go yet." Gina looks pissed and pushes dad's hand off her shoulder, not sure what he was trying to imply.

"Well, what do you want to do, Gina? You dragged us all out here and you think someone else is out here camping. Is the weekend over? Can we all go home?" Dad's now annoyed, and it's clear he could easily just go home.

Gina looks around and then looks back at Ale, who seems to have calmed down a bit. I walk over to Ale, and dad walks away. He goes back to the food to finish cooking. As he walks away, he yells back, *"Let me know what to do."*

I need to know what they saw. Ale shakes her head and walks away. I follow her as she walks towards David who is standing near the tent we are going to share tonight. Is she really ignoring me? I want to grab her by the hair when she starts talking to David. I don't understand why she would be mad at me.

"We heard someone laughing, and then Gina walked over to see who was there. I wasn't going to follow her, but she grabbed my hand, then jumped, and it scared me. I didn't see anything." She looks at me as I approach her and David. "I'm sorry, I needed a minute." She is now looking at me as she is talking. She looks terrified and confused. David's eyebrows furrow, expecting me to say something.

"Hey, if someone else is out there, we can't really do anything. David and I came across someone's stuff out in the woods earlier. Maybe it was them. Maybe we're bothering them and we need to just keep to ourselves."

"Why didn't you tell me?"

"There was nothing to really tell. We thought we heard something too, but came back and everyone was here. We got caught up in this." I turn to look at the family. Ale pushes past me. I can feel the tension from the way she pushed me. She's pissed. David shakes his head and walks with her towards the food. Ale turns, blowing out air and releasing the tension built up inside her.

"Are you eating with us?"

She must not be too mad if she's asking me to join them. We sit in silence, eating. It's awkward and tense and I'm not sure where all the tension is coming from.

"Mr. Perez, how is everything going with work?" David is the first to break the silence.

My father doesn't like to talk about work, and this is going to piss him off.

"It's good, you know, it's work. What is it you do?"

Did I miss something? I know he was vague in his answer, but he wasn't an asshole. He didn't badger David or give him an attitude. They go back and forth a few times, and before you know, there are more side conversations going on.

After we finish eating, David and I head out to gather more wood. Ale and Gina are off to the side. They are talking intensely and watch as David and I walk into the woods. My mom and Cat are trying to build a fire while my dad stands off near his tent, laughing at them. If he could lean on his tent without him falling into it, he would. That's the stance he's giving. It irks me to see him watch them struggle when he can easily head over and help them out.

I grab David's hand and ask him how he thinks everything is going. It is important to me that he doesn't see my family as the bat-shit crazy people they are. He's met them and hung around them enough to know them, so I do not understand why I am putting this kind of pressure on myself. David has stuck around me and my family long enough, I am sure he is going to be fine.

"It seems to be going ok, but what do you think is up with Ale and Gina? The way they came running in its like I want to believe them, but Ale said she saw nothing. So, I don't know, but where did you go? One minute you were there, and the next gone?"

My hope of slipping away unseen apparently didn't work. I didn't know where this weekend was going to take us, and I had snuck off to the car to grab the condoms I kept in the glove box. I shouldn't expect anything like that to happen, but I want to be ready in case. Not wanting to tell him this, I make something up.

"Ale wanted me to check for her lip gloss. I told her I would go at some point and figured I would run and check while they were gone. Slip it in her bag." I am not doing a good job with this lie. He does that thing with his eyebrows again. They furrow and one shoots up like he's thinking. He's trying to decide if he should believe me.

"I thought you went back to grab condoms and shit." He pulls me closer and starts to kiss me.

Embarrassed and curious, I wonder, *Did he see me? Does he know?* I still have them in my back pocket. He squeezes my ass as he continues to kiss me. Pulling away, I laugh. They are in my other cheek pocket. "Hey now, watch it. We're in the company of my family."

"Hey now, hey now, this is what dreams are made of." He breaks out singing that Hilary Duff song and shaking his torso like she did in the movie. His face turns pink and I'm embarrassed for him, for us, as I join in and repeat the chorus mimicking his moves.

We take our time together gathering up more wood and still singing but this time we've moved on to another cheesy but amazing pop song. We're now belting out *Rumors* by Lindsay Lohan, singing the chorus in tandem. There is a part of me that's curious and wants to head back toward that tent we saw earlier. I want to ask David if we should go check it out. Maybe whoever it was is there now, or maybe we can get the confirmation that they left and that is what Ale and Gina saw—someone leaving. Gina might have exaggerated the whole thing to scare us. I decide to ignore that thought and pull David in again to kiss him.

"You're going to need to calm down with all that. If we take too long, they are going to come looking for us and who knows what they'll walk in on," David says in a naughty tone that makes my heart race.

"You're right, let's head back." I am a bit disappointed because I want to stay out here, alone with him. We share one more moment, and this time our bodies are pressed hard against each other, and I can feel all of David. I can tell he is excited to be here with me and I am too.

Sometimes, I can't keep my hands to myself when I am around David, and sometimes, I'm afraid to even talk to him.

That's part of the whole reason why we were on again off again. We were so busy with school and other things that I just never knew where things stood. I know there were times I wanted to be with him just for sex and sometimes more. We both dated on and off and never discussed being a couple. I guess we were both trying to figure things out. I think it's almost better that we didn't seriously date, because if we were ready—as I suspect we both weren't—it would have ended, and I could have lost him, and we wouldn't be here right now.

We're interrupted by the sound of an animal's howl. It is at this moment I realize how dark it is, suggesting we get back. I adjust myself and bend down to grab the wood we dropped on the ground before we had one more make-out session. It's at this level I see David adjust himself too. I look up at him; this angle is hot. David winks at me and we gather our wood one more time and head off.

CHAPTER 24

ALE

David and Jayson head off into the woods without telling anyone. Seeing them walk away is a good sight. I know I give Jayson shit for the relationship they have, but I do want to see him happy and right now I am. I'd be a bitch if I didn't want my best friend happy. Would I ever find someone who makes me happy? Would I find someone who will do the things that David does to Jayson? My mind, now, won't shake these thoughts as I realize how lonely I've become over the years.

They're up to something, I know it. When it comes to Jayson, anything can happen, and I am not sure I want to be witness to it. I want to continue the conversation Gina and I had earlier. We have a lot to talk about, and this appears to be the perfect time for that. I remember what happened earlier and I am shaken from the interruption.

Gina has questions. She's going to want to know what I know about her father. She is going to want to know who he slept with and I am not ready to answer that. If I do, I will have to give more information about the situation than I want to, but don't want her prying. She needs to give her father time to tell them and does she really think I am sleeping with him—Gross. I still haven't had the chance to talk to him, but I hope I can. I shot off a few texts earlier in the day, but that was it. His replies and lack of replies told me all I needed to know and how I needed to do this.

I look over at him as I talk to G, smiling at him, making sure he notices, but he's staring at Cat and Mrs. Perez as they try to start a fire. They're struggling and he just stands there in a James Dean like pose. He's mildly attractive, and he's in decent shape. If he wasn't an asshole, or my friend's father, maybe I would have accepted his advances in the past. Who wouldn't want a little dad-bod action? Do I have daddy issues? Of course I do, and maybe he can fulfill them.

Returning my attention back to Gina, who's been talking the whole time, I find myself lost in the conversation. Her words echoed in the background as I thought about everything else that had gone on or what will go on over the weekend. I don't want to ask her to repeat herself, so I go in.

"G, I really don't want to go into this with you, not right now. I want to be able to answer your questions and talk to you about it, but I need you to understand that your father must do what's right. It's why we're all here, isn't it?"

I want to put this back on her the way I am putting this all back on her father. It's up to him to do what's right and make this better. I'm merely helping with that. He needed the nudge to make things right. At his core, I don't think Mr. P is a complete asshole. He needs to work on so much, but I see he has some love in him. He loves his family but is caught up in so many other things that it makes it hard for him to focus on the things that are important. Jayson told me how they grew up middle class and only achieved a better status in life as his father's company grew. It had changed his father, but he had some of the asshole in him before. It just wasn't as bad as it is now.

"Do you really think that is going to happen?" She raises her voice a little, but no one seems to notice. "He doesn't give a shit about us." Tears well up in her eyes as I see water collect in the corners, but it doesn't make its way down her cheek. Not yet at least. She's holding back her feelings and although I know she's hurting right now, she's holding it in. That's dangerous for someone, especially her. "I hate him!" A tear finally glides down her puffy cheek.

I am sure he heard her this time because when I look over at him, his face is long. I've never seen his eyes look that way. A slight tingle forms in my chest, maybe he is going to make things right. Maybe I finally got through to him. As soon as he catches me looking at him, his face changes. His expression morphs and I almost don't recognize the person staring at me. It sends shivers down my spine.

I know this whole weekend was about Jayson finally setting boundaries with his family. I know he isn't serious about telling them he isn't going to speak to them again. He's been saying this for years. We've had conversations about this. Each time he says he is going to do it, but he doesn't. I do agree he needs time away from them and he does need to let them know how much he's been hurt. Not only by his father but everyone else. Momma P is the only one who honestly has been his rock. They have a bond I wish I had with my family.

I haven't spoken to my father since that night. My mother I saw up until she passed away. Cirrhosis of the liver, a horrible way to go. I remember her last moments in the hospital. I didn't miss her or have compassion for her, because I had watched her deteriorate for days in the hospital. In her final moment, the only thought that crept through my head was "bitch". I was angry that she didn't come after me. I was angry she didn't stand up to my father, and I was angry at her for giving birth to me. I am filled with so much anger; it's why my therapist says I act out. It's why I'm so hypersexual. I am getting all my anger out in other ways she says. She doesn't know about the aggressive sex I have or the men I've let push my boundaries in bed. I've not shared that part of me with anyone and I am not sure I ever will. There are still a lot of unresolved feelings going on inside me, which is why rehab seemed like a good idea this weekend, but I needed to be here with my other family because my best friend needed me.

I feel badly for Gina who now is staring blankly at me. I must have stopped listening again. She doesn't seem mad, but she is waiting for an answer. I don't have one to give. I reach out and cup her face and squeeze. "G, you'll be ok."

I notice as I get up from the conversation that Ms. P and Cat are in deep talks about something important. Our tent is close, and Victor is sitting outside of it. Knees propped and head between his legs. I figure this is how I can get close enough to listen. I sat down next to him.

"What do you want, Ale?"

"Just checking on you."

"Lower your voice. I can't hear them."

He's being nosey just as I am. I put my head on his shoulder and whisper, "I want to hear too. What's going on?"

"I am not sure, but I heard the words: money, leaving him, and this weekend." He rests his head on my head, and I feel something wet fall on my face. It's at this moment I realize he's crying.

"It's going to be ok." He's crying, and I try to make sure he doesn't see that I'm aware of it, but as another tear falls on my lips, I lick them, tasting his salty sorrow. "I can sleep in your tent tonight." This is purely platonic. I don't want him getting the wrong idea.

"I'd like that."

I don't care if anyone asks any questions, and I am ready for their looks. I'm sure his father will say something. It's his mother who I don't want to upset. I'll either wait until she's in her tent or I'll sneak in after everyone's gone to sleep. I'll let Victor know this later. We don't need to figure that part out now, because I want to get back to listening to them.

I'm not able to hear anything more, as they start talking about how to get the fire going. They've tabled the conversation for later it appears.

The boys return with the firewood and help Cat and Ms. P with the fire. It's time to get the evening started. Victor and I remain seated, but I no longer taste his tears as he'd stopped crying at some point. He's gone through a lot, and no one discusses what happened to him when he was a kid. Apparently, he doesn't remember. When the family realized he had no memories of it, they decided they wouldn't talk about it. I only know because Jayson told me about it. They've all done a great job at erasing the memory of this. Jayson sits next to us and David's right behind.

"Are you guys ready to scare Gina?" Jayson looks excited. I'm sure he's been thinking of stories to tell to creep her out. I just wonder what he's planning on saying to really get to her. I want to stop him, tell him that it's a bad idea because I'm still shaken up from earlier and what we thought we saw. I just want to go home, but Jayson and his stories are really good, and maybe we didn't see anything, maybe we spooked ourselves or one of them tried to scare us and won't admit to It. Convincing myself to let it go, I decide to just go with it and not say anything.

Together we discussed tonight's plan and the order in which we'll tell our stories. Victor's mood shifted when he volunteered to go to the bathroom at some point only to come back just in time to scare everyone. This really feels childish, but what else is there to do? I think I am only going through with it because I'm trying to change the mood. A part of me kind of wants to be here. This family is my family. I don't have what Jayson has, even though what he has is broken. *A broken family is still a family*, I say to myself. I don't know if I believe it, though, because that family should never want to hurt you.

I see Jayson get up. I wonder what he is going to do because it looks like he is about to say something. My heart skips a beat when I don't know what's going on. Did he just change everything up? He looks around before he opens his mouth.

"So, what are we doing tonight? Who is ready for some scary stories?" I take a deep breath because for a minute I thought he was about to blow everything up and finally tell them.

We gather around the fire. Cat and Mrs. P get the things we need to make S'mores, and Jayson and David cuddle up next to each other with a blanket. Despite what happened a few years ago, Jayson has the courage to be open with his sexuality. I see the looks that his father gives him and I can see he's conflicted. Sometimes those looks appear to want to hurt Jayson, while others are compassionate. I don't under-stand what goes on in someone's head when they don't have acceptance. I always say what goes on between two people is between them, unless you're dreaming of what goes on in their bed. If that's the case, that is more of a reflection of you and your own thoughts than it is of them.

Surprisingly, Victor starts things off and is followed by Gina, who is a little too eager to tell stories of her own. Some-thing I am sure she planned before we got here. We go around with Mr. and Mrs. P skipping their turns. I told the weakest story of the bunch, as I am not good at this. Reading and storytelling are Jayson's thing. Writing is something he's also good at but does nothing with it. He says it's because it won't take him anywhere, but I disagree. He has a lot of potential he doesn't tap into. That's something I should work on with him, but right now, he needs to tell us a story because it's his turn.

CHAPTER 25

JAYSON

It's my turn to tell a story. I've read plenty of books and pulled from some of my favorite stories. I've been thinking about tropes all morning. Where do I want this story to go? I know I need this to be creepy because I need something that will scare Gina. While Ale and David smile, I know my task and they are ready for theirs. Victor has a role in this too. He'll wait for my cue to get up and go to the bathroom. It's up to him to time it perfectly and make sure he's back at the right time. I look around at my family who are all eager to continue with the evening's tales. I prepare myself and take a deep breath.

It was something the three of them spent their Saturday nights doing, meeting every weekend in the graveyard. They'd been friends since they were three years old, and growing up in a small town where there weren't many other kids, this trio bonded right away. Camilla, Isabella, and Mariana. It had been Camilla's idea to meet there. The town was small, with limited places to meet where their families wouldn't find out. It started because Camilla got in trouble for staying out late with the girls and ended in a week's long grounding. Camilla still wanted to spend time with her friends and asked them to meet up. The graveyard was the easiest but also the creepiest.

It was just another Saturday night, nothing out of the ordinary. Camilla shot off the first text to Mariana and then to Isabella, letting them know she could get out of the house. Camilla was no longer grounded, but her parents kept a close eye on her.

As soon as they met up, it was time to gossip. They talked about who was dating who and what they had done that day. They did this while making laps around the different headstones.

They would sometimes stop and make up stories about the markers in the graveyard. Giving a life to the people behind the grave. Camilla always made up the goriest of tales. Mariana kept the stories dark and depressing. While Isabella told stories with happy endings—with someone dying peacefully in their sleep unbeknownst to the individual themselves.

The entrance to the graveyard was off the main road and a black iron-rod fence surrounded it. The fence had pointed tips. If you could break off one bar, you'd be able to throw it like a javelin and pierce someone's heart, killing them instantly, while propping them on display.

The graveyard sits near the forest in an area where ninety percent of the land is trees and forest. The people of the town didn't understand why anyone settled here or why the area hadn't changed or redeveloped. It's pretty if you stay on the trails, but the graveyard is right in front of the densest area.

The trio never ventured their way into the woods before, because of the stories everyone told. Stories of alien abductions, a creepy cabin that appeared out of nowhere, or the axe murderer who lived alone with his inbred family. The forest goes on for miles, and there was always fear that if they went in, they wouldn't come out. It was easy to get lost, and it's happened *before. They would find the bodies of those who entered decayed, starved, and alone.*

"Let's go into the woods."

"Cam, are you crazy? Didn't you just hear that Sue from English class's cousin was missing for weeks and finally turned up dead? In these woods. I don't even know why we're here."

"Did you hear they found him decapitated?"

Isabella says this, interrupting Mariana, who looks stunned at this admission. They all look at each other but don't immediately say anything. You would think this would be the time they would leave.

"Come on, guys, you know he was into some nasty shit. That whole family has a history, you know. Who do you think sells the drugs to everyone in this damn town?"

The three of them don't argue this and finally give in to Camilla's idea to explore the wooded area.

"Look, we'll stay close, and once we can't see the graveyard, we'll go back. It's not that dense, so let's go in and see what's all going on in there for ourselves."

They agree and enter the woods.

I pause here to check and see if everyone is still paying attention and signal for Victor to get up. He makes his way into the woods for his bathroom break and to my surprise no one notices. He doesn't announce it, but he doesn't do it in a sneaky way. Everyone is focused on the sugary treats mom is making for us and the story I am telling. I think it's safe to return to the story. I look over to Ale and David to see if they noticed Victor leave, and they don't seem to have noticed. This is really working. I am not deep into the story yet, barely cracking the surface, so I am surprised at everyone's level of attention.

It isn't long before the three were deep in the woods. Camilla continuously checked behind her to make sure they never went too deep, but something was happening in these woods. It was almost like the woods were changing around them. Camilla was the first to notice and say something.

"Guys, stop, something feels weird."

"What's wrong?" Mariana looked around and now saw it. The woods didn't appear to look the same anymore. It was as if they'd lost track of time and ended up miles in. The dense forest around them allowed very little light through, and it was pitch dark. The flashlight they each held barely allowed them to see a few feet in front of them. They all looked around, each beam hitting a wall of trees.

"I knew this was a bad idea." Isabella panicked, her breathing now quick panting. Her chest moved up and down, and the other two didn't know what to do. She shook when they heard a guttural scream. That snapped them to attention.

They looked at one another, each afraid to move. Isabella was the first to take a few steps back. She was staring at the other two, fear in her eyes.

"What is it?" Camilla yelled at her. She tried to move, but her feet stayed planted firmly on the ground. "Isabella, you're scaring me."

It was at this moment both Camilla and Mariana turned to see what Isabella was staring at. When they turn back around, she was gone.

I look up and see everyone is quiet. No one is moving—they are waiting for me to continue. Dad looks invested in my story; I hope Victor is close because we are getting to the part in the story where he needs to jump out.

Both Mariana and Camilla couldn't move. They could only twist their bodies to look around. Fear had taken hold of them, and *then they heard another scream. This time they knew it was their friend Isabella.*

Victor comes in with a guttural yell, interrupting the story. "AAHHHHHHH."

I wanted to get just a little further into the story. The biggest part was just coming up, but it seems to have done the job because Gina is now screaming like someone has just tried to kill her. My mom's reaction was to shriek, but that turned into laughter, upsetting Gina.

"What the fuck, Victor?" Gina gets up, and she looks like she is ready to punch him. She gets really close when mom jumps in.

"Settle down you two." She says this in a stern voice, but then begins to laugh. Her laugh is infectious, and it's when she snorts, we all start laughing, including Gina.

"Ok, you got me. Did you guys' plan this?"

"Maybe."

I look over at David, who is smiling now. Leave it to him to admit and shift the blame. Gina can't be mad at him, but when she starts to walk over to him, I am worried she is going to smack him.

"I guess you're in. Welcome to the family." She leans in and gives him a hug and then playfully punches his arm. I look over and see my dad is even laughing. All tension now seems to lift, and I think to myself that this could be the moment where all things start to change. Maybe my family could be a family after all. Maybe I don't need to do or say anything this weekend. It's weird, but something is happening—something in these woods is changing us.

We spent the rest of the night making small talk. Dad's asking David questions about school and work. Mom and Victor are having their own conversation and laughing. The rest of us go back and forth, talking about nothing, until we begin to yawn. I look down at my watch to check the time. It's just after midnight, and I am tired and want to go to bed.

Mom and Cat are the first to get up and go to bed. They are sharing a tent, as Dad has his own. It doesn't surprise me that my parents won't be sharing. They don't share a bed at home, so why would they share anything like that out here?

Dad announces a bathroom break before he goes to bed. Ale gets up to follow. I say nothing as Gina gives her a dirty look. I notice this, but I don't want to know. I trust Ale enough that it means nothing. She just doesn't want to be out there alone. I don't trust my dad, but Ale can handle her own. If anything, he needs to be worried she'll kick his ass if he tries anything.

"I'm going to bed; you guys can wait for Dad and Ale to come back. Victor, you're staying up?"

"No, I'll wait for them to get back and then head off to bed. I don't want to leave these two alone in case something comes out for them. Isabella might come back and get them." His laugh is cut short when Gina punches his arm.

She gets up and heads off to her tent. It isn't long before both my dad and Ale return. I noticed that as they came back neither were talking to one another and were gone for only a few minutes. He heads straight for his tent and tells us all to have a good night.

Ale heads for Victor's tent. I am not sure what that's about, but then Victor gets up and follows. I don't want to go in after them and I don't call out after Ale. She's a grown woman, and he's a grown man, despite being my little brother. A part of me almost wants to grab the condoms out of my back pocket and chuck them at them. The last thing either of them need is a kid.

I look at David, a bit confused and relieved because now we'll finally be alone. We put out the fire with a gallon of water someone had gotten earlier. The area has some useful amenities but no showers or bathrooms. That is up to the forest to handle. I am not sure I want to even get to where I need to take a shit. Maybe I'll just get in the car and drive the thirty minutes back to town or head towards the gas station where I saw Enrique, the store's clerk.

After we put the fire out and make sure things are put away to avoid little creatures coming in the middle of the night, we head for our tent. I take one last look around when David pulls me inside. It's a bit aggressive, but his aggression does something to me.

I'm sitting there looking at him thinking that I am the luckiest guy in the world to have met a friend as good as him and even luckier that we're going to give this a chance. Now that we're alone, it's the best time to let him know what my intentions were for this weekend. I also want to let him know that I have changed my mind. I want to work things out with everyone because something is happening in these woods. Maybe Gina was on to something by picking this place. As I consider telling him, I don't know if I want to spoil the moment, because I want to kiss him. Instead, though, I decide to pass on both and get ready for bed.

He leans in to kiss me after I pull off my shirt and change into my tank top. I kiss him back and help him out of his shirt. We lay there kissing each other, our hands moving over each other's bodies. He reaches around to grab me again when he feels what's in my back pocket. I pull away embarrassed. I had forgotten to take the condoms out of my pocket and now he's found them.

"Jayson comes prepared."

"It's not what you think."

"What do you think I am thinking?"

"I didn't expect anything."

"Jayson, I am messing with you. We've had sex before and

we will have sex again. I just want you to know it won't be tonight."

"Oh." I'm taken back by this.

"I am tired because I couldn't sleep last night. I felt awful for telling you that I couldn't come the first time, so I stayed up all night debating if I should come or call you first, and then I had this wild idea to just show up. I am so glad I did. So, it isn't anything except I want to have enough energy to be with you. All of you." He seems genuine and apologetic that this is how the night will go.

"I love you, David."

"I've always loved you, Jayson. I wish you knew that a long time ago, but I guess it doesn't matter now."

That escalated quickly. I've never told anyone I loved them before. I am glad that he was my first. I think everything is going to be ok from here on out, and if it isn't, I always have David.

We finished changing, and while sleeping nude would have been preferred, we opted to sleep in our tank tops and our underwear because it is cold out. This is going to be an impossible night because David looks great with half his clothing off. We lay down looking at each other before we drift off to sleep, not talking or saying anything else. This is exactly what I wanted this night to be. We both smile at each other, and he soon drifts off to sleep. When I stopped at his place before picking up Ale, I didn't see his car, and I'm so glad he wasn't there. I had wanted to ask him again if he would reconsider coming with me, but it looks like he was on his way up here already. If he had been home, would things have turned out differently? Could I have convinced him to come? Looking over at him, I bite my lip wondering if I should wake him or just let tonight end where it's already ended. My eyes feel heavy as I continue to overthink everything and then drift off to sleep.

We're woken up by the sound of someone screaming. I can't tell who it is because I was in a deep sleep and dreaming of David and me somewhere on a beach. I scramble to put on my pants, knocking over the water bottle, the contents inside spilling everywhere. David is already dressed and trying to get out of the tent. I am putting my shoes on when I notice his feet are bare and dirty. I throw him his shoes and take over the zipper, but it's stuck on the tent. I try pulling and it only opens a few inches. How did this happen? I hear another scream when David puts his fingers in the opening and tears open the tent flaps, separating the teeth of the zipper. My initial thought is that he's damaged the tent, not that someone might need help.

As soon as we're out of the tent, I sense that everyone else is struggling in the same way as I hear grunting and the sound of everyone's tent zippers trying to be freed. It's dark out so I cannot see what might have caused them to get stuck. I rush over to where I hear my mom and sister arguing while dad starts swearing somewhere in the background. As soon as I reach them, I notice that the zippers aren't stuck. Someone had put zip ties on them, locking them in place, trapping us inside. Victor has his open and is stepping out with Ale and they rush over to Gina's tent.

"Who the fuck put these on the tents?"

"We're locked in here."

"No, just wait." I pull as hard as I can until they snap. I

am sure my fingers are red because it takes a lot of force to break apart the plastic trapping them inside. As I'm pulling apart the tent listening to the sound of the teeth break once again, Cat pushes past me to get out and falls on the ground.

"What is going on, who was that screaming?" Cat is crawling on the ground in a dramatic fashion like she just escaped from someone on the inside of her tent. I think this is an overreaction when we hear the scream for a third time.

"Is that Gina?" My dad looks worried and rushes over to help Victor and Ale, both of whom seem to be taking their time trying to open Gina's tent. I notice no movement on the inside. She is either fast asleep or something is wrong. Dad pushes them to the side and rips open the tent with one swift movement.

Ale screams and when I peer over her shoulder, the tent is filled with blood.

CHAPTER 26

I woke up in a bit of a panic. I checked the time, and it was still early enough in the evening. I was asleep for what, an hour? As I sit up, I hear the night and the hoot of an owl and it grounds me. The panic subsides. I only wanted to rest my eyes. I hadn't expected that I'd fall asleep. It had been a long day and an even longer evening, but I didn't want to miss my chance. I get dressed quickly, quiet because I don't want anyone to wake up. I need to slip out as silently as I can because the slightest sound can ruin everything out here. If someone is awake, they can hear me.

I walk around the campsite running my hands along the vinyl on each tent. The sound of my fingers caressing the material gives off the slightest sound of calm. I hear the owl again as it interrupts me. I trace my fingers alongside the zippers on the tent. Feeling the metal and the smooth bumps of the teeth. It's time to seal them inside.

I quietly zip tie each tent. Carefully trying to avoid any sound. The slightest noise may wake someone up, so I take my time, pausing after each click the zip tie makes until it is completely shut. I was afraid my breathing might wake someone up, so I hold my breath, releasing it at the same time there's a click.

I had been waiting for a sign on who would be the first to fall victim to what I had planned so when I heard Gina get up, I knew it had to be her.

I quickly try to find a place to hide. I first go behind a tree, but if she is about to head off into the woods, she'll run into me. I can't have her screaming. Not yet. I look around and see the boys' tent and decide to hide there. The woods are dense behind it, so I know she won't go this way. I watched her head out and walk around the fire pit. This was a good place to hide. The tent is big enough to cover me. I try to calm down, calm my breathing. My breathing is shallow, slowed. I take a deep breath to further calm myself down and exhale loudly. I tense, hoping no one heard that.

I watch her walk off into the woods. I think about following her, but I want to make it harder for everyone to get out. I quickly finish securing everyone's tents and go back to my hiding place. I work quicker this time around, not conscious of the sounds I might be making. I wait for her to return. She doesn't go straight back into her tent. Instead she sits near the drowned-out pit from earlier.

She starts to cry. Though my heart breaks for her, I am not having second thoughts. I want revenge. I am out for one thing—to finally help a friend.

When she's finally done crying, she heads back to her tent. I grab the closest thing to me. A rock. It was about two to three pounds with jagged edges. I don't want to kill her—not yet. I just need to get her away from here.

She's about to turn around and close the tent when we meet face to face. Our eyes lock. Her face is frozen in terror. I take the rock and swing it into her—it only takes one hit to knock her out. She falls back with a thud and not a single sound exits her lips. I glance around, checking to see movement from anyone else. The sound of the rock connecting with her face and the sound of bones breaking makes my blood turn to ice. I look down and see the blood pooling all around her. I take a deep breath and I drag her out of her tent.

CHAPTER 27

GINA

I woke up because I had the to urge to use the bathroom. Despite needing to go before I went to bed, I didn't want to follow Ale and my father, so I waited. Still unsure of what's going on and what Ale knows about him, I can't help but think she's involved. I'm sure she's up to something and I need to figure it out but first, I need to pee.

I put on my socks and shoes and slowly unzip the tent, making sure I don't make too much noise. Light creeps into my tent highlighting what little I brought with me. The moon is bright and there is just enough light for me to see the vague shadows around. The outlines of tents, trees, and our belongings. My body aches because sleeping on the hard ground is new. We haven't done this in a very long time. I stretch and wonder what everyone else is doing. Is anyone awake or are they all fast asleep? I want to go up to each tent and listen to their breathing. Check to see if they are in some dream state and not worrying like I am.

I look around the campsite and wonder how we got here.

How I got here and why my family is such a mess. All families have drama, but what about those families on TV? Why can't we be like them? I walk around the fire pit, staring at the remains of yesterday's fun, and then head off into the woods.

I come back and it's the same as when I left. Things don't change that quickly, I remind myself. My family won't change either. Not that fast, but maybe this weekend can be the start of something new.

I sit near the fire with my knees to my chest and hands under my chin. It's cold out here, and I feel something wet fall on my hand. I look up at the sky and put both hands out. It wasn't supposed to rain this weekend. That's when I notice I'm crying.

I take a few minutes, but get myself together and head back to my tent. This impromptu cry fest wasn't on my list of things to do this weekend. It's too cold and I am getting anxious and considering just leaving as I stand in front of my tent.

Taking off my shoes, I put them inside the tent. The ground is soft, and my feet sink into the dirt. I'm going to need to take those off when I get back inside. The last thing I want is to dirty my sleeping bag.

There's an eerie feeling coming over me as I sense someone or something behind me. My heartbeat begins to race and fear floods my veins. I turn around and am face to face with someone. It's hard to make out who it is. Frozen in fear, I open my mouth to scream. Then pain. Then darkness.

I wake up with a pounding headache. Raising my hand, I try to wipe my forehead but realize my hands are tied behind my back. I can't see what's in front of me, but I sense someone pacing back and forth. The person in front of me is mumbling something to themselves, making it harder to focus. Everything is blurry and I smell something metallic, the taste of salt in my mouth. My lips are coated with dried blood—my blood. My face is throbbing and feels like it's on fire. My nose feels like it's broken. Trying to speak, I notice my mouth is swollen, making the words sound muffled. When I finally get a few words out, the person in front of me stops and it gets quiet.

"Why are you doing this?" I wait for some sort of answer, but all I hear is heavy breathing followed by footsteps that turn into a light jog. Whoever was here was now gone and I'm alone. I scream and hear footsteps coming back. They are faint at first, and then the sound echoes like a stampede. I am afraid whoever is coming is going to tackle me, and then it gets quiet again. Whoever it is stops in front of me and I see the outline of only one person. Unsure if it's a man or a woman or someone in my family, I try squinting, hoping it would help my vision. Nothing takes shape or looks familiar because their face is covered, concealing their identity, making me feel like something is about to happen.

"Please let me go."

"Sssshhhhh."

"I don't understand." I start to cough and spit blood, feeling like I am choking on myself. The blood will not stop. It trickles down my face and into my mouth. My nose has to be broken. I feel them put their hand on my neck and I thrash back and forth. I am secured tightly in the chair by my waist. I can't make my way out of its tight grasp and feel pressure on my shoulders. I begin to scream, and when I finally am able, my voice breaks through. I manage one good scream before they squeeze my neck and what feels like breaking my windpipe. The pain is excruciating and I take a few gasps of air, but whatever energy was left in me is gone. All I can do is cry, and I feel the tears fall down my cheek. I can feel myself fading and I think I'm dying.

Whoever it is, is now walking away. I want to make sure they are far enough away before I try again to scream. I debate if it's even worth it since I cannot defend myself. About ten minutes after they walk away, I test out my voice and there is still some of it there. I need to get enough strength to scream again before I'm no longer able to. If I am going to die tonight, I'm not going without a fight. I get one test scream out which is louder than before.

I wait a moment, just to make sure I don't hear them coming back. Lightheaded after that last scream, I try to find some strength and feel some of it coming back. There might even be enough in me for one more scream, so I need to make sure it's a good one. I open my mouth and I do it. I know someone heard me this time. Everything fades once more. *That's it, I'm out.*

CHAPTER 28

I just wanted her to shut up and I didn't think she would wake up so fast. She was heavier than I thought as I dragged her out of the tent and threw her over my shoulder. Dead weight isn't just an expression—she felt lifeless, and it excited me. I tried running to the spot I had chosen earlier but was immediately out of breath. I should have practiced for this, who would have known that murder would be such a workout.

I quickly bound her feet together and tied her hands behind her back. I set the light on the ground so that I can see better. I brought chairs along with me to place each one of my victims in. I wanted them in a circle to be able to watch one another. I had imagined them apologizing and spilling their secrets like they were in round circle discussion. Each one telling their side of the story or whatever story they felt they needed to get out.

I think back to the night at the restaurant. I still couldn't believe it. How could they stand by and watch and listen to him and not say anything. I want to make my way back before anyone gets up and my hope is she won't wake up again. I had tried not to squeeze too tight because I didn't want her dead at least not yet. Once I feel that it's safe to head back, I take off running leaving the flashlight behind, illuminating her as if she was a doll on display, my work, my masterpiece.

I make it back to the campsite and it appears quiet. No one must have had heard her scream. I walk over and look inside her tent admiring the scene, it's such a mess inside. Her blood is everywhere and that's when I am interrupted by her scream.

CHAPTER 29

JAYSON

It's a confusing scene in front of me and I don't know what's happening right now. It's dark and I can see a small pool of blood in the center of her tent. A metallic scent fills my nose as Victor bends down and crawls inside. A part of me wants to stop him, but I don't and slowly back up as he calls out for her. He sounds like a little boy lost from his mother, his voice cracking out of fear. When he surfaces, he stands in front of us with a blank expression which sends shocks through me. My sister is gone.

Ale turns on the flashlight, shining it at him, and he's covered in her blood. It's a gruesome sight reminding me of Carrie, her blood dripping down the front of his shirt. I can see a sticky string of blood forming lines off the edges of his shirt, elongating before they fall onto the dirt as tears stream down his face in a silent cry.

"Victor, get over here." He's confused and disoriented, and I want answers as I call him away from the grim scene.

"She's not in there." Stuttering those words, he bursts into sobs, inhaling and exhaling as he goes into a panic.

"Where the hell is she? Gina!" I scream her name in hopes I'll hear something in return and we can figure out what's going on.

Victor slowly walks away from the tent and directly into Ale's arms. As he passes me, I don't know whether to smack him or push him as if it's his fault, even though I know it's not. Mom screams, and when we look in her direction, she's falling to her knees. David rushes to help her while Dad is standing there, not moving with traces of blood on him too. He must have got some on him when he pushed us to the side and peered into her tent, as I can see traces of it on the outside of it. Whatever happened here made a mess of everything.

Ale pulls Victor in as he breaks down even further, hugging him tightly. When she pulls away, she's covered in blood too. It's dark and almost everyone is now covered in blood except for me, my mom, and David. I don't know why, but I feel like something is wrong with this picture.

"We need to get help." Racing back inside my tent, I look for my phone but can't find it. I turn over my sleeping bag and rummage through the bags we brought with us, unsure of where I last put it. The last time I remember having it was when we walked into the area. Could I have set it down somewhere and have forgotten it? I call for David and ask him for his phone. He tosses it and when I frantically press the buttons, I realize it's dead. It's useless, and I toss it back to David as he clumsily catches it trying to power it on himself. When I look over, mom and dad are trying on their phones. Waiting for a response, they look at me and I know there phones have died too. I don't even wait for them to tell me.

Victor and Ale head inside the tent they were sharing. The sticky substance all over them is going to leave a trail over everything. Cat is all over the place when both come out trying to call for help on their phones. Looking pissed, it's obvious neither of theirs is working.

"My phone died as soon as we got here. I forgot to ask one of you for a backup charger before we went to bed." I can barely see her, only hear her from where she's standing in the dark. She offers this up before any of us ask her.

"We need to leave and get help." It's the obvious thing to do, but I do not want to leave my sister.

"I am not leaving Gina!" It's the first time mom says anything.

"I need to find her." Dad looks pissed. "And when I find out who did this…" He stomps his foot like a baby. "I swear!" He doesn't even finish his sentence as I'm sure he doesn't know what he'd do.

The way he says this sounds fake and forced. I was sure he would be the first one running. Maybe he should be the one to go to the car and get help as he's never added value to anything and I am sure he won't now. But would he come back? I want to suggest we split up—some of us go for help while the others go look for Gina—but I am not sure exactly where the scream came from. It is then I notice a backpack in front of everyone's tents. It looks familiar but I don't recall where I've seen it.

"What is that over there?"

Mom walks over and bends down, picking up a bag, as she beings to rummage through it.

"Bring that over," she signals to me, "I can't see what's inside."

I walk over and grab one of the bags as everyone follows. Ale speaks first as she holds open a piece of paper and shines the light on it to read it.

"Sometimes the past has its good memories, sometimes it has its bad memories. This weekend we will figure it all out.

At least some of us will." She looks up and glances around at all of us.

"Is this some kind of joke?" David's pissed and I've never seen him like this before. "Is this a sick joke?"

"This isn't funny, Gina!" Ale is screaming at this point.

"I don't think this is a joke; that blood didn't look fake, and that scream didn't sound fake either." We're all looking at each other, confused, not sure what to do.

"Gina said she had something planned." Ale's tone shifts to annoyed and is no longer screaming.

"Gina, you come out right now!" Cat, looking around, deciding which direction to go, "I am going to find her."

Cat walks off before I can stop her. I'm about to yell for her to come back when I instinctively reach out to stop David from going after her. If this is a joke, Cat might be in on it. The last thing I want is David mixed up in some sort of sick and twisted joke or even worse, getting hurt. I look at David and then back at the bag when we both realize what we're holding. This isn't the first time we've seen this; it was earlier today in that tent. I don't want to say it yet, but I want to talk to David because something is definitely off.

It's a shame no one goes after Cat, and I am pissed. Neither Victor nor my dad do anything. I look over at everyone and make a decision.

We all must be having the same thoughts right now. Someone needs to go for help and I'm not sure any of them are able or capable of that. When it comes to the sheer panic of the situation, I'm sure that I am the only one who can manage to stay calm in the face of terror and uncertainty as being gay has prepared me for that.

"Me and David will go get help. You guys stay here and wait for Cat to come back. It will take us less than 20 minutes to get to the car and drive a bit to get some service and charge the phones. We'll make the call for help and come right back."

I am speaking fast, but I hope they understand. "I have back up chargers in the car and in my bag. We might not even need to drive anywhere, but we just need to try." There's uncertainty as to whose phone had been tossed at me but I shove it in my pocket.

I go to grab David's hand when I hear dad going through his stuff and see him pull out a gun. He opens the chamber and checks to make sure it's loaded. They'll be safe, I hope.

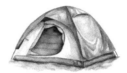

We take off running, flashlights in hand, beams bouncing all over as we try to remember which direction we need to go. We're halfway to where we think the cars are when I stop David.

"That's the same bag from the tent earlier, isn't it?"

"Yeah, it is. Who do you think is doing this? Why are they here, and what did your family do?" It's weird that David thinks someone in my family did something, but I wonder the same thing. The note suggests this is Gina, but the scream and the blood tell us a different story. I don't think this is a joke. I don't think Gina is trying to scare us into acting straight, not this way.

The contents in the bag weren't anything to suggest that she was trying to harm us or scare us. In fact, from the few things I saw, they were to make us remember we were a family. I saw a few pictures of us: beef jerky, the note, a t-shirt and a handmade picture frame with the words, best trip ever. She hoped this weekend was going to change us. There were a few more things inside the bags, but I couldn't make out what they were. I wanted to get to the cars quickly.

"I don't want to go back there. We need to get help and wait for them by the road. I know we said we'd go back, but I don't feel safe. Not with what we saw and what we heard. That was a lot of blood. I am not sure your sister…" He won't stop and I need him to calm down.

"Don't say it! Don't you say it!" I interrupt him, thinking that I was ready to walk away from my family earlier, but I wasn't ready to see them dead. There is so much going on that it's hard to concentrate and then we hear something. "Did you hear that?"

We look around trying to gauge where the sound came from and what it was. It sounded like movement nearby. We both turned in opposite directions, backs to each other, moving the flashlights over the terrain and hoping to get a glimpse of what it was. We turn up nothing. I can feel eyes on us now, and I am sure someone is out here watching us. I want to get out of here.

"Let's go!" We both take off running. It was a straight shot to the car and I'm surprised we didn't get turned around. It was dark and we could barely see in front of us. The flash-lights were no help in the pitch dark of night, and because we were running, the light bounced off everything, causing a bit of disorientation. I jump into the driver's seat and go through my pockets, looking for my keys. Panic erupts before I find them in my back pocket. It takes a moment to calm down and then I put them in the ignition.

"What's wrong?" David looks at me terrified. He's wondering why I am not driving off and so am I.

I turn the key repeatedly and nothing. It doesn't even try to start up.

"Someone did something to the car."

"What do you mean someone did something?"

"David, it won't start!" I look at him and the only thing I can do is bang my hands against the steering wheel, sobbing helplessly.

"Don't we need to go?"

"How, the car won't start." The words come out in a stutter.

"We can try someone else's."

"With what keys?" I snap back. "We need to go back."

I jump out of the car, and that's when I stop and notice the tires. Even if the car started, we wouldn't get far. I run around to each tire, inspecting for damage. All the tires appear slashed and we're trapped.

"Go check the other cars' tires." I yell to David.

"Why, what's wrong?" He jogs over to the other cars, and I do the same. Everyone's tires are flat except for one. The car that was here when we arrived. We still don't know whose car it was and I am thinking it wasn't anyone in our family anymore. It belongs to the person whose tent we found. Someone else was here.

I don't want to panic, but I don't know what else to do. It's at this point that I notice a shadow about a hundred feet away. Someone is standing not far from where we are. In their hands, I see something. It isn't a welcome sign, it's a knife. I shine my light toward the shadowy outline, and when I do, they turn and walk into the forest. David sees this.

"Who the fuck was that?"

"I don't know but we need to get back. I don't think we're safe here."

I go back to the car and look for something I can use as a weapon. Something to protect me and David. He jumps in the front seat, and I remind him we can't go anywhere. I tell him to look for something to help us in case whoever that was comes back.

"I don't think I want to go back."

"I don't think we have a choice; my dad has a gun and we're safer with them."

"Are we though? Do we even know what's going on?"

I am just as confused as he is. I don't know how to answer this question.

"I just figured out what this is between us, and I am not about to let whatever is happening stop that from figuring out what our futures hold. We'll be ok, we just need to get back." I am not sure why I am saying any of this because I don't believe it.

David reaches behind my seat and grabs hold of a tire iron. I had thrown it behind the seats when I had got a flat a few months back and forgot to put it in the trunk with the rest of the stuff. My carelessness ended up being a good thing because I cleaned out the trunk to make room for our bags this weekend. This easily could have ended up in my apartment. With a weapon at our disposal, we should be ok to get back to everyone else.

We get back to the campsite and everyone is there except for my father. The three of them are standing there looking at me, hoping I have good news.

"Where's dad?"

Victor is the first to respond.

"He left right after you."

"Where did he go?"

"He went after Cat, told us to sit tight and wait for help. Did you call someone?"

"The car wouldn't start and someone slashed the tires." I am about to mention who we saw when David interrupts me.

"Shit, the backup chargers!"

"There should be some in the bags. Ale might have some too."

"You could have mentioned that earlier." Mom interrupts, annoyed. I don't know how that didn't occur to me. Would it matter if no one's phone was working anyway? They are looking for the back up chargers to charge David's phone.

I see them fumbling with the cords and plug it in. We wait in silence for a few minutes. Mom is shaking. Victor is pacing back and forth. Ale is sobbing.

"It's turning on." David's face looks on in horror. The phone powers on and its fuzzy, but it's clear that it's damaged as he shows it to me, and the screen appears to display a distorted screen. We can't see anything, making it hard to place a phone call and we're not even sure if the phone would have signal. Everyone else checks their phones, passing around the portable charger and the ones that turn on yield no single and others just won't power up. We're stuck out here with no way of calling for help. We need to get everyone back here to figure out what to do next.

I am about to suggest something when we hear a gunshot, I look around. Everyone stops what they were doing. No one is crying; no one is shaking; no one is pacing. Just complete silence.

As time passes, no one says a word and I don't know what to do. I get up to grab some items when a hand stops me.

"What are you doing?" David places a hand on my shoulder. I pause and look up at him. He has tears in his eyes. I want to wipe them away. I want to erase everything that has happened in the last six hours. Everything except what has happened between us.

"I need to see what happened and go help my dad." I am about to ask him to come with me, but stop myself because I can't ask him to do that.

"You need to stay here with us." Ale is walking towards me when my mom's voice stops her in her tracks.

"Jayson, please help your father. I need all my children." The pain in her voice breaks my heart. As much as they've hurt me, I cannot see my mom in pain.

"I am going with you." I turn to David and give him a hug. What I am about to tell him is going to hurt him, but I don't get the chance to say it before he covers my mouth.

"Don't. I can't let you go alone. If you don't come back…" He doesn't finish as I sense he's about to cry.

Looking over at Victor, I wonder if he is going to say anything and then Ale speaks up. "Victor and I will stay with your mom. Get them and bring them back. Everyone!"

I grab what I think we are going to need and fast; I try to remember where the sound came from when I hear it again. Another gunshot. That's two. David and I take off toward the sound.

CHAPTER 30

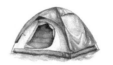

DAD

I need to go after my girls and can't wait for the boys to get back. What do they expect me to do? Sit around and wait? I've been an asshole to my family, but I won't let anything happen to them again. As soon as I opened the tent, the fear immediately came back to me. The emotion you get when you feel you've lost a child is something that sticks with you. Through all the arguments and fights, you never forget the feeling of a part of you never returning.

What happened to Victor when he was a kid is something we never talked about. Because of that, I am afraid of what could be happening now. It was one reason we stopped going camping. That is when I really felt like I started to change. Everything I did from that point forward was for my children, for my family. My family might see my actions and behaviors as something else, but I see it as building the perfect family—a strong family that no one can touch. It's not an excuse but that is why when Jayson came out, I overreacted. Not because I am against who he is, but the fear of change. The fear that what I built was now gone, and I wasn't prepared to handle it. I was afraid of what others would say and what he would have to go through. My initial shock and reactions were not my final reaction, but it was the reaction that pushed him away. My son, my creation, my legacy. Almost losing Victor broke me, and losing Jayson in the metaphorical sense is devastating, and my girls, I can't go through that. Once was enough with Victor and I still can't shake what happened all those years ago.

The kids were small, and we did a good job after it happened to control the narrative amongst the family—especially with the kids. It was easy to shield them from the terrors of the world and those twelve hours of hell. We never went camping again after for obvious reasons.

It was late afternoon, almost dinner time. It was the second day of a three-day camping trip. We spent the morning by the lake fishing and later Sack Toss. Nothing was out of the ordinary. My wife took the kids on a hike midday to wear them out, but of course, that failed. Kids were meant to play, and that's what they did. I wanted some alone time with my wife, so we sent them off to play.

The kids were not far from the campsite when we heard them calling out for Victor. My wife and I didn't know what to think of it. We thought it was a game of hide and seek, but when the calls became louder and more frequent, we rushed over.

I remember the panic I felt and the fear radiating off everyone when we met up with them. They were afraid at first to tell us what happened. They were playing hide and seek when an adult asked to play. We always told the kids to stay away from strangers, and I was sure that they would listen; usually they did. They told us the man left. Instead of coming to tell us about him, they decided to play another game. Since it was close to dinner, they knew the games would be over and we would all be settling down around the fire for the evening.

We suspect that whoever had asked to play with the kids was who took Victor. We didn't find him for 12 hours. It wasn't until early the next morning, with the help of police and the campground staff, that he was located just beyond the private campground we were at. We never did the wilderness thing again, or anything remotely close to what we're doing this weekend. Back then, we were at a more well-known campground with basic amenities. Across from there was forest and a private vacant piece of land.

When the police found Victor, he was asleep in the woods —cold and shivering. He didn't speak for days, so we didn't know what happened. Ever since then, he would fall into these dissociative spells. We took him to several psychiatrists and eventually it looked like it got better but I sometimes wonder if it did as I catch him staring off into the distance. We never spoke to him about it ever again because he seemed not to remember, and when we thought these dissociative spells ended, we just moved on.

We sat everyone down, fabricating a story that the children would believe. If he didn't remember, why would we bring it up? Why bring up the past and something that may never be relevant? Kids are easy to sway and manipulate, especially if you give them something. Since Victor didn't bring it up, the memory faded, and the narrative the kids know now is he got lost and stayed with the camp staff. While he was missing for those 12 hours, the staff kept the rest of the kids busy. They didn't really notice what was going on. I think as adults, they may know more just in terms of how serious it was, but no one brings it up.

Now my girls are missing, and I am not sure what is going on. Someone took my grown adult kid and my other daughter is off searching for her, and I was there with a gun in my bag considering driving off. Not to abandon them, but to get help.

The one thing we never told anyone was about the note that was left in my son's pocket. The police had missed it because when we brought him to the hospital to be checked; we had changed him out of his dirty clothes. When the police asked us for them, my wife forgot to give them his pants. She accidentally had given them a similar pair that she thought he wore that day. There was so much going on when we found him. We made mistakes throughout the process and when she found the note, it read, *I will come back for you one day. I couldn't do it now, but one day I will.* Those words on that paper burn a hole in my memory. They tell me that my kids, my family, could be taken and there is nothing I can do about it.

"Cat, Gina," I call out, hoping to hear someone or something, but all I hear is the dead of night. An owl conveniently answers my call with two hoots. I want to shoot it down, but what good would that do? It would only draw more attention to me, and that isn't going to save my girls.

The further into the woods I go, the darker it gets. The flashlight isn't strong and the weak beam it produces only lights the six or so feet ahead of me. Trees block whatever light the moon gives down to a candle's flame. The thoughts in my head are deafening as I feel vulnerable. I try to pay attention to my surroundings when I hear a branch break from up above. Shining the light, I go from branch to branch, hoping to catch what made the sound. I think, *could this be a distraction?* A tactic to divert my attention. I spin around in circles and cry out.

"Who's there? What did you do to my daughters?"

I wait for someone to answer but receive no response. Will the person who is doing this call out to me, let me know they have my Gina and Cat?

"Angelina! Catalina!" My daughters are important to me,

and I need to know that they are ok. I want to hear their voices. If I can hear them, I can get to them. If I go back to the others without them, I fail. I can't face my wife and two boys letting them know I couldn't find them.

There's an urge to take off running, to hide, but I am lost in fear and confusion. I keep going through questions in my head. Who is doing this? Why are they doing this? Is this my fault? For a moment I also wonder, Could this be some kind of sick joke or prank? There is no way. There was too much blood in the tent. The screams coming from my baby girl were real. The smell of copper and salt still waft in my nose. I have blood on me, my daughter's blood. I am going to kill whoever has done this to me and my family.

I turn, violently waving the gun as I hear someone laugh. In doing this I drop the flashlight. The beam is forward facing, and I see a pair of boots. They are large, steel-toed black boots. I've owned similar pairs in the past. I see the bottoms of a pair of jeans. No one was wearing jeans tonight. This is a stranger. I don't know who this person is, and I feel it is safe to take a shot. I fire once in the direction of the person in front of me. There's no steadiness when I aim, and I am not a great shooter. At the range, I hit outside of my target, never hitting near or at the bullseye. Instantly, I hear them take off running. I scramble to grab the flashlight. Fumbling with it, I don't know if I have just left myself vulnerable when I hear another sound. I turn again and find nothing but the night.

My gun has around fifteen rounds and I fired my first shot. I have about 14 more rounds left. The anger in me wants to fire off a second shot, but I don't want to waste it. I head off in the direction I heard them running. My sense is to run after them, but I need to be careful. One wrong move and I could end up hurting my family instead of helping them.

It feels like I am walking for a long time as I make turn

after turn trying to follow the sounds in front of me. The trail seems to widen and narrow several times as I make my way through the trees. A mosquito bites my neck and I smack at it hitting myself with my gun. I need to be more careful before I shoot my own head off.

The creek must be near because I can hear the flow of water and I can see light as I enter a small clearing. There's a shadow off in the distance near the creek and I take another shot. The gun wavers in my hand and the recoil has me unsteady on my feet. I am not used to shooting a gun. I only bought it because it was something I thought I should have in case I ever needed to protect myself and my family.

There was a time I thought about killing myself. In recent months, as finances have grown out of control, I have thought that this could be my only option. A way to free myself and my family.

My aim must have improved because the shadow is gone. Making my way towards where I think they went I continue to scan the area for signs I might have missed them. As I get closer, I see someone crawling on the ground and I yell. Their movement is slow but they are still alive.

"Stop, stop right there!" I am feet away from them, but it is still dark. I aim my flashlight towards them when it conveniently stops working and I toss it aside. I sense them still moving and yell again hoping that this time they will turn around. I don't want to have to kill them with their back to me. "I said stop and turn around."

It's at this moment they pull themselves far enough into the moonlight and turn over. I freeze because I recognize them and hear them say.

"Daddy."

CHAPTER 31

CAT

My thoughts are torn between this being a sick joke or that something terrible is going on. There was no need to wait there, and I need something to do so I left. My distrust for my family is showing right now. My last words to them were that I was going to go get her and that is what I intend to do. I am not coming back without her, and when I do, we're leaving. Family or not, we don't leave anyone behind.

Growing up, my family may not have always been there for each other, but when one of us had a problem, we would show up for them. We would bond in these moments of protection from each other and sometimes from people on the outside. My brothers have stuck up for me and I've stuck up for them, but Gina rarely needed our help. She was the tough one. That is why in this moment if anyone could make it out here with whatever is going on it would be her.

I am immediately thrust into pitch black darkness. I fumble for the switch on my flashlight and look for my phone. I remember it's dead so there is no point in checking.

My hands are shaking and when I finally click the light on, I see movement in front of me. It looked like someone was up ahead, and they went through the trees. It could be Gina; she could be lost. Instead of calling out for her, I head in that direction. My flashlight bounces off the trees, and then the bushes, and finally a small animal. My heart races at sight of a field mouse racing across the ground and into some bushes.

It's been about ten minutes and I feel turned around. Unsure of where I am or how far I've wandered, I wonder how long will it take to get back? I can't see much in front of me or behind me but hear the hoot of an owl in the distance. The faint sound of water is up ahead so it must be the creek. I figure I will head in that direction, even though I don't see movement in front of me anymore. Maybe my eyes are playing tricks on me and there was never anything there. Being lost in the woods with someone else is one thing, out here on your own is terrifying. If my sister is alive, I hope I can find her. There are so many sounds out here that are unfamiliar but there was one I recognized, the sound of someone close to me.

"Angelina! When I find you, I am going to kick your ass."

"No, you're not." I turn around as soon as I hear the voice, but my flashlight is knocked out of my hand, and I stand there stunned. Silenced as a hand covers my mouth and a blade touches my torso. I fear that if I make one wrong move, even to get away, the blade will cut through me. Instinct tells me to run but my senses tell me to stay and listen. I cannot see who is in front of me.

"You know why this is happening, don't you?"

I shake my head because I have no clue. I don't know who this is or what they want from me or my family.

"I've been watching you all for a very long time. I've been in your houses and in your life for some time. I am surprised you never saw me as we've met before." There's a slight laugh when he says this. "We've been in the same places. Ate the same foods." He looks at me and I can see he sees the confused look that turns to horror.

"I don't know who you are. Please let me go." Cat pleads.

"I can't do that. You see something happened a long time ago. I need to right some wrongs. I need to rewrite history."

I have no idea what this person is talking about. They whisper and I can't make out their voice, I can't identify anything about them, nothing sounds familiar. They are short like me, their frame small. Nothing indicates who it is, so my mind goes racing through names and people I have met. People who have met my entire family. My memory immediately goes back to camping when we were young and the incident with Victor. I don't know why I didn't realize this sooner. I don't remember much but I do know that something happened, and my parents were weird about everything after.

"You were there, weren't you?"

They nod.

"Why now?"

"Because it's time to make things right. I can't keep watching you hurt each other. I want to hurt you all and free him from you."

Why would he need to free him from us? I am confused but I think about this statement for a moment. Do we need saving from each other? Are we really that bad? A sound off in the distance interrupts us and I use this opportunity to take off running. I kick and make contact. They fall and groan in pain. I run towards the creek.

Branches and twigs smack me in the face as I run through. I can hear them behind me, grunting in pain. Whatever I did must have done some damage because I am gaining distance as I run. I take the opportunity to duck and crawl near a few trees that create a shelter from whoever this is. I try to slow my breathing as I don't want them to hear me. Once they are far enough past, I can go in the opposite direction.

As they approach, I hold my breath. I close my eyes and count. One. Two. Three. I stop because I can't tell if I am counting out loud or in my head. I am afraid if I keep counting, they will hear me even if my mouth isn't moving. I lean back against the tree. My back is pressed so hard against it that I feel like I'm sinking into it, becoming one with the tree. If I could dissolve into it and away from everything that is happening right now, I would.

I don't see the direction they went, but I know I've been sitting here against this tree for a few minutes. I slowly get up when I see movement in the distance. There is no way they made it that far, but if they did, it's my chance to create even more distance. I can't see whoever is heading this way, so I make my way towards the creek.

Standing feet from the creek, I hear someone.

"Stop. Stop right there." I consider taking a step forward contemplating if I should turn around or run. My instinct is to run but I don't even have time to turn around when I feel a sharp pain. Falling to my knees I begin to crawl.

We learn to crawl as babies, and we grow out of that and use our legs. My legs don't feel like they are working anymore, so I crawl. I want to continue to put as much distance between me and whoever shot me. I think about my mom and use the strength I have inside me to pull myself a foot forward. I think of my dad, and I move another foot forward. I start to think of my siblings, and I want to continue. It's getting harder to pull myself forward and my lower half feels like dead weight. I hear them get close.

They are standing over me, and I turn over to see his face.

"Daddy."

CHAPTER 32

Watching him shoot his daughter pissed me off. I was standing in front of her and could have ended her right there which I really wanted to. I pressed the blade against her taut stomach tracing a figure eight with the tip of the blade. Her eyes told me she was trying to understand what I was doing, if what I was tracing was a clue to what was happening. Was there a hint of recognition in her face. I pushed it in just a little so she knew I was serious, piercing her skin just enough so a trickle of blood slipped down her abdomen. I wanted her to know that this wasn't a game and that this was going to happen. I still wanted to get them all together and in one place.

When I heard him, I lost my grip and the moment passed. It was a painful kick in the knees. Her aim was good and caused a shooting pain to radiate through my body. Her father had missed me earlier. What a loser. What a cheap shot. Why buy a gun that you can't shoot? It seems his daughter might have better aim.

There were two of them near me and I didn't know how I would take them both down. She was a lot closer than he was and I didn't want to keep looking for him because he was a bigger threat with that gun despite his poor aim. She looked like she was headed for the *creek, so I made my way. I hid as best as I could away from the light of night.*

She stopped running when he called out and my hand went to my mouth covering the urge to laugh and to hide my breathing. Everything from that moment went in slow motion. He raised the gun, took aim, and fired.

Watching her crawl like a baby in front of her father didn't upset me. Watching him watch her crawl away like he shot some game animal tickled my heart. He had no idea what he had done at first and just watched her. That made things even more intense from the view I had.

The face he made when she called his name almost made me burst out laughing. My hand was still holding my mouth closed when a muffled laugh escaped my lips.

As I sat there and watched, rage coursed through me. He killed her and not me. This was supposed to be my victory, not his. The difference between his shot and mine is that mine would have been a victory. He was in pain and torment because he just shot and killed his daughter.

I took off running. I needed to run off some of the feelings I had coursing through my veins. Killing him right now would be easy and I wanted a challenge.

CHAPTER 33

JAYSON

I didn't want to go after them, but the look in my mother's eyes broke me. My family and I have a complicated history of manipulation, love, pain, and togetherness. Just thinking of them still confuses me. When I decided to come this weekend, all I wanted to do was walk away from my family. Not for good, but for a while. I wanted to find myself and make them see that the way they've treated me and treated each other needed to change.

My father's acceptance was important to me my entire life. My sexuality was never an issue for me growing up. I didn't even know who I was or what I wanted but my relationship with him was always tested. I think it's a universal experience to want acceptance. We go through it with our friends, our co-workers, and peers. It's harder and more hurtful when you don't get it from family, and you don't know why.

No surprise that my coming out dinner didn't go as expected. Knowing how unpredictable my family was, I should have planned for different outcomes. I planned for weeks, maybe even longer on what I would say. I didn't think about the reactions, what they would look like, and how I'd respond. My therapist and I worked on what I would say but never the other parts. As someone with anxiety, I thought that I would ruminate on the details. It turns out I just perfected my coming out speech. Spending weeks working on what I would say, my responses and reactions. It didn't surprise me that I walked into it over prepared.

When I knew that I wanted to come out, I knew I had to tell my family. There are times that my family still surprises me. I don't know why because when I look back, I should have anticipated their reactions. I think it's everything that happened after that shocked me even more. My father became even more distant. The coldness I felt from him and my siblings froze me. I felt the ice every time I entered the room down to my core. Our relationships were never great or strong, but this new dynamic was isolating. It isn't what a newly *out* person wants. There were moments I had with the family after where I heard apologies and excuses. I sometimes felt better and sometimes worse. Is it worse to get an apology when you don't think it's genuine, or is it worse to never receive one? At least if you don't get one, you know they don't care. The one I got from my mom was heartbreaking.

"I am so sorry, Jayson; I love you so much, but you know how he is. I've accepted his hate for me for years because of you kids. Please know I am not like him; I don't believe the same things he believes." She pleaded with me on the phone. She knew I'd had enough, but I stayed around for her. Walking away from them meant I might have to walk away from her. I sometimes wish they'd separated, but she always said things would have been harder for us. I think I would have been happier and she would be too.

My father has strong opinions, and the opinions he shared

that night were hard to digest. It was like a punch in the gut or eating bad take out and wanting to violently purge all night. The pit that formed in my stomach after that dinner stayed with me as I replayed his words. Does he believe them? Even to this day? I don't know what he believes because this weekend he was acting so strange. Not just with me but with David, Ale, and my mom. There were times he seemed off, distant. Other times engaged, connected. He was always confusing, but he was even more confusing this weekend.

"Jayson, I don't know which direction to go! I don't know what to do! We should just go and get help!" David is panicking and I feel like I am on the verge of it too. "We can go back and explain to everyone that this is stupid, and we need to get out of here. I know you want to help but…"

"I know that, but did you see my mom? If I go back without my sisters… I need to find them." I can't finish the thought. Finishing it might mean that I am admitting that it's over and that they are not coming back.

"I don't understand any of this. What did your family do?" The blame that came out of him shocked me. I looked at him, stunned. I want to defend them, but I know he is right. Someone might have caused this. It's no secret that my father built his business off lying and cheating, and who knows, stealing. I don't want to argue with him, so I respond in the form of a rhetorical question filled with sarcasm.

"What did my family do? That's the million-dollar question, isn't it? Why did my dad bring a gun?" We never grew up with guns in the home, at least not that I was aware of. My dad was a man who would have bragged about it or flashed it around. This wasn't like him. I knew he bought one, but I don't know why.

"I thought that was a little strange. I know it's legal and all, but I am sure you would have known if he carried it because when you saw him pull it out, you looked scared." David stops like he wants to give me time to say something but continues and I wonder if it's his admission of what he's feeling right now. "Not confused but scared."

He was right, I did look scared. I have just never seen him hold it and I have never seen him load it. These things were different—he seemed different in the moment. It also looked too easy for him. Watching him confused me because he shouldn't look so confident and eager. I want to distract myself from where my mind is going because I don't want to think he has anything more to do with this. I just need to find my sisters and get us all the hell out of here.

"Do you remember where that sound came from?" I look around as if I am looking for a sign to point me in the right direction. David is doing the same and we both come up with nothing. He doesn't seem confident but offers up something.

"Honestly, I thought it came from over there." He stops and looks both ways and then continues. "But then it sounded like it came from over there the second time." He is now pointing in two very different directions and neither really follow a path. We're not splitting up and there is no way that I am going to go in a direction that isn't marked.

"I noticed that too, which makes me worried." Was he chasing someone? Did he catch whoever it was? Was that even his gun? I rapidly fire off these questions in my head when David pulls my arm bringing my thoughts to a stop.

"We'll find them." He looks at me in a way I find reassuring.

There is always comfort in being around David and I hope he finds that same comfort in me. Leaning in to give him a hug I stop short when we hear a loud sound.

BANG.

It's a third shot and we both look at each other. This time we know the direction it came from and take off running. It isn't long before I feel lost and completely turned around. Panic rushes through me and I swear I am about to faint. I can feel the blood in my veins almost thicken. My chest feels tight and my head is about to explode. My vision is getting fuzzy when my name is called.

"Jayson, look!" David is pointing at the tent we saw earlier. We both look at each other and freeze like two statues staring blankly at an object we expect to see do some type of trick. We're awestruck at something we find so familiar and terrifying. We don't know if we should hide or go through the tent again looking for answers. My instincts are to hide when I see David stride towards this lone tent on a mission.

"Maybe they have a phone? Maybe whoever grabbed Gina did something to them?"

"David, NO!" My instinct is to throw my flashlight at his head as he turns and to look at me and shrugs.

"What?" His response is adolescent, as if he just did something he knows he shouldn't have and was caught by his mother. David is going to be a handful if we ever get out of this.

"What do you mean what! You're going to get yourself killed!"

"I think that's all of our fates this weekend if we don't get out of here."

I rush towards the tent and nudge him as I go past. I can't let him die before me. I can't watch that. I crawl through the tent, looking around for something. I look at the bag. This time I know it is the same one that was left outside of our tents. How did one of these get out here? When we found them earlier, it was obvious that Gina had put these out for us. But why would one be here? Is this Gina's tent? Is this her idea of a sick and twisted game? Or did someone get a hold of one of these bags; or worse, was Gina taken as she was putting these out? It would explain the scream we heard and how quickly she was gone.

I come out of the tent holding up the bag. The look on my face must be of pure terror as I see the color drain from David's face, and he is no longer just staring at me. It looks like he might start shaking. I toss it at David, hitting him in the chest. He grabs it before it falls to the ground and starts going through it, tossing contents on the ground.

"It's the same fucking bag! Why is it the same fucking bag?" He's now holding up a note that looks a lot like the note from earlier. The flashlight sits between his chin and chest while he reads it over. "Do you think it's Gina?"

"I don't know what to think anymore." I grab the bag from him and toss it on the ground kicking the contents out of my way and swearing under my breath. I lean against the nearest tree and slide down. I can feel splinters going through my shirt, stinging my back. I plop down and sit under the tree. There is a feeling of blood on my back and it reminds me that I am still here and alive. My whole entire life starts to flash before my eyes. I see me with my family, I see a flash of me at funerals. I see myself in my own coffin and David leaning over me. With my hands on my head and knees to my chest, I start to cry.

"It's going to be ok. We'll…" David is leaning over me, and I look up at him. Those eyes stare back at me and are filled with rage, fear, and comfort. He bends over trying to comfort me.

I look up and lean towards him and kiss him to shut him up. I am sure he can feel my tears as they fall down his cheeks. The kiss isn't passionate it feels more like a kiss good-bye. As quickly as we found each other I feel like we're losing each other. I don't know if we'll really make it through the night. It feels like nothing is going to be ok, and nothing is going right. I need comfort and kissing him right now brings me that. He sits down next to me and that's when I hear him —he's starting to cry. We just sit there with our hands intertwined, motionless, and with tears streaking our dirty faces. He is just as afraid as I am and there is nothing I can do right now other than feel everything that I am feeling. Fear, heartbreak, and anger.

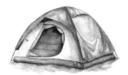

"Get up!"

"Excuse me?" I don't have the time for his attitude right now.

"This isn't going to happen! Not this weekend and not to us!" David appears pissed off and angry with me. I've never seen this side of David before, his assertiveness yields confidence.

"We have an advantage," he says looking down at me.

"And what's that?"

"There are way more of us than whoever this is." This sounds more like a question than a statement.

"Are you sure about that?"

"I am not sure of anything, but if there were a bunch of folks out here coming after us, then I think we would have been picked off sooner."

"Ok, so what should we do?"

"Keep moving. Keep looking."

"That's your plan?" I don't want to laugh, but when David first stood up, I thought this was going to be some motivational speech, something to get me going and keep me alive. Instead, it seems like it was more to make him feel safe and comfortable. He needed this boost, but I can feed off this. I can keep this going.

"Did you see anything else in the tent? Anything at all?"

I make my way back inside and find nothing else. There are just some random items and a few beef jerky wrappers. I come out of the tent and show them to David.

"That doesn't mean anything except that a bunch of people around here eat that crap." As he snatches it out of my hand, I can't tell if he's annoyed with me or the situation. I don't want to think that what we just started is now crumbling. He's right, though, this doesn't mean anything. I hope it doesn't.

We hear someone approaching, so we grab our flashlights and kick the contents of the bag out of the way and into the bushes. Panicking, we rush behind a group of trees while holding hands as we watch someone come into the clearing. It's hard to see who it is, but it is not Gina.

CHAPTER 34

VICTOR

Watching my brother and David take off made me proud of Jayson. Despite everything, he has been the brother anyone would want. I am sorry I didn't do a better job of letting him know this. It isn't until you are in situations like this that you have these types of thoughts. I wanted to go with my brother, but I don't know what I could do to help. I have always felt useless in my family. I would say I'm the black sheep, but doesn't everyone say that at some point in their life?

When I heard the commotion outside of the tent, my initial reaction was, *Here we go*. I didn't hear the scream; I only heard everyone outside and what sounded like panic and terror. Ale and I had a great night together. We stayed up talking for a while. She told me that my dad had been cheating on my mom and had gotten someone else pregnant. She didn't want to tell me anymore than that, which I found annoying. I always say, don't open a door you can't fully close. I am always going to want to peek to see what's on the other side.

I tried to get more out of her, but that only led to her stubbornness, which I found to be a turn on. I've had a crush on Ale since she first started to come around our family. We're not that much different in age now. When we were younger, she wouldn't give me the time of day. Now there is a flirtatious banter between us. I've seen her body and curves and she is a beautiful woman. She's walked in on me changing before, so the embarrassment of our naked bodies in front of each other is something we don't need to worry about. I just wanted to make love to her.

We talked for about an hour before we passed out, only to be awakened by the horrors outside of the tent. I regret not making a move earlier. But if I know one thing, it's don't be too pushy, or you will push a woman away. And someone like Ale had options. My regret mainly stems from seeing my sister's tent and knowing that I may die a virgin. The scene inside of it was awful, and I can't get the image out of my head. There was a lot of blood and when I was inside, I kept slipping on it as I searched for her inside. The sticky thick substance coated my clothing. Even though I changed my clothes, she's all over my skin. No amount of water and soap will erase the memory of what I saw, what I slipped in. I can still taste her coppery life in my mouth.

Since earlier I've been having weird flashbacks, but I know that these things haven't happened to me. It isn't just images flashing in my mind, it's feelings too. Feelings that I know are mine, but I don't have memories to go with them. I feel scared, alone, and disoriented. I can see myself wandering in a clearing. Near a wooded area, cold and alone.

Ale is just sitting there trying to comfort my mom who is inconsolable. She's crying and blaming herself.

"I'm supposed to protect my babies. I am not supposed to see them go before me."

"They are not gone; Jayson and David will find them, and

we will all get out of here together." Ale tries her best, but mom doesn't seem convinced. She cries louder because she knows Ale is wrong.

I am still not convinced that this isn't just a sick joke by my sister who thought it would be funny to bring us all out here to play a prank. Pranks are her thing. We've all been victims to them growing up, but this is the worst she's played, and I am not enjoying it. I am scared, and these new feelings I have are causing me more and more anxiety.

"Ale, come here." She gets up slowly and a bit confused. She doesn't want to leave my mom's side, but she kisses her on the head and comes over to where I am.

"What's going on? Your mom needs someone right now."

"I need to go after them. I should have gone, and they should have stayed here. Jayson is better at handling my mom. She needs him. I am going to go and send him back with David. I think you guys should go back to the cars. Maybe find a way to get us out of here, even if it's driving on slashed tires. Once you're on the road, it could be easier."

"You've never been good at whispering, Vic, so we're all going." Mom stands up and she isn't crying anymore. She looks determined. She starts looking around the campsite trying to find something.

"What are you looking for?" Ale starts to help her but doesn't know what she is doing. It's obvious as she awkwardly picks up bags and places them back down in the same spot.

"Anything to protect ourselves from whoever is out there doing this. Vic, I know that you want to help, but we are going together, and I don't want to hear another word or else I'll start crying again and make you feel really bad." She says this as a demand, an order that we must follow.

At this point I hug my mom close because she knows she

can manipulate us with her tears. This makes me laugh—we don't all hate each other.

I start looking around for something we can use as a weapon and see something on the ground. It's the tire iron Jayson brought back from the cars. He didn't take it with him. Mom and Ale both pop up at the same time. Mom with metal skewers and Ale with a bag of marshmallows.

"Are we making S'mores?" It isn't time for humor, but we all look at each other and begin to laugh. Fear makes us do weird things, including using humor in tense situations. Humor can also give comfort in situations where fear is the motivator and right now we need all the humor we can get.

Ale pops a marshmallow in her mouth. "It's for energy." I notice she has blood on her hands. It glistens in the moonlight. We're more connected now than we ever were. When Ale started coming around, Jayson let us know she had a troubled past. My mom accepted her because she accepts everyone as her own. It's a trait that I love about my mom. We are all her children.

Ale and my mom look ready to go with skewers and marshmallows in hand. It's still a ridiculous sight but what else do we have? I think it's dumb for all of us to go, but it is equally dumb for me to go alone. There is no right or wrong about this situation. We just need to get everyone together and get my sisters back. Everyone is out there now and who knows what's going on.

"Which way do we go?" As Ale questions our plan, we hear a third shot ring out. It's obvious now which way we are going, and we head that way.

CHAPTER 35

ALE

"It came from over there." I stand there pointing through the bushes. My gaze fixed on an area we can't cut straight through. We'll have to take the path around. We're not familiar with the woods, so we don't even know if it will make a loop, but I don't want to go off the path. It will be even easier to get lost that way. Spending days in the woods would be terrifying. The last thing I want is to starve or freeze out here. It's a crazy thought, seeing that it isn't that cold and tomorrow will be a new day. If we even make it that long. Victor and his mom look like they don't care about going through the bushes. Getting lost isn't important to them. I can only imagine how lost Mrs. P is without her daughters. They just want to get to their family. I am hoping that one of them says something because I am about to go the other direction down the safer path.

"Toss me one of those energy puffs and let's go." Victor is the first to break the awkward silence but not to tell us what to do next. He's afraid. Last night we spent some time talking.

I thought things were going to go in another direction, but as we talked, he seemed a bit lost. I don't know what is going on with him, but I know he isn't doing ok, so I didn't even bother making a move.

I toss Victor a marshmallow and he catches it in his mouth. His mom asks for one next. Is it weird that we are sharing these sweet morsels at a time like this? Wiping my hands before I toss anymore, hoping not to get any blood on them, I launch one in her direction. Surprisingly she's a good catch. The puff hits her chin, and she catches it, and it looks like she's juggling with it before she pops it in with a smile. She places the sugar puff into her mouth, grinning with it inside revealing a mouth of marshmallow teeth. This is cute and makes me laugh. The humor we are throwing around is making me appreciate the family. It's in moments like this that you need a good laugh, and right now we need this.

Mrs. P was welcoming when I first started coming around. She may have had opinions about me or my family, but if she did, she kept them to herself. Unlike everyone else who blustered about my family's misfortunes, she was respectful. From what Jayson told me, she had a similar upbringing as mine, so she understood. I used to hear Jayson's father talk about me. As much as it hurt, I know it wasn't directed at me exactly. My family wasn't nice to anyone. They used people and then discarded them. I am sure both Mrs. P and Mr. P both had some type of problem with them in the past.

"Let's get going. Wherever that shot was, someone's either hurt and needs us, or they are already gone. We need to hurry."

It sounds rational when Victor says it, but why does it scream danger to me? When I decided to come on this trip, I had my own intentions that went beyond supporting Jayson. I wanted to get through to Jayson's dad that he was about to lose his son. I wanted to tie up loose ends with my aunt, his maid. He still doesn't know that she is my aunt. She's the one family member who managed to stay out of trouble and I am grateful. I was only close to two of my aunts growing up and she was one of them. My other aunt—the one who practically raised me—stopped talking to the family and moved away. That's when I got closer to Tia Patricia. When she started working for Mr. P, I was shocked. I didn't even know they knew each other until she filled me in about their past and history. Our families are connected in more ways than I want to know, and I was going to confront Jayson's dad about his son this weekend.

I started blackmailing him about his affairs, and I was working my way towards the kids, but then all of this happened. I knew it was wrong to blackmail him, but I was in a tight spot. I was going to lose my apartment. Since I had no family, I took advantage of Jayson's dad. I have many regrets and I am starting to regret this now. Even though his dad is an asshole, what's happening now is making me feel like I am hurting my own family, not just his father. When I look at Victor and his mom, I realize they have been my family this whole time. For years they have taken care of me, and in many ways, I took care of them by keeping their son around. Jayson had many dark moments growing up and, in his journey to find himself. Without me, there would be no him, and, honestly, without him and his family, there would be no me.

"If we hurry, I am sure we'll catch up to them. They've only been gone twenty minutes." Victor seems to be gaining confidence and ground, and I find this attractive.

Victor's great, but I shouldn't be thinking about a future with him. He is someone I could settle down with and he's only two years younger than me, but Jayson would have a fit. I know he'd understand and would want what was best for me and his brother, at least I hoped. He was just becoming a teenager when we met, so I never saw him in that way before. But as a man, he is sensitive, sweet, and sexy and a lot of Jayson. If Jayson hadn't turned out to be gay, I'm sure I would have ended up with him, but I am glad that we're friends. At least we have that.

It's not that I haven't tried to be with Jayson. But with his subtle rejections growing up, I couldn't tell if it was me or his sexuality that repulsed him from me. He was a late bloomer and didn't come out until he was past his teenage years, even though I think he always knew. Conscious or subconscious, isn't it something that is born within us? Doesn't Lady Gaga have her whole brand based around the idea of being Born this Way? Lyrics Jayson would change and belt out *Born This Gay*. I think about myself, though, and my sexual fluidity. I don't subscribe to one gender or one sexual preference. I am who I am. I myself, was *Born This Gay*.

We head towards the path and as we move further away from the clearing of the campsite and deeper into the woods, it's getting darker and darker. The only light we have is from the moon and what little comes through the trees. Our flash-lights are weak and only illuminate what's directly in front of us.

The sound of an owl makes me jump. When it hoots twice more; I am afraid it's signaling our end. I want to ask it to shut up, but that wouldn't change anything. I look up trying to see if I can lock eyes with it, but I can't find it. Maybe it would be able to sense the danger below and stop. To be that bird sitting in that tree with a bird's eye view of the forest gives me an idea. I am about to suggest one of us climb the tree when Mrs. P calls out.

"Angelina! Catalina!" Her voice quivers as she calls out again. "Jayson!"

Immediately I want to yell at her for screaming but hearing his name makes me want to scream for him too. I came out to support him and not lose him. I am about to start yelling for them when Victor shushes us.

"Quiet, do you hear something?"

We all stop and try to listen. We do hear something. It's off in the distance but I can hear it. We see a dim light and I swear I hear crying. "Is that your father?"

"I think it is." Victor is convinced it's safe to go because he immediately starts walking in the direction of the sound. We follow because there aren't too many options right now. It's this or continue the direction we were going to go, which is just slightly to the left.

The dim light we saw is gone and the sound of someone crying has stopped. I hear what sounds like water now. We must be near a creek or a body of water. It's faint, but at least it means there will be more empty space and we won't have to worry about someone ambushing us. Slicing off our heads or stabbing us in the back. Victor starts to jog and I see a clearing up ahead.

As we make our way through the woods, I can hear the sound of heavy breathing. It's Mrs. P and she is out of shape, but she is trying to keep up with us. I want to call out to Victor to tell him to slow down, but I can see the water from where we are and feel like there is help or hope waiting for us. There is light and I want to get to it as soon as possible because I want to feel safe again and I know I will once we're there.

We're about five hundred feet away when I can see the shape of a body lying on the ground near the edge of the water. I cannot make out who it is except the outline of a petite frame. I start to panic as I think we've just found Gina. As we get closer, I am sure it's one of Jayson's sisters. The clothing is familiar, but I don't remember who was wearing what as we've all changed from our day clothes to our evening clothes, and I don't remember what either of them was wearing.

"No! No! No!" Victor sounds broken as he picks up speed. I am about fifty or so feet behind him and Mrs. P is about a hundred feet behind me. I want to stop and shield her from what we are about to come up on. I can hear her breathing become heavier as she picks up the pace. She is closing some distance now.

"INA" is all I can hear. I am not sure who it is, but I know now that it is one of his sisters and I hear a blood-curdling scream from behind me.

"My baby!" Mrs. P passes me and almost knocks me over.

I am standing over her and Victor as they both shake the body of his sister. I still can't make out who it is because both are over the lifeless body and are crying and screaming. It's a scene that breaks my heart. One, because I can feel their pain, and two, because I feel like I am losing one of my own sisters. This family is my family, and I am afraid to see who is lying on the ground. I turn around and start to pace and try to calm my nerves.

Going through my pockets in search for a Xanax, I can't remember if I have any on me, but I know I am going to need one right now. I can feel my chest tighten and hear echoing in my head as if I can feel the blood coursing through my veins. Everything around me feels like it is closing in. The pressure is building, and I can feel myself starting to cry. I need to keep it together because I don't even know who it is or if we can help them. I don't know what the situation is in front of me because I cannot bring myself to look.

When I turn around, I finally can see who is on the ground in front of them. Victor is crying and holding his sister's head in his hands. Mrs. P is laying across her daughter's stomach as she lifts her head up to the sky with a guttural scream.

CHAPTER 36

JAYSON

"I killed my daughter." Shock coarsens through me as I hear these words.

I look over at David and quickly raise my hand to his mouth while my other hand immediately shoots behind the back of his head. He is now sandwiched between my hands, and I am squeezing tight. I need him to stay quiet because I am still processing what was said. At first, I wanted to call out to him, but hearing my dad's words, I knew I needed to keep David safe. It was the first time I've ever seen someone's eyes go as wide as David's. His pupils dilated in terror and shock proving to me that what I heard was true.

"I killed my daughter." The words are on repeat now as he continues like a broken record.

He keeps repeating this phrase over and over as he has the gun in his hands. He stops and stares at it. Hands shaking. I am so confused right now because I saw someone else earlier, and seeing dad right now makes me think he might have something to do with this. Why would he shoot his daughter and which one? Is it Gina or Cat? I nod at David, and he shakes his head. He knows I want to approach my dad and find out what is going on, but if he just killed my sister, would he turn the gun on me? David and I are no match for a guy with a gun. Especially in the position we're in.

I see David reach for a rock off the ground. I don't understand what he thinks he is going to do with it when he tosses it behind us. Leave it to David to come up with something, but I don't get it.

"Who's there?"

It finally dawns on me what he is trying to do. David is causing a distraction; he wants my dad to think someone is coming this way, so he'll leave. He lifts his gun in the direction we're hiding. Understanding his reasoning for doing it I am a bit confused as to why he did it so close to us.

"Who the fuck is there?" With the gun raised and his hands still shaking, it looks like he's about to fire when another distraction comes.

David tosses more rocks and dad appears confused and the expression of his face starts to show terror. The man with the gun in his hand doesn't appear as confident as he would hope he did despite a raised gun in front of him.

This time David tossed them off the side in the direction we wanted him to go. Away from us and away from where we might have been headed. He takes off running but not before firing one shot into the air. I tense at the sound of the gun firing so close that I can smell the gunpowder. We sit looking at each other for a few more minutes before we slowly creep out of hiding.

"Your dad killed your sister! Did you hear what he said! He said he killed your sister Jayson!"

"I know, I heard him." I am stuttering the words. I am afraid and angry. None of these feelings are towards David but at my father, at myself, and at my sister. I feel like we all could have stopped this by staying home. If one of us just decided to not come on this stupid trip, I think that everyone else would have followed, dropping out and opting for peace. Coming to these family vacations isn't for us anymore. Now, the motivation is to please each other. No one has ever missed one of these, so if I or someone else announced staying home, I think this whole trip would have been canceled and I wish that person would have been me.

"Why do you think he did it?"

"I don't know. I just know when my mom finds out, it's going to break her."

"Do you think it is Gina?"

"I don't know. If he had anything to do with this, yeah, it could have been."

"We need to get back and we need to get out of here."

"There's still the problem of the cars." I can't believe I need to remind him of this.

"At this point we need to just hike it back to the road. We're not completely in the middle of nowhere. The main road was a distance away from where we parked. Twenty minutes or so of a drive, so what? An hour walking, maybe less. We just need to get the hell out of here. If we would have just done that the first time, we would be halfway to help."

David has a point. We miscalculated some stuff earlier. If we would have just headed for the road, then maybe help would be on the way. I guess now we just have to find our way out and hope we aren't lost. If it wasn't for the darkness of the night, we would easily be able to find our way. But because it is pitch-black out, I am not sure which way is which anymore.

"You don't think we should follow him? Maybe we could find out who it was exactly."

"I love you, Jayson, but that is how people die. We need to get out of here."

We start to grab what we might need and head in the direction my dad came from. I figured David would not want to go the other way. Although if Dad has anything to do with this, the way he went could be the way out.

We haven't been walking for too long when I realize we've made a complete circle. We are back where we started. At the mysterious tent where we heard my dad confess to killing my sister.

"How the fuck did we get here?"

"I don't know, I felt like we were walking in a straight line. There is no way we looped around."

I look at David confused, going back over in my head the steps we took. I could tell when we were headed downhill, and I could tell when the ground leveled up hill. In the night it's hard to tell if you're turning though. Especially if it's a subtle turn and shift. But to not notice you would think we would have needed to walk for hours to end up in the same place. It seems like we were walking for fifteen minutes.

"We need to keep walking. We had to have made a weird turn or something. Got confused."

"Yeah, it's most likely we're too anxious and scared. We need to calm down and focus. I know there is a creek nearby. I heard it earlier when we were out walking. It was farther off but I know the sound of water. You know the area where it felt like we were walking down? We need to keep going in that direction. I felt like we made a slight right."

"Yeah, that's because the woods got denser." I am not trying to get lost, but David seems to know a little more about the outdoors than me.

"OK, but what if that turned us around? I am not sure, but water would continue to be downstream. Isn't that how that works?"

"I don't know. I failed limnology." I never took the course, but I know what it is.

"What the fuck is that?" David looks so confused.

"The study of lakes and water. You literally act like you know what you're talking about, so I assumed you took a course."

"I doubt that's a real thing but yeah, no."

I take one last look around and everything looks the same. I remember Dad's words just a little while ago and they haunt me. He killed my sister. He really killed her.

We head back in the direction we were going the first time. When we get to the area I mentioned and are headed down a little slope, I see what David was talking about. We did head off a little too much. In fact, as I pay attention this time, I can see the path splits and there is another turn that looks like it directly takes us back to where we were. We must have missed that due to the shock of the night.

David starts to make his way through the thick of the trees. There is room for us on what turns out to be a small path. You can tell it's a path made by people going off on their own. It's dense and hard to get through, but with so many people going through, it isn't that hard. I'm scratched by a tree branch as they slap against my legs while branches smack me every so often in my face as David leads the way.

"Damn it." I fall onto my knees and feel a sharp pain both in my ankle and my left knee. I feel warm liquid drip down my calf as I stand up putting pressure on the leg. It doesn't feel broken, but it hurts. David turns around and rushes towards me.

"Are you ok?"

"I don't know, I twisted my ankle on the roots of the tree. I lost my footing." David uses his flashlight, and my knees are covered in mud. I can't tell if I cut myself, but I can feel liquid running down my leg. I try shaking off the pain by stretching out my knee but, the pain comes back.

"Are you sure? We could…"

"Sit here and wait for help?" I laugh because I don't know what he expects me to do.

"No, I was going to say we can wait a few minutes, or I can go up ahead and save you the time of going down, just to come back up. You know, you can sometimes be such a jerk, Jayson."

I know he's right, but it seems like his goal this weekend was to prove something to me and my family. Prove that he is a good guy but that was never something that I questioned about him, and I don't believe anyone in my family has either. Right now, my patience is running out, I'm in pain, scared.

"I'm sorry."

"It's ok, are you sure you can walk on it?"

"Yeah, once we get going, I know I will be fine. Wait! Quiet! Do you hear that?" It was faint, but when there are no other sounds, the faint sounds tend to get louder when you focus. You just need to pay attention and when I close my eyes I hear it.

"Crying. I hear someone crying." David points in the direction we were going, and we see a faint light off in the distance.

"Let's go." I feel a wave of strength and my knee no longer hurts. It's almost like the cries we heard somehow made everything I was feeling go away. There is a sense of hope that I begin to feel. I don't know what we are walking towards, but if there are people over there, then it sounds like it is a safe place to head towards.

The more we walk, the more the sounds around me become clearer, and the less my knee hurts. The limp I have is not as noticeable as before, but I still feel a sting in my ankle every time I step on it. I guess it wouldn't matter if my dad shot me, or if the stranger who took Gina murdered me. Twisting my ankle is the least of my worries right now.

We see a clearing and someone is tied to a chair. A flashlight is placed on the ground shining directly on her. David falls to his knees and immediately starts to untie her. It's Gina, we found her. She shakes her head, and we hear it. Someone is coming.

I grab David and apologize to my sister. The look on her face is of heartbreak and understanding. A single tear falls down her cheek. Although she's been crying the whole time, this one tear seems isolated and slowly trickles down the side of her face. I wipe it away and quickly kiss the top of her head. The understanding on her face sends shivers down my back. There isn't enough time, but I will be back. I will not leave my sister here.

"We'll be right back, we promise."

We take off running. We manage to stay close in case she needs us. We find a spot where we can keep an eye on her. I can't see her that well, but from here I can see that David was able to untie one of her legs. The rope is hanging half off. If whoever did this notices my sister, we may end up dead. I nudge him and point to Gina and down at my leg. David looks horrified. He jumps up like he's about to go back, but I hold him down as someone approaches.

CHAPTER 37

All this back and forth is tiring, but I feel so alive. It took years to get to this place, and I'm living out years of built-up anticipation and revenge. Revenge for someone who hasn't been able to fight and stand up for themselves and revenge for myself. There's a movie going on in my mind from what I had witnessed earlier, and it's being replayed over and over again.

"He killed his daughter! He killed his fucking daughter!" I catch myself saying this out loud in both an angry and yet very amusing way.

It's hard not to be upset when I want to do it myself. I didn't come all this way to have the job done for me. Though, I did find joy in his pain. I know that he didn't mean to do it. He thought he was shooting at me, I'm sure. I've never seen a grown man cry, but I got excited from that too. There is a muffled plea coming from her. I turn to her and hold back the urge to slap her. What overcomes me is adrenaline and rage and it's a battle to not react.

I look at the girl tied in the chair and position myself, so I am eye level with her. She is beautiful. I'm not into girls, but if I was, would she be my type? There's blood streaking down her cheeks, which reminds me of candle wax that's dripped down the side of a burning candle. It looks soft and I bring my thumb to it and check its density and smear its thickness across her. I go to wipe her hair from her eyes so I can see if she's hurting. When she snaps at me, it makes me laugh because she thinks she can intimidate me.

There were two reasons why I came back. She needed to be checked and she needed to know what her dad had just done. I bend down to grab the flashlight off the ground. It's still in the same position as it was when I left it. With her family running around the woods, I am surprised no one's come across her yet. Her useless sister is gone now.

"Your daddy killed your sister. She tried to crawl and get away. You should have seen her," I whisper into her ear.

She starts shaking to get herself free when I slap her. It feels good when my hand connects with her face. I feel a jolt go through me as new adrenaline surges through me. I want to do it again but stop myself as this wasn't the time to get carried away. I lower myself again, so we are face to face.

I whisper into her ear again. This time I take my time drawing out the words. "Daddy." I take a pause and continue. "That's what she said to him after he shot her." I make sure my lips brush against her earlobe.

She starts crying which makes my insides tingle. This is getting to her and she's having a hard time keeping it together. She's mourning for her sister and the pain from my most recent smack to her face. There is a bit of surprise at how quickly she's become saddened by the news though. I was sure there would be a bit of joy because she's never got along with her sister. I've been watching them for a few years now, and they never seemed to go out or have girls' nights together.

"I took one of those bags you made. You put a lot of thought into it didn't you. It was cute that you wanted to bring everyone together." I try my best to mock her in hope to further get under her skin.

"How did you?" She can barely get the words out. Her voice is raspy. I guess that happens when someone has their hands pressed against your throat.

"I've been to your house."

"I've watched you for a long time."

"This wasn't random, Angelina."

The horror is written across her face. I know she's questioning when I was in her house. How many times, and if I have seen everything. I know everyone's secrets. In order to make this work I had to spend a lot of time following them.

"I need to go but I will be back." I want to go check on the body. I should have dragged it away. I watched him for a while, and then when he walked away, I considered following. I let him go. The chase would feel better. I stop and look at this girl in front of me. She doesn't really deserve this, does she? I reach around my back and pull out a small blade. She sees this, and in an instant her eyes widen. I plunge the blade in her side and laugh as she screams.

"That feels good, doesn't it?"

CHAPTER 38

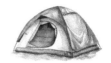

MOM

I push my way past Ale when I realize who is lying on the ground. I drop to my knees, grabbing the body close to me. Victor was at her head trying to talk to her. I couldn't believe I was holding my daughter's lifeless body. From the front, I couldn't tell what was wrong. She didn't look injured, but when I tried to lift her, I felt blood on her backside. I wanted to turn her over, but my fingers grazed past what felt like a circular opening.

"What happened to her?" I don't let Victor know that she was shot. Telling him would also tell him I think it came from his father.

Ale is pacing behind me and is adding nothing to the situation. I know she is panicking. I look back and see her fumbling in her pockets for something. She is avoiding all eye contact with the body and the situation in front of us. I can't do anything else but call for my daughter.

"Catalina." When I say it, I can feel pain coming through. Every time I say it, I get louder, and the words are a bit harder to get out. The only thing I want at this moment is for Cat to open her eyes, lunge for me, and call out to me. I need her to hug me and tell me everything is going to be ok.

"Catalina, Catalina, no." There is no movement. She is dead. A mother should never have to hold the body of their child this way. My chest hurts, and in this moment, I swear I can feel the pieces of my heart breaking off and traveling through my blood because I hurt everywhere. I feel stinging throughout my body, and I hate it.

I feel a hand on my shoulder and Ale is now kneeling next to me. I can see the shock and pain in her eyes. She starts crying and rests her head on my shoulder. I can't imagine what this looks like, the three of us around her body crying. Victor starts shaking as his sobs are getting louder. It looks like he's about to have a seizure with the way he starts to shake. I shove Ale off me gently as to not upset her and look over at Victor. Pulling him close I kiss the top of his head several times. I hold him tight as his sobs grow louder and violent. He needs to calm himself down because I don't want us to be heard. Whoever did this, his father or someone else, could come back if they weren't already headed back. I can feel him slowly starting to calm down as I tighten my grip even more. There are breaks in between each sob and gasp for air.

Ale comes around to the other side of my son. She knew when I pushed her away it wasn't because I didn't want her to touch me—it was because my son needed me. I needed him. She wraps her arms around Victor and me. I look at her and mouth, "Thank you." We are all hugging. I am glad that she is here because I don't know if I could do this alone.

It takes some time before we can break away. We all stand up and stare at my daughter. She looks so empty. I expect her chest to rise and fall at any moment and it doesn't, which makes me want to cry all over again. We're all looking at the body and have the same questions running through our minds. In unison, we ask.

"Who did this?" The three of us just go back and forth looking at one another, waiting for an answer. I think about holding back what I felt behind her, but I can't.

"Your father shot her." This admission has no truth, so I correct myself, "*Someone* shot her."

"How do you know that?" Ale jumps in.

"I felt something on her back. It felt like a bullet hole or something. Since there were no visible wounds from the front, I am assuming it didn't come out the other end." Victor starts to bend down, and I stop him. I don't want to see her body moved again. Not right now. "Victor, don't."

We couldn't stop Victor as he leans down ignoring our pleas. It's better for us to know for sure, even if we don't know who did it. He bends down to lift her body and my daughter's head slumps forward. I jump back as it hangs there. As I stare at it, I am waiting for her to lift it. The next thing I see is Victor lowering her again.

"There's a single bullet hole. I don't understand why he did this. What did she do?"

"We don't know if he actually did it—" Ale starts to say but Victor jumps in.

"He brought a fucking gun, who else could have done it?"

"Who could be doing all of this? Maybe someone else has a gun, maybe someone else is out here, or something happened to your father and someone took his gun? I don't know, I don't know anything anymore." Ale is crying again and bends down hugging her knees. She slumps onto the wet ground and just sits there. She looks like a child, and I expect her to start rocking back and forth, but she doesn't.

"Please don't fight, not now. We need to move your sister somewhere safe."

"I don't want to move her. The police…"

I cut him off because I don't care about the police. I don't want anything eating my daughter's body while she is out here. It is bad enough she'll be alone out here. Did she die alone? Or did my husband sit with her? I can't live with myself knowing that she's been nibbled on by nature's creatures.

"I know you don't want to move her, but we have to. We cannot leave her out here. Who knows what's out here and how long she'll last?" When I say it out loud, I see the looks on their faces. They know exactly what I mean. I can imagine that they are picturing it in their heads right now. Their sister, half-eaten by whatever wild animals are out here. I don't want to think about it, but I do. It's morbid, but it is my daughter.

I look at Ale and she knows why. She is going to have to move her with Victor. I'm too weak, and I won't be able to do it. Ale and I can try her bottom half, but Ale will have to do most of the work. Victor will have to take her by the head.

Ale stands up, and together we all approach Catalina again. We take a few moments to stare at her. Under my breath I say a prayer. We aren't a religious family, but I feel like I need the strength of something bigger than me, bigger than us, to help me get through this.

We position ourselves and bend over her body. We're about to lift when Victor stops and takes off his shirt and is left in a black tank. He tears it at the seam and drapes it over his sister's face. I don't think he can look at her while he moves her. He is trying his best to disconnect from this moment, and I understand why.

My son was never good at funerals, and I always wondered why? He stayed away and towards the back never trying to get close enough to view the dead. Was it something he saw when he was taken from us all those years ago? He never was able to tell us what happened or what he saw, if anything. The note we found indicated that someone took him.

When we got him back and I found the note, I was afraid he saw some horrible things or someone tried to do horrible things to him. The doctors examined him and said he was fine. Dehydrated and tired, but he was ok. He didn't talk for some time after, but when he did, he didn't say much. He didn't even know he was missing or was taken. We tried asking about the note, but he didn't know anything about it. We decided that we would pretend this never happened, because if he didn't remember, why bring it up? Why force him to relive whatever happened to him? Now I am so sorry I failed him.

"Thank you." I see him tear up. He stands there pausing for the briefest moment and then bends down. We take his lead and bend down too. She's a lot heavier than she looks and I am barely lifting. Ale is struggling, and with the way the body is tilted we are not doing a very good job.

"Where do we move her?" We didn't plan this very well. I nod towards the trees behind me away from the water and moisture. We'll prop her up against those trees where it looks dry. We'll make sure we tell them where she is so they can come back for her.

We're positioning her against the trees when we hear faint voices approaching us. My instinct is to hide. We have no idea who this is or why they are coming this way. Could it be whoever did this to my daughter? Is someone else out here in the woods? Before we even have time to react the voices are on top of us and I turn around in time as someone enters the clearing.

CHAPTER 39

DAVID

There's regret about coming as I think about what's been happening. When I decided to come, it was to be with Jayson. I wanted to tell him how I felt. I was prepared to leave if he asked me to, but things didn't go that way. I also wanted to spend time with his family and get closer to Ale. I've met them all before and I do enjoy their company. They're a bit dysfunctional but so is my family. Jayson hasn't met them because I keep them away. I don't like people getting too close to me in case they hurt me. Here we are though. The scene in front of me playing out makes me regret the decision to come. I should have just called to talk to him. Now, we are fighting for our lives.

Sitting here hiding from an unknown killer wasn't on my bucket list. Especially if that killer could be one of them. The thought crossed my mind several times. Nothing has ever happened when we were all together. When we woke up to the screams and found Gina gone, one of them could have easily done something. We've spent so much time away from everyone that I don't know what to think anymore. I don't know who I can trust. With Jayson's hand in mine, I know that he is the only one I do trust.

This person pacing back and forth in front of us still doesn't convince me it isn't one of them. I have questions. If Jayson's dad shot his sister, is he part of this? I don't know much about his dad, but I am drawn back to the moment where he pulled the gun out of his bag. Then to the moment where we saw him talking about killing his daughter. He's clearly capable.

It's tense and uncomfortable watching Gina get slapped. It's also heartbreaking. Watching her eyes well up when he told her that her sister was dead and her father was the one who did it, broke me a bit. I can't imagine what it would be like to sit there, tied, bound to a chair, and having a murderer tell you he watched as your father killed your sister. I see all the pain she is experiencing, and I fear for our lives, not only hers. We sit here watching, hoping that he doesn't hurt Gina anymore.

Just when it looks like he's about to leave her alone, I watch as he lifts his shirt. I grab Jayson's hand because I don't want him rushing them. I don't know if he's going to scare her or if he's going to use the knife. The silver shines in the moonlight; it's not a long blade but it can do damage. The black handle reminds me of kitchen knives, but the blade seems more like it's for hunting. It took all of five seconds for this to play out, but these five seconds stretched to five minutes as we sat there unable to help. The next thing I see is the knife go into Gina's side. She screams and it's over. Her head is slumped and he's walking away.

We both cover our mouths as tears spill down our faces. We don't make a sound because we don't want him to come back. Silent crying is the worst. Your stomach aches as you hold in the pain. We try our hardest to muffle the few sounds trying to escape our mouths. We need him to get away from here so we can see if we can help Gina.

We don't wait too long before I see Jayson already untying her. I can see he didn't want to waste time. I race towards them to do the same. Jayson has Gina's head in his hands. He's trying to wake her up.

"Gina, we're back. It's going to be ok. Gina."

I saw this on TV once and it was worth the try. I take my knuckles and press hard against Gina's sternum. And make a quick circular pattern pushing her as hard as I can. I feel like I might break her when she takes a deep breath and shrieks. I quickly covered her mouth.

"He just left; we need to get you out of here. Can you walk?" With my hand on her mouth, she shakes her head. "Gina, are you sure?" She mouths words, *I don't know*. I stand her up and see she's weak. There is blood coming out the side of her shirt. It's a lot but I don't think it's too much. I tear off one of my sleeves and apply pressure. After a few moments I realize that there is no way to keep this pressed firmly against her and try lifting her pants high enough to keep it in place. Jayson's looking around when he grabs some rope tossed on the ground and uses it to wrap around her waist. After her wound is secured as best it can be given the limited resources I ask her again, "Can you walk?" This time she nods.

We put both of her arms around us and started heading away from the place Gina might have spent hours in pain. She must be relieved because she can only say *thank you* as we carry her.

"Shit!"

We hear it and we know who it is, so we pick up the pace. He's coming back and we don't want to be here when he does.

"Quick, over there!" We need to hide and there isn't much time or a good place. We take a chance near some trees off the path where the forest starts to get dense. I push both Jayson and his sister through the trees. I must have pushed too hard because she winces in pain. There isn't going to be room for all three of us, and if we're all together, there's less of a chance for one of us to help each other out. I lean in and kiss Jayson and he knows what this means.

"No! No! No!" He is reaching for me.

"It's going to be fine. He grips my hand tight and then lets it go, knowing that if I don't find a place soon, I won't be safe. There is pain in his eyes, and it feels like when he lets go hours pass as our hands disconnect.

As soon as I turn and walk away, I feel empty and afraid. I scour the area and see some bushes, forming an idea. I crouch down as low as I can, hoping that I am covered enough. There is a part of me that thinks this could work.

CHAPTER 40

"Shit!" I forgot to shut her up. The last thing I need her to do is to start screaming. I thought about gagging her or taping her mouth shut. It was spur of the moment as I wasn't planning on doing it. Something came over me, and in an instant, I was stabbing her. When I reached for the blade behind me, I didn't expect for me to react so quickly. It wasn't Gina in front of me when this happened. I saw someone else and that made it easier. Not that anything this weekend seemed hard, but there was no hesitation in this action.

It had been quick. I brought the blade around me and plunged it into her side, she screamed, then fainted. She's been through enough and I don't need her around. It was time I ended her and better that she was out of the way. I couldn't have her calling for help. Her father could be nearby—or someone else. Seeing that her sister was out here and now dead, they could all be wandering around.

Last I saw her father, he was by the creek, but he could be anywhere now. I should have stayed longer to watch and see where he went, but I'd wanted to get back. I'd wanted to check on her. Share the news of what I'd just witnessed. I am not sure how much longer we have until day breaks. My watch broke earlier in the struggle, but I assume it's around 3AM. I'm only halfway to the creek when I realize all of this and turn back. I need to pick up speed and decide to sprint the rest of the way.

I feel turned around now. I don't know if it's panic or excitement, but I feel like I should have come up on her by now. Everything looks like it should, but I don't see her, and I think I'm lost.

I enter the clearing where I am sure she should be, and I spot the empty chair.

"FUCK!"

Rushing to the chair, I kick it over, hurting myself in the process. How could I be so careless and stupid? I begin hitting myself repeatedly. Calling myself different names over and over. It's calming somehow and something I did as a kid. My parents saw this once and thought something was wrong with me and maybe there is.

Pacing back and forth there's a realization that someone is nearby, and it could be any of them. I need to be careful and stay guarded because I can't screw this up.

I consider for a moment what it would mean to give up and get out of here. I don't want to risk getting caught or killed myself. Their father has a gun and might want revenge on me, and things have just gotten complicated.

"Ginnaaaaaa!" There's rage filled with years of revenge built inside of me and comes out in the most jarring way.

I need to find them. I take off in the only direction I think they could go. If I find them, I will just get it over with.

CHAPTER 41

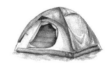

JAYSON

It's unclear as to what David is trying to do, but he can't be our hero. I need him. He needs to hide somewhere. I see him looking around. His glances back and forth are confusing. Watching him is like watching a chicken with its head cut off. I start to feel dizzy, and for a moment I think his head is going to detach from his body. The way his body jerks from side to side as he tries to decide where to go looks like different parts of him want to go in their own directions.

We can hear whoever is responsible for everything happening; they're upset and cursing. David stops and I can hear him listening too. I hear them head in our direction. I look and see David is still out in the open. He's easy prey at this point. I don't know if this is his plan, but if it is, it's a bad one.

"I'll fucking kill you!"

He's angry. David needs to hide. I whisper over to him hoping he can hear me, "He's coming." He looks over at me and lifts his finger to his lips to shush me and mouths, "I know."

Suddenly, I see David moving towards some bushes. He can't possibly think that's a safe space. I don't know what he is thinking but he is not thinking clearly. I hope he knows what he's doing. In an instant, the stranger is here.

I watch the stranger burst through to where we're at. It causes me to jump, and my heart stops. I look over and pull Gina close. She starts to shake, and I pull even tighter. I raise my hand and cover her mouth and look into her eyes. I'm afraid if I squeeze too tight, she'll make a sound. Her eyes speak to me. It's as if she knows that she's breathing heavily. She blinks, and then closes her eyes. I don't know what else he may have done to her, and I don't want to know. I want to get out of here with my family. All of them.

I see them pace back and forth. He raises his flashlight, shining it through the trees and bushes. I am afraid he is going to spot David because I can see him. I don't know if I really can, or if I am imagining it, but where he chose to hide is not inconspicuous. He can easily be spotted, and I am afraid that if he finds David, he will hurt him. Looking at Gina tells me all I need to know about what this man is capable of.

I feel something wet all over my hands. It's warm. I look at Gina, and though it's dark, I see something shine across her face and on the back of my hand. I realize that Gina is crying, her tears streaming down. In the moonlight her tears give off a sparkle that under normal circumstances would look comforting.

Still covering her mouth, I close my eyes and hope that we get through this. Feeling her body relax more in my arms, I open my eyes and see her energy draining. She doesn't have the same light she did when we found her. Something is wrong. I am not sure she is going to make it.

"I swear when I find you, I am going to kill you! Starting with you, you little…"

Out of nowhere I see a rock being tossed. It's coming from where David's hiding. It's just to the left of him. I don't understand what he's trying to do. He must have tossed it thinking his aim was a lot better than it was. Whoever this is now heads towards where David is hiding.

"I know you're here."

Another rock this time a little further away. I think back to earlier. He's a genius. I don't know if she knows what's going on, but her tears have stopped. I whisper into Gina's ear.

"David's got us." She looks over toward him, trying to see. She looks confused. We see another bigger rock this time. I see it because I know what we're looking for. This time with it being larger he tosses it farther. Suddenly, whoever this is, stops.

"Where are you?"

I think to myself that he figured it out. He turns around, shining his flashlight directly where we are hiding. For a moment, I think he's about to come towards us. My heart starts to race. I realize I am squeezing Gina a little too tightly because she wiggles in my arms. I release my grip just a little. He turns around and then takes off in the direction where David was tossing the rocks.

We sit here for what seems like forever. I don't see any movement from where David's at. Gina and I are wondering if we should come out. I don't want to stay here hiding forever. Gina doesn't have forever. I'm about to call for him when I feel someone touch my shoulder.

My reaction is to scream and knowing that David just risked his life to distract them, I need to stay calm. I turn around hoping that who I see is David.

"He's gone."

"How did you…"

"Don't worry how; we need to go."

I swear David was just over there, and I don't know how he made it over here so fast and without us even hearing him. I want to press him on the matter because he has skills. What else could he do without me knowing? I hope we have a lifetime to figure it out.

We pick up Gina, and she feels like she's gained weight in the time since we last carried her. She's losing steam, and her weight is exhausting as life drains from her. We need to get her somewhere safe, and we need help fast.

"Help me." I lift Gina and her face tells us how much pain she's in, but she doesn't make a sound. I don't think she has the energy to do that anymore. At what point is someone in so much pain they stop feeling it? Is that a thing? If we're going to get out of here, she's going to have to help us a little. If we do all the work, it will take us even longer to get out of here.

"Gina, can you walk?" Her chapped lips move. I can see dried blood and a string of saliva through her open mouth.

"Please leave me here." She's defeated.

"I am not going to leave you here. We didn't come all this way to just leave you here. Listen to me. I love you and we are going to get out of this." With her body weight on me, I feel a wetness on my side. I look down and see it. Blood, it never stopped. Her shirt is soaked and it's now soaking into her pants. Now it's all over me. I wipe my sister's blood on me. I am reminded of the scene inside the tent. She's lost a lot of blood tonight.

"David, we need to go. She needs a hospital. Now." David spots our blood-soaked clothes and I see the worry in his face. He doesn't try to hide it.

"Where's mom?" She sounds like a little girl when she asks this.

"I don't know, but she was safe with Vic and Ale when we last saw her."

"Can we find them?" It's faint when she says it, but I am afraid she's asking because she wants to say goodbye to them. I would want to. I don't want to think that is how this night is going to end. I know my father shot my sister and his reaction from earlier tells me she's dead, but I am not sure. She could just be hurt somewhere.

We lift her up and I can tell it's hard for her. We toss one arm over each of our shoulders and do our best to lift her as we walk. She is trying her best, but we do most of the work for her. I am sure she looks like she's gliding. A ghost in the night. I want to make sure she knows we got her, so I lift her just a little higher to relieve more of the pressure off her. I cannot leave my sister out here like this, not in this condition.

I have no idea where I am going, but I know one thing—it isn't in the direction where whoever that was is headed. We don't communicate with each other which way to go; we just start dragging Gina away from here.

It isn't long before we are out of breath.

"What's wrong, babe?"

Babe? David has never called me that before. Gina looks at David and smiles.

"Oh, so he's babe now!"

"Shut up, Gina." I say playfully.

"I just need to rest for a minute or two." As I say this, Gina jumps in.

"I can try and walk." We look at each other and then at her.

"Gina, I don't think…" She takes her arms off from across our shoulders and then starts to take a few steps. It must be too much for her because her legs start to wobble. We rush forward before they completely give out.

"I guess I have sea legs." My heart breaks. It's a reference to her favorite movie. I feel like we're losing her.

"I just need a minute and we can go."

"Jayson, I don't think I can go much further. I don't feel good. Just leave me here and go get help. I will be here when you get back."

"Gina, I am not leaving you here. There is no way I am going to leave you. What if he comes back? What if you…" I don't want to finish the sentence because I don't want her to know what I am thinking.

"You don't want me to die alone. Jayson, I've lost a lot of blood. I know what's happening. If I don't get out of here soon and get some help, I won't make it. I don't feel good already. I don't want to slow you down. Please."

"Come on, let's go. I don't care." She throws her arms around me and kisses my cheek. I want to push her off me; this isn't a goodbye.

"I love you, big brother." It's a whisper but I know I need to save her.

"David, give me a hand." We launch Gina back into position and start walking again.

"I have no idea where we are going." David looks confused but doesn't stop moving and neither do I.

"We'll eventually run into someone or something." That's when I spot a light off in the distance. I hear water.

"Look!"

David spots it too and is now pointing. Gina looks up from where her heads been slumped down. At this point I didn't even realize we were dragging her. I look over my shoulders and see a line in the dirt. Her legs start to move, and she has some strength left in her. She doesn't feel as heavy anymore as she has just gained some momentum and is pushing herself to walk on her own. I hope she doesn't take off running.

"Who do you think is over there?" Gina has her voice back. I notice it's raspy. I don't want to ask why but my mind goes to dark places.

"I don't know but I see more than one person," I reply.

"Mom!" I see her smile and I squint because I don't see her. I don't know who it is. There is more brush we need to get through. As soon as we are through, we see all of them. They are in front of my sister, and she's slumped against a tree.

"What's going on?" I speak. Gina leaps from us and into my mother's arms.

"What happened? Are you ok? Are you hurt?"

My mom is all over Gina and Gina is crying in her arms. Ale comes over and hugs me.

"Where have you been?" She punches me in the arms in between hugs. She grabs David and pulls him into a group hug and kisses his cheek. I hear her whisper in his ear.

"Did you take care of my boy?"

"Yes," he whispers back.

We're all hugging when we're interrupted by panic.

"Gina, what's wrong?" Mom's panicking as she struggles with the weight of Gina.

Mom is trying to hold her up when Victor, out of nowhere, is trying to help my mom lower her to the ground.

We've been here maybe three minutes, and then I realize something is wrong. In the sheer excitement of seeing everyone I finally notice Catalina hasn't moved. I see her lifeless body placed against the tree. I look down and see them trying to wake Gina. It's at this moment I realize two of us are gone.

I pace back and forth because for the first time tonight I am losing it. Both of my sisters are gone. I knew my father shot my sister because we heard him say it. I know Gina was stabbed by someone, but she survived. Until now.

My mom is not crying—she is screaming. A mother's cry is worse when she's crying over the loss of her children. Her scream is filled with pain. But we need her to quiet down.

"Whoever did this is still out there. He could be coming. We need to get out of here."

"Not without my daughters."

Victor hasn't said a word up until this point and when he does, he sounds cold, emotionless, and disconnected.

"We can't carry two dead bodies."

"Gina isn't dead," David says as he is kneeling with his head against her chest. "She's still breathing and there is a pulse." He lifts his head up and slowly says, "It's faint but she needs help."

"How will we get her that help?" I can't believe he sounds like this. Does he not care? I'm angry and not in control of my emotions anymore.

"What's wrong with you?" David questions.

"Nothing, we just found our sister dead and you want to ask what's wrong with me! Then you bring Gina over and she's dying in front of us! I can't take this!"

There's a sense of chaos I can feel in the air mixed with confusion and fear. I don't know what's wrong with him but maybe he's right. What did we expect? I don't know what's going on anymore. I don't know if I can deal with this anymore. I see my brother looking off in the distance. He's disconnected. He looks like he's trying to calm himself down.

Ale heads over to him and wraps him up in her arms. She is saying something to him when I see his body shake. He's sobbing. He is clearly not ok.

"Is there anything we can do for her?" I bend down to check on my sister. David is still trying to get her to wake up. She's lying there unconscious.

"I don't know. She needs help now; I don't think she has much time left. If any at all."

I look over at Ale and Victor and he's getting angrier. I've seen him lose his temper before, and then it happens.

CHAPTER 42

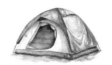

DAD

I stayed with her until her last breath. There wasn't much life left in her when I got to her. Her face and those words as she turned over broke me into a million pieces. *Daddy.* Her last words. My daughter, gone. And I did it. I sat there and held her for what seemed like an eternity. I ran my fingers through her hair as I spoke to her, apologized, and asked her to wake up. But she never did.

Holding her reminded me of the day she was born. I had cradled her in my arms then and now sat here doing it again. The end of her life. I rocked back and forth crying. Holding her tight until the last breath left her body. Then I kissed her and gently placed her on the ground.

I looked around for something to cover her when I looked into her lifeless eyes. I expected her to blink at any moment. When she didn't, I bent down and closed her eyelids. Whispering goodbye. If this happened to me, would my kids say goodbye to me? I'm sure they would. We may not always get along, but we love each other. It's the one thing I tried to instill in my family. Despite everything, we come together when one of us needs each other. Except that one night at dinner. I don't think we ever came together to talk to Jayson, to help him and be there for him.

So much was going on and I didn't know how to react. I know my reaction caused him a lot of pain. Suffering myself in the process, I never tried to reach out and repair things. Now we're here and I don't know if I will get the chance to fix things with him. I'm thinking of Jayson now as I stand over my daughter. I think about all my kids and their lives. When faced with death—either yours or someone else's—you think about life. In this case, my mind goes to Catalina's life.

I think about her life growing up. The things we did right, the things we did wrong. All the things she did. All the things she wouldn't do. I wouldn't get the chance to walk her down the aisle. I wouldn't get to hold her kids and watch them grow. I will never get the chance to hear her kids call me grandpa, that's if she ever decided to have children.

My aim isn't good, but I didn't mean to shoot her. I thought I was shooting at him whoever he was. I don't know what's going on or who this is. I think back to when Victor went missing. Could this have anything to do with that? The note and the fact that they never found anyone tells me it might.

Is this my fault? I've made some bad decisions with the business, and I owe some people money. Then there is Ale, Jayson's friend. The blackmailing. I know she's into drugs or at least I suspect someone like her would be. She's asked for a lot of money, so I assume it's for a drug habit. Did she set this up? Did someone follow her out here? If they want her, I will give her to them. She isn't part of this family despite how everyone else acts. She may be close to my son, but if she's why this is happening, I will gladly hand her over.

I check the gun to see how many bullets I have left. I

should have more, but I dropped the gun, after setting it off again by mistake. I couldn't remember if the clip was full to begin with when I had taken it out to check and dropped it, bullets spilling out of the clip. I tried to grab as many as I could, but it was dark, and I heard someone coming. I thought about hiding but something told me that I needed to get far away from here. I didn't want to end up dead. I needed to find my family and get them safely away from whoever this was.

After saying goodbye, I look around for someplace to hide and nowhere seems safe, so I run off. Now I'm lost and all I can do is think about my daughter.

"I killed my daughter."

I repeat this over and over. I can't get these words out of my head. I'm pacing back and forth, and I just want to rewind time. I want to go back, way back. Back to the day Victor was taken. Back even before he was taken, to that morning. I would have spent more time with the kids. I would have played hide and seek with them. If I did, maybe this wouldn't be happening right now.

"Who's there?"

I'm lost but I am not alone as I turn around, looking to see if I spot anyone. There's a sound of rocks scuttling across the ground. Someone is nearby, watching me. It's dark and I can't see. The moonlight isn't bright enough and the flashlight is a dim light. It shows me what's directly in front of me, not what's off in the distance.

"Who the fuck is there?"

I raise my gun and scan the area. I hear something off in the distance. Whoever it was or is seems to be heading away. I don't want to hide anymore, so I hurry off after the noise.

I recognize the area as I continue forward in the direction of the sounds. I know I am close to the camp. The noises stopped a while ago, but I just need to keep going. Whoever it was is now back at camp or I've lost them completely. I left everyone here, so I hope when I get back, they are still there. I don't know how I will face my family. I don't think I can tell them exactly what happened. I could always lie and say someone was shooting at me. I'm sure they heard the gun. I could easily say someone shot my Catalina but that would only take me as far as when police investigated everything and then I would have to answer to them.

I thought finding the campsite would have taken a lot longer. I got lost a few times. Everything looks the same out here in the dark. I start to really recognize the area and stumble right back to the campsite.

When I get back, the campsite is empty. I go through the tents hoping that maybe someone is hiding in them. I don't know why they would still be here. My hope is that they went to the cars and found a way out of here. A way to get help. Jayson is resourceful. If someone was going to save this family, it would be him. I never gave him the credit he deserved for being such a good son. If I was him, I would not have stayed put for as long as he did.

I've been a shitty father, husband, human. I don't deserve to live. I don't deserve the family I have been blessed with. If I was going to end my life, today would be a good day to do it. I could spare my family the trouble of dealing with me. Maybe I should try and save them first before I decide to end my own life.

I'm standing in front of Gina's tent, and peek inside. It's the only one I haven't checked. I don't know if I can stomach the scene again. When I saw them trying to get her tent open earlier, I grew frustrated. I needed to see inside. Now I don't want to look but I feel like it's something I have to do. I pull open the tent slowly and peek inside. The smell of iron stings the inside of my nose, and I feel like it's going to be stuck there. It looks awful and there is blood everywhere.

I bend down and touch the surface of the tent. The blood is sticky, though it's starting to dry and feels pasty. Is this how it's supposed to feel? I realize that this is my daughter I am touching the blood that was once in her body, running through her veins and giving her life. I hear something behind me and turn around quickly, drawing my gun.

CHAPTER 43

JAYSON

My brother needs to calm down. I am about to say something when he shoves Ale, and she goes down hard. Everything around her seems faded in my eyes, and it's almost like her journey to the ground is a long one. She bounces as she lands on her butt. Her hands dig into the dirt and the look on her face is pure rage. Her color has changed slightly. It's hard to see it in the dark but I notice. I've known her for a long time, so I know what's coming. She's going to go off on Victor.

I notice bullets on the ground near her. I see them because they glimmer as we flash our lights to assess the damage my brother might have caused.

"Fuck! What the hell is wrong with you!" She says this as her hands claw the dirt, her fingers brushing one of the bullets as it rolls away from her. She doesn't notice. I see now that there are quite a few on the ground. I can't really tell if they are just the casings or the whole bullet. We haven't heard enough shots, so I am sure they are the full bullets. Why would they be all over the ground?

Victor stands there with a blank look on his face. He looks disconnected. He doesn't look like himself right now. I see David rush over to help Ale. In one swift motion she is back on her feet, brushing off her pants and backside. She approaches Victor, who is still standing there stunned and hasn't said a single word. Snapping her fingers in his face, she yells again.

"Hello? Victor, what was that for?"

He seems to snap out of whatever trance he was in, shakes his head, and storms off. I hear him mumble something under his breath, but I don't know what it is.

"Victor, where are you going?" I call out to him but it's too late; he's already headed off into the woods. I stop David before he heads off after him. I need him here.

"David, let him go."

I don't want him to go but I also don't want him here. We must figure out what to do with both of my sisters.

"What happened to Cat?"

"I don't know, we found her like this. I think it was…" My mom stops mid-sentence. I look at her and I can see that she knows what happened.

"Dad shot her." It's an admission that I need to explain. "We ran into Dad. We didn't know who was coming at first, so we hid. When we realized it was him, we were about to come out, but we stopped when we heard him say he shot Cat."

"Why did he?" Ale steps forward and wants answers. She looks scared.

"He didn't say. He just kept repeating to himself over and over. 'I killed Cat. I killed my daughter.'"

"How did you get away?"

"David tossed some rocks to get his attention and he fled. We haven't seen him since."

Everyone is staring at me as I tell the story. Mom has stopped asking questions and sits there with her head hanging. When she finally speaks, I am shocked at what she says.

"I should have left him a long time ago." She looks up at us. "I was planning on leaving him after this weekend. Your sister knew."

"Is that why this is happening?" David's questioning my mom now. I have the same questions, but he's beat me to it.

"I don't know."

"He's been cheating on you."

I look over at Ale. How does she know? Is she sleeping with him? "Ale, what did you say?"

Suddenly it seems like my family wants to start spilling their secrets and I find it annoying because this isn't the time for that. Before I have the chance to say anything, Ale continues.

"He's been sleeping around for a long time, and it gets worse."

"I know." My mom stops Ale before she says anything else. I want to know what else could be going on and what she has to say, but my mom wants to speak.

"I've always known. I stayed because of you kids. I wonder if I hadn't, would things be different? Would any of this be happening?"

"Mom don't do that to yourself. It isn't your fault." Watching my mom blame herself for his actions and for all of this is upsetting.

"Isn't it?" My mom is blaming herself for everything right now. She is carrying the entire weight of our family's problems on her shoulders, and it is crushing me. We've all played a part in this destructive mess of a life we have. Yeah, my dad is an asshole, but could he be doing all of this?

I look over at Ale, who is just watching my mom. I think she has something more to add but is not saying it. I don't think it makes a difference at this point. We need to get out of this mess, and we need to go.

"I've been taking money from your dad too. Someone took some of it. I think it was Cat."

Mom's confessing to more secrets and I begin to wonder just how many more she has when Ale speaks up.

"Do you think that's why Mr. P shot her?" I want to slap Ale for asking that. Of course, it isn't. If it was, it isn't my mom's fault, but of course my mom immediately breaks down. She's already blaming herself for everything. I know Ale didn't mean for her words to have the impact that they are having on my mom.

"It's all my fault. I should be the one..." She can't finish her sentence as her sobbing has now escalated to a complete breakdown.

I don't know what to do. I feel like things are getting worse with every minute that passes. My mom is still sitting next to Gina. She's holding her hand and I see her fingers rubbing against my sister's. It's something she used to do when she wanted to calm us down. We would sit there with her, and she'd hold our hand rubbing our fingers. It brings me comfort to see this.

Gina still hasn't moved. I bend down to check her pulse and I feel nothing. During the two minutes that Victor had his temper tantrum until now, my sister has passed. My mom is still crying when I put a hand on her shoulder.

"She's gone." I put my other hand out to stop Ale from saying anything. I nod and sit next to my sister, opposite my mom. I grab my sister's other hand and mimic what my mom is doing.

We all sit there for what feels like hours, but only a few minutes have passed. David and Ale are sitting around us too. I look over at my sister slumped against the tree, eyes closed. I am too shocked to cry anymore, and I am afraid that one by one we are all going to die. I look over to my mom.

"What should we do?"

"Put your sisters together and let's go get help. I don't want them out here long and we need to get away before something else happens to one of us. I've already lost two of you. I won't lose you and your brother."

David and I move Gina and place her next to Cat. We lean them next to each other. It feels eerie, and a chill runs down my spine as I step away from them. Looking at them, I feel a rush of sadness. It feels like I posed them for a post-mortem photo, the kind families would take of their loved ones after their passing, sometimes with the living. But this isn't a photo, this is real life and my heart breaks.

I closed my sister's eyes as she passed with them open. When I do this, I say goodbye to her. When I came this weekend, I was ready to say goodbye to them. But I didn't want it to be forever. Then I had changed my mind midday. I figured maybe there was a way through everything. It's obvious we care about each other. We just don't know how to show it. I go back to that dinner where everything changed, but did it really? But now's not the time to reflect on that. We need to find my brother and get out of these woods.

CHAPTER 44

VICTOR

Every minute that passes gets harder and I can't stand here anymore. Ale is holding me tight and all I want to do is get her off me. I smell her perfume mixed with the scent of iron. My sister's blood, the scent we both now have on us, and I need to get away. Before I know it, I am pushing her away.

She lands hard on the ground, and I immediately regret it. I can see the look of rage on her face. I am prepared for her to get up and punch me in the face. It's what I would do in this situation, except she doesn't. David looks at me shaking his head. He lifts her up off the ground, and I am immediately filled with regret. It's happening again, I can feel it. I'm no longer present; I've disconnected from reality. I'm now some-place else.

Everything around me is cold; I am laying in a field and shivering. I see the shadow of someone hovering over me. I don't see a face, but I hear a voice I don't recognize. Other memories form, blending with this one. Each memory is a little clearer. I have been having these snippets for some time, and right now I feel like they are all coming together, forming something that is starting to make sense. I have a memory of me playing with my siblings. Another one comes to mind, a strange man asking to play with us.

I remember playing hide and seek somewhere. It's at the campground we used to go to as kids. We were playing and it was my brother's turn to seek so we all hid. I found a spot a little farther than my parents told me to go. There's a memory of smelling flowers and pulling grass up from the ground as I sat there. I could hear them looking for me. I was about to come out because I knew too much time had passed and I was getting hungry.

Making my way out of the hiding spot, I froze in fear when I heard someone creep up behind me. Danger is all I sensed, but I didn't know what to do. I wanted to call out because I could see my brother from where I was. The same voice hovering over me was behind me asking me to play again. It happened fast. A hand covered my mouth and then another hand wrapped tightly around my waist hoisting me up in the air. I wanted to scream but everything turned black.

All these memories are coming back quickly, and I cannot tell them apart. They feel real; they don't feel like they happened to someone else. I don't think I am confusing them with anything that is my memory. This happened to me, but why has no one ever talked to me about this?

"I can't do this to you. I thought I was ready, but I am not."

It's the only thing the shadow says to me. I feel them put something in my pocket, but I am too cold to check, too afraid that if I move, something bad will happen. I'm searching for more memories when I'm snapped back to reality by the sound of Ale snapping her fingers and yelling something in my face. Shaking my head and regaining focus, I walk off.

Not knowing why, but knowing I needed to get away because I am so confused. Staying there to help is what I should have done but walking away is what I needed to do.

"Did that happen to me?" It's the last thing I say under my breath as I walk away from everyone. I need to be alone.

I hear my brother call after me and I am expecting someone to come chasing me down, stopping me, before I end up the next dead person on this trip. No one does and I am alone. Alone like I was in that memory in the field. What was that?

I know it was real because I've been having these flash-backs for as long as I can remember. Except I was never able to piece them together to make sense of it. Since I loved horror movies, I always just thought it was my imagination processing something I had watched. Back there though, it was the first time more pieces came through. Something happened a long time ago and I don't know why they've kept it from me for all these years.

I want to go back and ask them about it, but I can't look at my sisters again. I'll eventually get out of here and get help. Following the creek for some time, I realize it seems a lot longer than I thought. The time on my watch hasn't moved since this afternoon, so I don't know what time it is. I think about the last time I changed the battery, and I don't think I have. It's not like knowing what the time is would help.

I've been in my head and thoughts for too long. Thinking about the watch and the battery I forgot or never changed was a distraction. A much-needed distraction.

I am considering walking back when I hear something off in the distance. I look around and the creek is gone. There is no way I just walked around for that long and ended up in some unknown part of the woods. I don't hear the water anymore. I don't hear the faint cries of my mother. Silence—except for feet walking quickly nearby. Scanning the area, I quickly hide because I don't know who it is. Turning off the flashlight, I can't see because it's too dark. The light was the only thing giving me any sense of direction. If the person who is out here doing this sees me, I might end up victim number three, or is it number four, because at this point who knows where my father is.

I see a shadow of someone walk past. They look like they know where they are going. Determined and on pace for something. I consider jumping out and chasing after them. My hand brushes against a large rock. I could take this and smash them over the head. End everything.

Deciding that's the best plan, I grab the rock, rolling it in my hand a few times. It's a good size. Big enough to hold and grip, and heavy enough with a few jagged edges to pound someone's skull in.

I don't know when I became violent, but I imagine this rock coming down hard on whoever caused this. Blow after blow, I want to get revenge for my sisters.

Not going after the shadow right away, I decide to wait two minutes.

One, two, I am going to count until I get to a hundred and twenty and storm after them. *Twenty*, I think about my mom and all the pain she is going through, Jayson who has been through a lot already, my sisters who were murdered, and I can't believe what is happening. *Fifty-four*, not much longer and I will finally figure out what is going on. My mind flashes to my father, why I haven't thought of him this entire time. None of us are close to him, but I do love him, he is my father. Should we really love someone just because they gave birth to us? Our only bond is our blood. *One hundred twenty.*

I try to walk as quietly as I can. I do not want to disturb the ground too much and give myself away. I can see the shadow and hear their footsteps. They are walking heavily, and they are also as determined as I am right now. I am sure they are who murdered my sisters. I am gaining distance because the shadow is growing larger and larger.

I start to recognize the area as I am following this shadowed figure. I think I am headed back to camp. A part of me wants to turn around and find my family, bringing them back. If I do whoever this is gets away with everything. They could be heading to their car now and we could end up screwed and lost until another group of campers show up, and who knows when that will happen. I am still so surprised we ended up the only ones out here. It's a national park; then again, it's the Midwest and who camps out here? National park or not this isn't the most ideal place to be for the weekend, but I do find beauty in nature.

Whoever this is knew where they were going. Hanging back, I watch, still unsure of their identity because I can only see their backside. They look around and I decide to creep in. They are now kneeling in front of my sister's tent and I'm walking towards them with the rock raised above my head with every intent to bring this down on them and crush their skull.

CHAPTER 45

"Where the fuck are you, little girl?"

I call out because I know she couldn't have gone far. I hadn't been gone that long. Someone else had to have been here and helped her. There is no way that she would have been able to get free on her own. Things are starting to fall apart. I am not doing this for me—this is all for him. That's what this whole weekend was about. From that day in the restaurant all I wanted was to get revenge for him. Seeing that he couldn't stand up for himself, I felt that I need to do it for him. Watching his father tear him down in front of his family, an entire restaurant was hard to watch. It's frustrating me more that no one stood up for him and no one did a thing that night.

My thoughts become distracted by a noise off in the distance heading my way. If it's her, I want to catch her before she gets away, and make sure she knows that what she did was a mistake. Scanning the area, I see there isn't a good place to hide. The bushes won't shield me, but they'll have to. Crouching as low as I can into the smallest possible form, almost folding in on myself, I make sure that I can still see because I need to know who passes.

I see a shadow pass and then another a minute or so behind. Could there be more people out here? I still don't know why she chose this place, but it was to my advantage. This place has been closed to visitors all summer. I know she knew that because I followed her here and saw when she took down the no trespassing sign. When I got home later that day, I saw the online posting about the park. The flooding earlier in the season caused some overgrowth and bacteria in the creek. As a precaution, the park was closing for the summer while the area was tested further. According to the latest testing, it was all clear, but with the season ending, they decided to keep the park closed for the summer only opening for the fall season and it isn't fall yet.

It would work to my advantage because I could leave the bodies, and there would be almost six weeks for them to decompose. A win for me. Unless someone found them sooner. I still had some time on my hands.

I decide to follow the shadows and see who these two are. Two against one. I can easily take them. My confidence has really started to take off since this all started.

All trails lead back to the campsite. Where the first attack took place. I see him looking through the tents. Then I see him. He's got a rock over his head.

"Is he going to do it?"

I cover my own mouth because I can't believe I just said that out loud. This is going to be so much easier than I thought. They are going to end up killing each other and I won't have any blood on my hands. Except for that bitch.

I eagerly wait for the rock to come down on his head. He's feet away, and somehow he hasn't tipped him off that it's about to happen.

CHAPTER 46

VICTOR

I feel the adrenaline coursing through me. The blood running through my veins warming my body in the night's cooler temperature invigorates me. I've never felt this way before. There's rage built up inside me, along with the memories I've been having. I'm angry because for a long time I thought they were dreams, but I am sure my family has been keeping something from me.

There is a lot going on as I approach him readying, myself to take him out. I am feet from him, and he hasn't heard me. Suddenly, I step on a twig, snapping it in place. I know he's heard me because he stands and turns around as I am about to announce my presence.

CHAPTER 47

JAYSON

I don't want to leave my sisters. Leaving them here makes me feel like I am abandoning them, and I already wish there was something more that I can do. I know my mom doesn't either, she's staring at them quietly. The thought of them being alone out here doesn't sit well with me. I don't think we have many options though. My brother is gone, and I feel a loss of control. Ale pulls something out of her pocket. A marshmallow. Did she just have a bag of marshmallows in her pocket? I watch her plop one in her mouth and notice my stomach rumble. This isn't the time to think about food, but I can't help it. My mind goes back to my brother—he's alone now.

We need to catch up to him before he ends up lost or like my sisters. I should have gone after him or at least let David go. I don't know why I stopped him; it was most likely fear that he would end up dead. Then why did I let my brother go? Was it to have him suffer the same fate as my sisters? David on the other hand, has helped to save me twice tonight already. He also has a way with words, and I am sure he would have been able to get Victor back here.

It's now Ale, my mom, David, and me. I can tell no one wants to leave, but we need to if we're going to make it out of here. Ale has said little and has been staring at my sisters the entire time. I see her wipe her tears, and then I hear her swearing. Words like "fuck," "shit," and "bitch" are commonly used words for her and I'm hearing them now. Surprised though, I also hear the words "sorry," "scared," and "help." She's scared and so am I. Sorry wasn't something that she should be saying right now. Unless she's done this to us or had someone do this, there's no need for that. She's my best friend and there is no way she's involved.

My mom walks over to my sisters. I am not sure what she's going to do, but she bends down and plants a kiss on each of their cheeks. Then another on top of their head. My mom's a strong woman. She runs her fingers through their hair and says her last goodbye. As she stands up, I hear her whisper something. I don't know what it is, but I know she needs her space, so I turn around and give it to her.

I feel a hand on my shoulder, and when I turn around, she is standing in front of me. The look on her face is determined. She wants to get out of here and she's pissed. There is no look like the look of a mother's rage.

"Let's go."

We grab the flashlights and get ourselves ready. It's been about ten minutes so he couldn't have gone far. Maybe he just needed a time out. We could have all used a time out at this point including myself, but the clock is ticking and we're dropping like flies on a hot summer day. In need of something to eat, I walk over to Ale asking for a marshmallow. She reaches behind her and pulls out a small bag of smashed marshmallows. Popping one in my mouth starts a buffet and everyone is there grabbing one.

"Where do you think he went?"

Mom pushes through us after popping one in her mouth. She's in charge now and takes the lead and we follow. She seems to know where she's going like it's her mother's intuition guiding her. Instead of asking questions I'm glad someone else is calling the shots and taking the lead—and for once it isn't me.

"I want to find my son and get out of here."

We head off in the direction where my brother went. The woods are dense, and I keep getting smacked in the face with branches. I am directly behind my mom and she's moving quickly. We enter a clearing and I see her stop and look around.

She hasn't spoken since we walked off leaving my sisters behind. I want to ask about my father. She hasn't mentioned him since I told her he shot Cat. I think she's over him at this point. I would be too if I found out he killed my daughter.

We're no longer by the creek. We are now in the middle of nowhere again. Mom doesn't look as determined as she did a little bit ago. She looks like she is lost. I'm about to ask if we should change directions when I hear it. Off in the distance we hear someone approaching and the sound of twigs breaking under the weight of someone's feet. Someone's headed towards us and my heart races into panic. Waiting for instructions from my mom she turns around and finally gives us direction.

"Hide!"

"What do you mean hide?"

"Jayson, I love you but listen to me and hide."

I don't want to argue, and my mom is clearly no match for whoever this person is coming this way. You don't argue with mom though.

"Ale, come with me." Mom grabs Ale by the hand and

drags her off. I want to stay together but maybe splitting up is going to help us.

My mom ducks behind some bushes which doesn't appear to be a good plan. She's going into hiding and looks at me like I should know what to do next. She begins to swat at the air, signaling me to go, I sigh in relief, grabbing David's hand and try to find a place to hide.

A shadow passes by and I think it's my father. It happened so fast I wasn't sure if it was him or not. I want to go after him, turn him around, and punch him in the face for what he did to Cat, to us. I decided not to in case it wasn't him.

"Did you see who it was?"

"I was just going to ask you; I thought it was your father."

We sit there looking at each other, then in the direction of whoever just walked past.

"Wait, someone else is coming."

It wasn't long before we see someone else. We hear someone behind us, and I think we're surrounded. I am sure there is more than one person now. Pulling David down lower, we stare at each other not sure what to do. I see the bushes move over where mom and Ale are. I see one go one way and the other go another. It looks like they are splitting up. I wonder if David and I need to do the same.

"My mom and Ale are moving, should we?"

"I don't think we should. Just wait it out."

There is no way I can wait this out. I want nothing to happen to them. Trying to get up, I'm pulled back down by David.

"We don't know who is out there and we don't know what's going on. I care a lot about you, but don't be stupid."

It is the first time since all this happened he hasn't said "I love you" and instead says "I care about you." I knew this would happen. Somehow things would get screwed up. I think he knows what I am thinking and pulls me in for a kiss. As I pull away from him, he tightens his kiss.

"I love you." He pulls away and I am in shock. My mind went from I'm losing him to he loves me, and then he's gone. This whole weekend has been filled with confusing thoughts. There are even more as I sit there, not stopping him as he walks away from where we're hiding. He's confident and determined. I think I should go after him, but I don't. I don't know why but at this moment all I can do is sit here and watch the man I love head off towards danger. When I see him look in the direction my mom went, I know I'm going to go looking for Ale. I see him turn around as I stand up.

"I'll get her, wait here."

"I am not waiting here."

I can't wait. We need to find them. If we both hurry, we'll make it back here, together. I jump up and hurry after David. He stands there waiting for me to catch up to him. Pulling him close I need to let him know I care.

"You go get my mom and I will go get Ale, just hurry and get back here in five minutes, ten tops." He taps his wrist signaling the time, but his wrist is bare. We have to find a way to track time without any means of doing so. He nods and kisses me one more time, this time it's quick.

"Be careful."

"I love you."

"I love you too, Jayson."

I watch him walk away from me and I am standing in the middle of the woods alone. Looking around, I take in my surroundings. I thought this weekend was going to end up very different. I thought I would finally talk to my family. Tell them how much they have hurt me and start a new life. Seeing David walk away both scares me and excites me. I am afraid he's going to end up hurt but I am so excited that he is here and that he showed up.

When Ale and I pulled up earlier and I saw him, everything changed for me. I knew we were finally going to get the chance we deserve at being together. Now all of this is happening, and I don't know what is going to happen.

I turn and walk off in Ale's direction, and I know that if I am going to get out of here, I need to find her and try to make it back before ten minutes, preferably five. Not having a watch or a phone, I need to time it somehow. I can count but I have always been good at figuring out things like time, never once being late for an event my entire life, I won't be late coming back to David. My goal is to be back in nine minutes, hopefully with Ale.

CHAPTER 48

VICTOR

"It's me."

With his back turned I didn't recognize him at first. I could have really hurt if not killed him. The rock positioned where the jagged edge was most prominent could have done some damage. Just one blow is all I needed. I could take him out and end all of this. With way too much confidence in the moment, I had raised the rock a little higher, prepared to strike. When he stood up and turned around, I saw who it finally was.

"I almost smashed your head in." He doesn't lower his gun. He is staring straight at me not saying a word. I immediately think about Cat. He shot her and now he is standing in front of me with the gun pointed directly at me. The next thing I see is his hand shaking a little.

"Dad, we've been looking for you. Gina, she's dead, and Cat, you?" His eyes widened.

And then it happens. I feel a sharp pain.

CHAPTER 49

ALE

I came with Jayson this weekend to support him, not to cause trouble. But when I was texting his father on the way over, I knew I had made some mistakes. Now with everything else happening, I hope I can try and fix things.

I've always been one to screw things up and even blame myself for what happened on the last night I saw my parents. I was tired of the abuse, but I still blamed myself. Am I to blame for this weekend too? If I would have said something sooner, maybe I could have helped them fix things.

There was never a time I was good at fixing things. I'm good at destroying things, and I am afraid I did more to hurt this family than help them. It should be me laying against the tree back there, not his sisters. There is a desire to survive tonight. I want to do things differently. I look over at Jayson's mom and I see the mother I wish I had.

"Ale, come with me."

"Where are we going?"

I don't know why she would think that splitting up was

the best thing that we could do. I want to make it through this, not put a target on my back and die. So far, every time we have split, someone ends up dead or hurt. I don't want to be next or left alone. I want to stay with my best friend, the person I always feel safe around.

I want to protest. Stomp my feet to the ground and demand that we stay with them. Instead I let her drag me away. The grip on my wrist is tight, and I am afraid it's going to leave a mark.

"I vote we stay together." It's all I can get out as I'm being pulled away from my comfort.

I feel like I have to go with her. My ability to choose was taken from me. The look on Jayson's face said it all. He wanted us to stay together too. He doesn't argue with her or challenge her enough. I wish he would because this could be all over for me. I might not make it out of these woods.

"We need to hide."

We both look for a place that would cover us both. Somewhere that would be hard for them to get to us, but easy enough for us to get away if we need too. As complicated as it sounds, I think she knows. Before I can protest anything, I am dragged behind some bushes where we can still see. I guess the advantage is that maybe they wouldn't come looking for us because who would hide in such an easy to find spot.

Crouching down as low as I can, Mrs. P shushes me every time I try to speak. I feel like I am being scolded every time I open my mouth, but she's right. I need to stay quiet.

We hear something faint in the distance, and I am worried it's him and he's found us. I hold my breath waiting for someone to come. When the first shadow passes by, I feel like I am finally able to breathe. A sense of relief rushes through me. Getting fresh oxygen in your brain can clear your thoughts. I see Mrs. P exhale, so I know she is feeling what I am feeling.

I am ready to get up and go find the boys when we hear it —another sound. We turn and look at each other confused because this whole time we thought there was only one of them, but maybe there are two.

The chance of survival is slim when you're dealing with one crazed killer, but two makes the chances impossible. I'm now worried that being split up only shaved time off our life. Whatever time we had left is now cut in half. I reach down and grab Mrs. P's hand and squeeze tight. She squeezes back.

After the second person passes, I start to think of the boys. Are they ok? Are they just as worried and scared as we are in this moment? I want to get up and find my way back to them, but the thought of leaving Mrs. P alone doesn't feel right. She just lost both of her daughters, and what would that tell her if I left her right now. Alone and unable to really defend herself.

I see this woman in front of me as strong, but I also see her so sad and lonely. Living with her husband had to have been a nightmare. The way he's treated them is just as bad as how my dad treated me. It's abuse but a different type. I am about to suggest we go find Jayson and David when she has another idea in mind.

"We need to split up."

"We need to split up? Are you serious?" I can't believe this woman. Is she trying to get us killed?

"You go that way and I'll go this way. We go find our way back and then we get the hell out of here."

"What was the point of splitting up in the first place?" I ask because her plan seemed flawed from the very start, and now she wants to do what I wanted to do in the first place.

"I really don't know what I am doing, I was just thinking that if we saw the other being hurt, we could come from behind or whatever and kick their ass. Catch them by surprise." She motions her hands in a way like she is mimicking an attack. I want to laugh because this little woman in front of me doesn't seem like she would be capable of fending off an attacker, especially with a weapon, but she looks convinced, and I am buying what she is selling.

She has a point though; it does make sense. If whoever was doing this saw one of us alone, they would think they had the advantage. If we were close enough to each other and able to keep an eye out, we could easily help. It's funny how you come up with these things after but in the moment your mind goes blank. I appreciate her for thinking a few steps ahead, but now we have the difficult task of finding our way back to Jayson and David—but on our own.

"Are you ready? Ale, look at me, are you ready?"

"No, I don't want to go alone."

I want to stay here and wait for help. I want to wait for them to come to us. She doesn't wait for an answer and makes a demand.

"Go."

She's gone before I can respond.

I look over at where the boys are. I can see Jayson and I know he sees us. It's dark but I guess you can see better when you know what you're looking for, even in the dark. I go in the opposite direction of Mrs. P.

I still don't know who it was that hurried past us, but I want to get back to Jayson. I see a clear path to him but it leaves me out in the open and I still don't know if it's completely safe, so I crouch down and work my way through the forest taking the scenic route to safety.

The shadows gave no clue who went past. I wonder if it was Victor or his father. All I saw were shadows. There were two of them close to each other, but each one looked like they were following the other one.

I realize I may have taken a longer than expected detour

and panic. I look around and hear the hoot of an owl and jump. My hand clutches my shirt just above where my heart is. I take a deep breath out when I hear a twig break behind me.

I stop, hoping it's Mrs. P. I don't want to turn around, but I feel like if I don't, I'll sit here frozen. Slowly I turn around and see no one standing behind me. You hear things when you're out here, and under pressure it's even worse.

I am about to turn around when I feel something hit me over the head, immediately grabbing my skull feeling warm liquid. It's dripping down my face. I'm immediately dizzy and feel unsteady but before I can yell or scream for help, I feel a bag over my head. I feel a tightening around my throat as if someone has just wrapped a thin rope around my neck. It feels like I am being crushed, my airway collapsing. I can still breathe but it's getting harder to do it.

My feet drag with my back against whoever is behind me. I try to wiggle my way out of their grip, but I can't get my footing under control to stand up. Each time I try, I am dragged further and further away, and my feet kick in front of me. My weight is what's hurting me in this situation. I don't know what is happening, but the more I try to fight my way out of this, the more I feel like I am going to lose. Feeling weak, my instinct is to not give up, but I have nothing left to give and go limp.

CHAPTER 50

DAVID

We just need to find them and get the hell out of here. I saw where his mother went and headed off in the same direction. I know that we can get through this if we just stay together.

I find her and rush towards her. At first, she looks like she's about to run when she sees me. I can see her looking around for Jayson.

"We were coming to you," she says eagerly.

"It's ok, Jayson is looking for Ale." I can still see her looking for him.

I grab hold of her hand and we head towards the previous spot we were at. I told Jayson to meet back here; I made it back quickly and hope he does too. His mom was already almost to us, and I wonder if we should have waited. I am tempted to head toward where Jayson was going, but I know that if I did and he came back, we would end up missing each other. I can't risk us going back and forth looking for one another when I could just stick to the plan.

"Get down, he'll be back soon. I told him to meet us here in ten minutes."

She crouches down and we sit, waiting. I don't have a watch or a phone, so I am counting in my head, losing track a few times. I was never good at keeping time. Something that annoyed Jayson because he was very punctual. I am not sure where that came from but he was never late for anything. In fact, on our first date he showed up an hour early. I know because he told me about it later.

I wish I could rewind time and go back to that first date. We chose a movie. I picked it out because he would pick what we would do after. I was nervous so I figured that if we were in a dark theater and weren't pressured to talk, I would slowly break out of my shell. Jayson claims I am filled with all this confidence, but I'm not. We ended up at a bar after the movie, watching some drag show. I learned that night that Jayson was social despite saying he was a homebody.

That night I also learned I was a jealous person because every few minutes someone was coming up to him and talking to him. It was nice seeing him outside of college because at school he was very different. There are many sides to Jayson, and I love getting to know each of them.

"He should be back already." Becoming increasingly impatient, I pick at my fingernails as she watches me.

"I don't think he's coming back." She places her hand on mine to stop me from pulling off a piece of loose skin I've been tugging at.

"He is. Just wait!" I say it with all the confidence that I have in me, but it isn't enough. I can tell she fears she's just lost her son.

We come out of where we're hiding. I feel defeated. I don't know what to do.

"What are you doing?"

"Waiting."

"We can't wait here."

"Watch me."

I want to sit on the ground and wait with her, because I know I can't go look for Jayson. If I leave her and something happens to her, I wouldn't be able to live with myself.

"You look like you make him happy. I think he's always been happy around you."

I turn around and I am already crying. His mother has always approved of him.

"Why is your husband like that? Jayson told me what happened at dinner a few years ago."

"Did he tell you he hated me too?"

"No, he didn't, he feels sorry for you. He wishes you would have left his father a long time ago, but you stayed for him, for your kids."

She's shocked. That might not have been the thing to say to her. When I look at her again, she starts to cry. I feel horrible for doing this, but I think this is something that we both need right now. We need closure and we need to come together and bond. I just didn't think I would be bonding with his mother over the death of his sisters and maybe even him. I sit here holding her hand.

"If we make it out, just take care of my son."

I will take care of him, but I want her to know that she is going to be around too. I can see she is the mother I wish I had. She's the type of mother who is everyone's mother. There is nothing about this woman that screams evil or mean.

"You can take care of him, us."

She looks happy when I say this. I can see that there is some hope left in her because there is some hope left in me.

I reach down and lift her up.

"We're going to get out of this and we're going to go find Jayson." She needs my confidence right now, but I wonder if I am trying to convince myself of that too.

I don't know how we're going to get out of here, but we will.

As soon as she's off the ground, I know something is about to happen. I don't even have the time to get my words out.

CHAPTER 51

MOM

Jayson did a good job finding David. He is nothing like my husband. You know you always end up with someone like your father. I know this because I did, and that I regret, but not my kids and my family.

Sitting here getting to know David was a distraction and I enjoyed it. I just wish it was under different circumstances and someplace else. Well, I don't mind the setting, just not the mood and atmosphere and murderer out there. Getting to know your son's partner shouldn't happen in the middle of the woods while you wait to see if someone has killed your son or not.

I've never met someone Jayson was interested in before. He leads a private life when it comes to stuff like that. I am so proud of him though. I am proud of David too, even though I don't know that much about him. He seems like he is a private person too. He's come around before but was always introduced as a "friend." A mother knows. I think I always knew, and I was ok with it. Maybe I should have said something that night at dinner. Maybe things would be different.

If I could change anything, I would change staying with my husband after all my kids were born. I wouldn't change having them. They are here because of their father. We were happy at some points in our marriage, but I just think we weren't ready. I wasn't ready because I chose the wrong person. He wasn't ready because he's a pig.

When his family didn't really accept me, I should have taken that as a sign. When you're in love though, you don't care about those things. He always told me we didn't need anyone else. He would tell me it would be me and him until the end. Then we started having kids and I noticed some changes. Subtle changes at first. He would spend more time away from the house or avoided spending time with me, especially during the pregnancy. He was worried about money, and he wanted to support his family. A horrible husband and father, but a great provider.

David is so kind. He sits here holding my hand while we talk, but it's time to go and we need to find my son. I watch him get up and dust the dirt off his pants. Noticing that they are my son's pants, I look up at David and smirk. He shrugs and we both understand the moment we just had. My son and this boy in front of me are going to be so happy together. It doesn't matter where David comes from or who his family is, I just hope I get to meet them. David is part of my family now. Accepting him and their relationship relieves me. One of my kids is going to have a happy ending.

David is lifting me up when it happens. I see him come out of nowhere and watch in horror as David is struck over the head by what looks like a tire iron. I watch in shock, and I know he saw the look on my face. He knew something was about to happen.

David falls to the ground and doesn't move. He goes down hard, face first into the ground, blood seeping, pooling next to his head. I want to drag him to safety, but there is no time. I see the man coming towards me and his weapon is raised.

I try to back away and trip over my own feet twisting my ankle. I turn around and crawl away. My hands don't move like they used to, and my carpal tunnel slows me down. I feel a foot press against my back, which puts pressure on me and my wrists. It feels like they are about to snap. I cry out in pain when I feel his entire weight on my me. He grabs a fist of my hair and raises my head up and smashes it into the ground.

I try to pull his hands from being entwined in my hair, but there is no use. He's stronger than me and I have no way to fight him off. I try to pull my body away. I crawl another foot in front of me. He's amused.

"Where do you think you're going?"

My head raises a little higher, and then my face is smashed back into the ground.

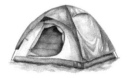

I wake up not knowing where I am, or how I got here, but everything is fuzzy. My vision has never been blurry before and my head is pounding. I can feel pain in different spots on my head where I am sure I have bald spots. I am unable to see what's around me or who is around me. My hands are tied to a chair and my feet bound tightly. There is tape over my mouth. The tears and blood running across my face make it impossible to see and I can't wipe anything away. I start to feel dizzy all over again as my breathing is labored and panic overtakes me. I squint and I see him walk off. I can feel myself about to lose consciousness when I hear him.

"I'll be right back."

CHAPTER 52

I watched the scene unfolding in front of me. As he got closer and closer, I was sure he was going to do it. I wanted to watch but I felt a second of hesitation, so I headed in. As soon as he stood up, I knew he wasn't going to do it.

I guess it's a good thing because now I get to do what I came here to do.

He doesn't notice me at first, but when I leaned over getting ready, he saw me, and his hand started to shake. I wanted him to see me, so peering around Victor's shoulder was just my way of taunting him. Letting him know I am still in charge.

I miss the bullet and I am grateful, but he's proved he has horrible aim—as evidence by his daughter's death. I feel the knife in my hand and raise it quickly, stabbing his son directly in his side and leaving the blade. He goes down crying out in pain. I run towards the tree and take cover. I toss a few rocks to distract and confuse his father.

He's approaching with careful skill, gun still raised and aimed directly in front of him. He's moving side to side like some cop in a movie. I hold my breath as he slowly passes in front of me. I wait a few seconds while he checks to see if it's clear.

As soon as he's just passed me, I creep out. I take the tire iron and simultaneously hit him in the head as the hoot of an owl can be heard in the distance. It only takes one strike, and he goes down. He's out.

I drag his father back to his son, tossing him next to him. He doesn't move and just stares. Victor leans over and checks to see if he's breathing.

I pull two chairs around and place them next to one another. He watches as I tie up his father, not trying to get away or even stop me. He just asks questions.

"What are you doing?" he yells, "Who are you?"

"Taking care of Jayson." I laugh only because he has so much confidence right now. *"Don't worry about it."* I want to end him right now as he's starting to annoy me.

I don't have time to argue with this kid or go through all the reasons this is happening. I need to get them tied up, but his dad is heavy. He works out and at over six feet tall, he would tower over me when standing. Knocked out, he looks and feels feeble and weak. It's one reason I needed to get him from behind. A man of that strength would be hard to take on from the front. I look over to his son who continues to watch me.

He's in a lot of pain and I would almost prefer if he had put up more of a fight. He came off as the weak one out of the bunch. You get to know a family when you spend a few years watching them. Studying them and getting to know them. I wanted to make sure they really deserved it. I also wanted to give time for Jayson to do it on his own. Not kill them but tell them how he feels.

Victor seemed like he was sorry after that night. I could see changes in him. It was mainly in the way he interacted with his father. I look over at him and shake my head in disgust. It looks like he's all but given up. I take him and tie him up next.

I empty one of those stupid bags his sister packed for them. The contents spilling across the ground. He's looking at me but can't say anything. Once he's tied up, I head off looking for the rest of them.

It doesn't take long to find her. She looks pathetic out here alone, lost, and helpless and an easy target. She just might be the easiest one. I open the bag. It's one of those gym bags with the drawstrings. I don't have time to react because things are moving quickly, and I don't want to miss this chance. I need to get her back and them all together so they can face each other.

I slowly creep up behind her, trying not to make a sound. I duck out of the way after stepping on something that breaks under my feet. She doesn't immediately turn around, which buys me a little more time. I slowly circle around some bushes as I see her looking in the direction I was just standing.

She turns back around and it's happening. I strike her and quickly place the bag over her head pulling on the strings and start dragging her back. She puts up a brief fight but gives up faster than I thought.

She's easy to drag back. She weighs nothing compared to the boys. Surprisingly, I still have enough strength after dealing with Victor and his father. I am going to be sore tomorrow, as this all feels like a workout.

When we get back to the campsite, I quickly make sure the other two are still there. I didn't want them to get away like his sister did, so I double tie them and recheck everything again.

I quickly put her in a chair and make my way out again. Five down, three more to go. I don't want to hurt Jayson, but I will if I have too. I just want him here, so I make my way to grab me another. Jayson has to be the last one.

Finding them quick, I don't think they even realized how close they were to getting away. Jayson isn't with them, but I need to get them alone or separated. I decide my best shot is to get him down and then I can easily work on his mother.

It was cute watching them bond. I almost cried listening to them talk to each other. It's clear they both love Jayson. They both want what's best for him.

I see him lifting her up off the ground. Now is my chance. I run up behind him. The look on her face tells me she knows it's over for the both of them. I hit him and he goes down. She trips trying to get away. I hear her ankle snap when she goes down. This is going to be easier than I thought. She tries to crawl, and I feel bad for what comes next. I started to like this one a little. I lift her up by her head and smash it down into the dirt. She goes limp and I do it again just to make sure.

Looking back, I check on David and he's out cold. I'll come back for him. I just hope he is still alive when I get back.

She's lighter than the rest. And I feel bad for her. Like Jayson, she doesn't need to be in this family. She was planning her escape, which ultimately helps me plan my getaway.

She doesn't wake up as I strap her into the chair. I was sure one or all of them would be awake by now, but they all sit there, heads down. I check each one to make sure they are still breathing. Victor's breath is labored and I see blood underneath the chair. I need to get them all back for this to work. I still want them all alive and awake.

I make my way back to where I left David. I am getting more and more excited because this is all going to be over soon. Both for me and for Jayson. I am thinking is this justice really for him or for me? That day in the restaurant, I was taken back to when I came out to my family. Watching the scene in public made me grateful that my embarrassment stayed within the four walls of my home. The looks on everyone's faces. I was ashamed of this family.

When I get back, David is gone. There's just blood on the ground. Nobody, no sign of where he might have gone and who helped him. I am sure Jayson found him. I am thinking maybe I should just go back and kill the others and let Jayson and David live happily ever after. Would that be enough for Jayson? Does he need to confront them like I needed to confront my family and never did? Is this more for me or for him at this point? I take off in search of them to get justice and revenge for us both.

CHAPTER 53

JAYSON

Ale isn't anywhere and I'm thinking that I'm lost and that I won't get back to David in time. It's been over ten minutes and I'm usually good with time. It's a blessing and a curse. For one, I am never late, but then sometimes I am early.

Like our first date. I showed up an hour early. I was so nervous. I was so used to seeing him in school that when we decided to go out, I was excited and didn't want things to go badly. It didn't; we had a great time and ended up at my favorite bar watching a drag show. I think he saw the real me that night.

I end up wandering around for what feels like forever when I recognize the area. I see the bushes where David and I had been hiding and see where my mom and Ale were. Entering the clearing to where we were supposed to meet, I don't see anyone, not at first. And then I see him—David sprawled out on the ground.

"David, wake up! What happened?"

He's groggy at first and immediately pops up asking for my mom.

"Where is she? She was just here, we were just here, and then..."

"No one else is here."

Helping him up I feel myself begin to panic. He's wobbly as he tries to gain balance. His head has an open wound. I don't know what's going on, but everyone is gone.

"I couldn't find Ale." It comes out as a plea.

"Jayson, we need to go. Something doesn't feel right. I know you love your family, but we need to leave."

"Alright."

I don't argue with him because at this point he is right. There is nothing more that we can do. We lost my sisters. My brother is off somewhere, and now my mom and Ale are missing. For us to make it out of here alive, we need to get far away from here, and we need to get help. We can let the police help us. I can see that morning is approaching. I can feel dew in the air, and I can see a little better than I did earlier. We have about thirty minutes until sunup. If we hide and head out in the daylight, we might have a better chance. But I am not sure if I want to risk it.

"Alright?" It comes out as a question.

I don't know why he's questioning me. I just want to get out of here and to be as far away from here as I can get.

We get up and head back the way I came even though it might not be the right way. We're about to turn right when I stop.

"I just came from that direction."

All of a sudden we hear someone groan off to the left. We take off running. I hope it's my mom or Ale.

As we enter the clearing, it's an odd scene we stumble on. My entire family—at least the ones who are still alive—are sitting in chairs in a circle. They are facing each other, bound and their mouths covered. It was my mom groaning. She's in pain and crying. When she sees me she starts to move trying to free herself.

"Mom, what happened?" I kneel and start to untie her feet. David is doing the same to Ale. Victor and my father look bad. Victor is almost lifeless.

I pull off the tape from my mom's mouth. It comes off easily. Her saliva and tears have moistened the glue on the other side.

"He's coming back," she says.

"Who is coming back?" I yell at her, wanting to shake her. The way she told me he was coming back was like she knew who this was.

"I don't know." She's still crying when I start to untie her arms. David is behind me, and I can hear him struggling. He hasn't been able to undo any of Ale's ties. I stand up and am about to ask him to switch places so I can help Ale and he can get my mom up and out when we hear yelling, I think he's coming back.

"Go hide. Get out of here."

"I can't leave you, Jayson."

"Go. He clearly left you out there, maybe it's just us he wants." It must be. Why else would he have left David out there?

"Just go." I push him away and he takes off running. I turn around in time to see him standing in front of me. A stranger.

"Where is he? I went back for him, and he was gone." He begins to yell taking a step towards me.

"Who?" I try and play dumb because I don't think he saw David just now. If I have any chance of at least protecting him, I need to make him think I don't know where he is.

"Why are you doing this?"

"Why am I doing this?" He repeats back.

I don't like the back-and-forth questions. We're out here and my family is hurt. My dad and Victor are now awake. The family all sitting across from each other. I see the gun in his hand. We're not going to make it out of here.

I see my mom trying to untie her hand when he comes up and strikes her. She stops moving.

"Mom!" I scream out.

I am about to rush towards her when he raises the gun. He directs me away from them and points to an empty chair. I take my seat. I don't know what he wants.

He walks around taking the tape off everyone's mouths. Dad and Victor are swearing at him. My mom is half awake and Ale is just staring blank faced with tears streaming down her face. I see two more chairs off in the distance. The chairs for my sisters. Either he wasn't expecting David to be here or this chair I am sitting in was for him. I look up and he starts to speak.

"Let's talk, shall we?"

CHAPTER 54

He needs to hear it from his family. I want them to apologize and beg for forgiveness and their lives. It's why this is even happening. I had a similar experience to Jayson, and I just want justice and revenge.

I came out to my family when I got home from school one day. It was high school, and I was younger than Jayson was when he came out. I'd just had one of the best days at school when I walked in the door and felt like something was off.

I hadn't chosen to do it. I was forced. My father had found the letters in my room from the boy I had been writing to. We had been writing letters back and forth for weeks. I took a chance writing the first letter, and when I got one back, I had fallen for him. With the first letter there was hesitation. We both knew what we wanted, but we both came from families where we knew that it wasn't going to be accepted. College would be starting in another year. We had decided we would go away together. We didn't want anyone to know about us, so we kept everything a secret and, the letters continued.

Seeing my parents in the living room along with my brother and sister I knew something had just happened. They had tears in their eyes, and they looked scared. Mom was crying, and dad had the belt lying out. I saw the box where I kept our letters.

"What are these?" My dad yelled.

"It's obvious what they are."

"And who are they from?" My mom jumps in, wiping away her tears.

"I am sure you know since we're all standing here."

I look to my family, and everyone is just staring back at me. No one is saying anything. It looks like my brother and sister already got theirs. Dad was abusive, and I was sure I was about to get the worst beating of my life. He was going to beat the gay out of me and make them watch. And he did. And no one did anything to help me. I tried to defend myself, but it did nothing. I avoided the worst of it by taking off and I never saw them alive again. The next day the news reported that they all died that night. I can't say that I wasn't upset. I was mad at everyone in that house.

After I left, I ended up on my best friend's doorstep. I told her everything about what happened when I got home. I had been keeping everything about the letters and the boy a secret. I finally opened up to her, and I told her, but never told her who the boy was. She wouldn't forgive me if she knew. It was her boyfriend. I didn't mean for it to happen, but it did, and I didn't regret it. I only stayed with her for a few days because I was under 18.

I moved in with other family members and because of what happened I never got to be with him. I tried to call and write to him, but he never responded. I don't know if his feelings changed for me or if he was afraid of being outed. We never wanted to have a relationship while in high school for obvious reasons. The first being we weren't ready, and the second we still had not figured out what to do about his girlfriend, my best friend. We didn't want to hurt her, but we knew that she would hate us for the rest of our lives.

College was postponed a few years, and when I finally attended, it was hard to find myself. I never could get over what happened and how my family ruined my life. That day had stuck with me.

*I told no one how I went back to the house that night. My inten-
tion was to grab some of my things. I wanted the letters the most,
but when I saw the empty box lying next to the fireplace, I knew
that my dad had destroyed them. I don't remember much after that;
I just remember being filled with rage. I walked through the house,
closing all the windows, and opening the bedroom doors. I broke the
gas line behind the stove and left before I was affected by what I had
just done.*

*My friend never noticed that I left the room that night and when
we saw the news the next morning, everyone had been grateful I
had spent the night there. My alibi was perfect, and no one ever
questioned me.*

I look over at Jayson's father. "Tell them."

"I cheated on your mom."

"Go on." *That's not why we're here. I knew he cheated, but I
want him to apologize. Hasn't he figured this out yet. Gazing at him
I give an order,* "Apologize."

He looks at me so confused.

"I am sorry. I have another son." *He hangs his head as he said
this.*

"Stop playing with me." *I raise the gun and aim.*

"I love you, son, and I am so sorry. I was afraid and—"

*I don't want to hear anymore. Aiming directly at him, I fire off a
shot.*

*I look around to make sure everyone knows how serious I am.
They look on in horror. With their arms strapped into chairs, I see
fists clench and claw openly in the air. The slutty one is crying so*

much I am tempted to just get her death over with because I can't stand to hear her whimpering.

"That's what happens when you play games." I walk over to his brother. He doesn't look well. I am about to ask him to speak, but I will wait. I want his friend to talk.

"Now, you. Tell him."

"I was blackmailing your dad, Jayson. I am so sorry. I knew he was cheating. It was with my aunt. And he has a kid with her. I am so sorry."

"What is with you people?" I raise the gun when she screams out.

"Stop please, stop! I know you took my son a long time ago. I know it's you." It's Jayson's mom who jumps in.

"What are you talking about?" I raise the gun because I just want to shut them up. None of them are getting this. "You all sat there and watched while your son poured his heart out and came out to you. He needed your love and acceptance, and you all just ate your food and let your husband say all that shit to him."

"You were there? Who are you?"

I need to explain to them that I am no one. I'm a stranger, triggered that day only to become obsessed with them. All I wanted was to eat a meal in peace at my favorite restaurant. But I was subjected to a horrible scene that played out somewhere that should have been private.

"Honestly, Jayson, I am no one. I am nothing to you and you are nothing to me."

He looks so confused.

"But I have been following you and your family for the last few years. I have gone on some of the other vacations with you too. I'm just good at hiding."

I stop talking because I hear something behind me.

CHAPTER 55

DAVID

We've been through a lot in the last twelve hours, and I am not leaving without Jayson. It's more than I ever thought we would have to go through. Especially so early in the relationship but I need him in my life, he makes me a better person. I get the courage together and make my way, I might be about to do something stupid. He stops and is about to turn because I am making too much noise. I had been circling the campsite, trying to find the best place where I could sneak up on him.

"You're not the one who stole my son?" Jayson's mom starts talking again in time to bring his focus back to them.

"Mom, what are you talking about?" Jayson is as confused as I am.

"When you were all younger, the last time we went camping, someone took your brother. He was gone for less than a day, and when they found him, they told us he hadn't been hurt. He didn't remember anything, so we decided to just leave it alone. We didn't want to make a big deal out of it."

I cannot believe what I am hearing. Who would keep this from their son, their family? How did they not know about this?

"You guys were with the camp staff, and they kept you busy. When he was found, you didn't really ask questions, and since Victor didn't remember, your father and I decided to just leave it alone and pretend it didn't happen."

"I knew it." It's the first time Victor has said anything since being tied up.

"I've been remembering. I think I always remembered. I just didn't know it happened. I thought I was having weird dreams, nightmares. Didn't you take me to get help?"

"We did. We took you to a few therapists, and when they couldn't get you to remember, we just left it alone. I am so sorry."

I see him pull out a beef jerky tearing open the packaging. He looks like he's just as interested in this story as I am. Jayson's family is really fucked up. He takes a bite and tosses the rest onto the ground. I hate those things, they smell, but Jayson loves them and apparently this guy. I still can't believe everything that I am hearing.

His best friend is blackmailing his dad. His dad has another kid. His mom was going to leave him. Victor was kidnapped as a kid, and they hid it. Do I really want to be with Jayson?

"You guys are really messed up. Do you see why I did this now, Jayson? You need out of this family. You need to get away from them. I am trying to help you, free you. The way I freed myself from my family."

"What does your family have to do with this?" Jayson isn't buying what this guy is selling.

"My dad did the same thing to me. He didn't accept me. Your dad doesn't accept you." As he says this, under different circumstances I would feel sorry for him.

"Yes, I do." His dad isn't dead. He looks like it; his breathing is shallow.

"I do, son, I love you, and I am so sorry." And then it happens. Two more shots. His dad and brother are gone.

"I am sick of this shit! Now, where is your little boyfriend?" He points the gun directly at Jayson.

"He's gone, he went to get help."

CHAPTER 56

JAYSON

He didn't leave when I told him, and I can see him. David never listens, and I am glad for it, because looking at him gives me hope that maybe I can think of something. Maybe he can help distract him. I am not bound and tied like the rest of them. Why haven't I tried to rush him? A part of me thinks it's because he's right: I am confused about my family, and I want answers. I want explanations.

Hearing the confession that something happened to my brother is shocking. I remember those camping trips and I remember the last one. Nothing seemed out of the ordinary. I remember Victor wasn't around for part of the day and we had to stay in the rec center. We painted and played with other kids. When I look back, I can see some signs that something was off. Mom and Dad were gone for almost the same amount of time that Victor was and when we got home, mom got a little obsessive. She didn't want to let us out of her sight. Dad became even more withdrawn.

I wonder how much this man knows and how long he's

known it. He looked a bit shocked when he heard the confession. To buy me some time, I decided to ask him. I see David and I think he has an idea.

"Did you know about my brother?"

"No, I didn't."

"Now, tell me where your little boyfriend is."

"I told you, he left."

He looks at me and laughs.

"I told you he left!" This time I yell it.

"I was going to let you two live. Maybe I am not sure. I am sure he has secrets too. Everyone does. No one is honest, and no one cares about people like me and you. They only want to hurt us."

I think about it, could he be right? I have been hurt before. I've been hurt by the people around me, the people I love, but he's wrong about David. He is the only person who hasn't hurt me.

"He hasn't."

"But he will—they all do."

"Maybe that has more to do with you than me."

It's a risk to throw that out there, but I am running out of time. I can see he is getting impatient. That's when I see David coming closer.

"He will never hurt me. He cares about me."

I see David creep up slowly. His arms raised, and I see something in his hand. He's got the tire iron, and he swings.

The stranger ducks out of the way almost as if he knew it was about to happen and raises the gun. I reach down and grab a thick log we found earlier. It's thick enough for me to get a grip. I can feel the bark chipping as I pick it up. It's got to work.

"Oh, you're back." He sounds angry, gun raised.

"I never left." David sounds confident as he backs up a little.

"Well, this will be easier then."

He shoots at David at the same time I bring the log down on him, directly hitting him and causing the gun to drop.

David crawls towards the gun as I bring the log up for another blow. The man turns around.

"I just wanted to save you." He barks out.

I am ready to bring the log down over and over, killing this man. Make him pay for Catalina, Angelina, and my father.

"I don't need saving." I hear David trying to fire the gun behind me. Click, Click. There are no more bullets.

"You thought it would be that easy, didn't you."

He pushes me off him and quickly rises to his feet. We're face to face only feet apart. I see my mom in the background reach into her pocket with her free hand. She tosses something at David, and he catches it.

"I killed my family. Now I am going to kill yours, and I think I'm going to let you live."

"Why would you do that?"

"I don't know, Jayson. You and I are the same."

I want him to continue, because I don't think we're the same, but I don't have the time. David has the gun and it's pointed at the man.

"Get away from him."

"What are you going to do?"

I don't know what David thinks he's going to do. He's standing there with an unloaded gun. I see him pull the trigger.

CHAPTER 57

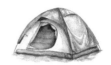

JAYSON

I free Ale while David is working on getting my mom untied. He's still having a hard time despite me getting most of it done earlier. Ale rushes over to Victor and is untying him. He slumps over into her arms. I know he's gone. I haven't seen him move since he was shot.

"How did you..." I can barely get the words out. Did he know how guns work? I don't. I have never held one in my hand before. It wouldn't shock me if he hasn't either.

"Your mom." I turn to look at her. She's staring at Victor and my dad. She's not crying. I assume she's all cried out. She watches Ale.

"They were by your sister when we were moving her. I honestly didn't know what I was doing when I grabbed them."

She's still not facing me until I tell her.

"You did good, mom."

She turns around and smiles. I am proud of her. I have always been proud of her. She's always done what she could for us and she always will. I look down and watch David.

"What are you doing?"

He's going through his pockets. Pulls out a wallet and flips through it. He tosses it on the ground. I am afraid to open it. I am afraid to see his picture and his name.

It's empty except for some cash and a wrapper for beef jerky, the same kind we like to eat. Inside his pockets are a phone and a set of keys. The key looks like they belong to a Camry. I recognize the brands name on it as we all owned the same car at some point. The car in the parking lot must have belonged to him. I was so distracted after we got here and assumed it was one of my sisters.

As I stand over his body, I see something familiar, but I don't know from where. Maybe he was telling the truth, and he was at the restaurant. Have I met him somewhere else? He knows a lot about that night at dinner. He was right though. No one stopped my father, no one stood up for me, and that's why I have had so many issues from that night.

Ale still has said nothing and has moved very little. It's unusual to see her like this. She's in shock. I would be too after witnessing all of this. I just hope she still wants to be friends. Looking over at her, her face says it all, but she still feels the need to say it. She rushes me, giving me one of the biggest hugs she's ever given me. I feel so much comfort in this moment. She whispers in my ear.

"I'm sorry."

Pulling away I gaze into her eyes. I pull her in again for another hug.

"It's ok. We can talk about it later." She knows what I'm referring to. I have more questions, and only she has the answers. She also knew my dad was cheating and who with and that he has another kid. I want all of this explained to me but not now. Right now, I just want to get out of here.

David tosses me the phone. I turn it over in my hand, looking at this old flip phone, I power it on. There's a moment I pace back and forth as I try and work my way through it. The signal didn't immediately catch and what surprises me most is it works. With a few weak bars indicating it has signal I am relieved as this saves us the trip out of here and making our way to help. I can't imagine driving out of here on four flat tires. David calls to me and then tosses me the keys when the call connects.

"911, what's your emergency?" I am too stunned to speak. I feel a sense of relief, but I still can't get the words out.

"911, is someone there?"

We're getting out of here I think to myself.

"911, did you need help?" The dispatcher repeats.

I try to explain as quickly as I can. The 911 operator wants to stay on the phone, so I tossed it over to Ale who takes over. They wanted me to check on the other two, and I do, but I can't find a pulse on either of them. I think about my sisters who are sitting upright against a tree. I still can't believe they are gone, and now I've lost my brother and my dad.

Ale eventually hangs up on them, and we decide to wait for them where we parked the cars. I don't want to be anywhere near this guy.

I turn around and take another look at the scene in front of me. I see bodies and an empty campsite. I look over at Gina's tent and picture the blood inside. David places a hand on my shoulder for comfort. There's an urge to nudge it off, but I leave it there.

"Let's get out of here."

"Are you sure you're ready Jayson, if you need a minute." David is always putting me and my feelings first, it's why I am in love with him.

"No, I think I'm ready."

I turn around but not before rushing back to my tent,

retrieving my favorite book. Reading is as an escape, but I didn't have the chance to do it this weekend. When I come out, they are all staring at me, waiting. I look down and turn the book over in my hands, reading the title and decide that I want to leave it behind. The past is the past and I am ready to move on, find a new book to love. This one is damaged and I'm not so damaged anymore. I am ready to start healing. Walking over to my brother, I place this book at his feet, it's symbolic of our relationship. Not just the relationship with him but also with my sisters. I whisper goodbye to him and look out into the woods saying my sister's names.

By the time we make it out to the car, the police and ambulance are pulling up. Vehicle after vehicle enters. There is so much going on. So much chaos that I find it hard to concentrate on anything. I have a hard time talking to the police and detective who are trying to ask us exactly what happened. We told them everything we could. There are things I don't know and details I am already having a hard time remembering because I think the shock is setting in.

The detective seems frustrated when I can't tell him who did it. He looks confused.

"There's a live one here."

I hear one of them yell and a bunch of responders take off

back towards the campsite. Victor was dead, and I was sure that whoever that man was had died too. My interview ends with the detective, and he takes off with everyone. I am sure he'll be back with more questions.

We sit there, waiting for them to bring out whoever it was. They are rushing us into other ambulances when I see someone off in the distance. Through all the chaos I don't know who it is, or if it's just my imagination, but someone walks out of the woods and across the lot. They disappear into the woods. It was brief. The ambulance door shuts, and I am left confused. Despite being ok to drive, they strongly suggest that we don't. We couldn't even if we wanted because the tires on the cars have been slashed.

They are carrying a body out on a stretcher, but there are too many of them to get a good look at who it is. I dodge my head in and out between the crowd trying to catch a glimpse as the doors to the ambulance shut and the vehicle is moving. I can see them rushing the person inside another ambulance, and we ride off to the hospital. I know for sure that four of us made it out of the woods alive. Maybe five of us, but I don't know who yet.

EPILOGUE

JAYSON

It's been six months, and I'm still having a hard time believing what we went through. I still don't understand why it happened or how it got to that point. As a family we were broken. I was ready to give up on them, and sometimes I feel like I did. We're still broken but with fewer of us. We're missing pieces that we'll never find. The pieces that remain are trying to find ways to recover and find peace amongst our pasts.

Ale and I patched things up. We didn't talk for a few weeks after because I needed time to try and understand why she couldn't come to me. Why she felt that she had to hide those things from me. We used to talk about my dad. I told her I thought he had been cheating. The way he talked to other women in front of my mom made it obvious that he didn't respect their marriage. When she finally apologized in what seemed to be a three-page text, I knew I had to forgive her. She wasn't good with her words, so she either spent time working through what she wanted to say or she hired a ghost writer. The text was filled with heartfelt words and ended with the simplest two words in the English language. "I'm sorry."

Hearing my dad say that he was sorry and that he loved me right before that man shot him stings. In therapy, I learned that sometimes someone's first reaction isn't their final reaction, despite how mean someone's first reaction was. I will never get to understand why my father was so afraid to tell me, because he was shot right before he was able to explain. I imagine he was just afraid of change. Afraid that me being gay was going to change his idea of what he thought a perfect family can and should be. It stings because it was there the whole time. He had the answer but was afraid to say it. His words. At least I think those were going to be his words. His love and acceptance. It's what I always wanted. I think I got it in some ways. I just wish he could have expressed it before he was forced to. It's most likely a product of his own upbringing. I wonder what would have happened to us if this stranger hadn't come into our lives that day.

I still can't bring myself to say his name—and I am not sure if I ever will—but what happened got plenty of media attention. I couldn't go anywhere without someone staring or pointing.

It's going to take some time to heal from everything and move on, but I am trying. I have the support of the remaining people from that day, my family.

We're all sitting around at home. The five of us. I must have imagined someone crossing into the woods before the ambulances took off because they found his body. He died. David killed him. I guess I will never know what I saw or didn't see. I was worried about the rest of us. The ones who made it out.

Ale is laughing and sitting on the couch with David. They've gotten very close since everything happened. I'm glad because they are the two most important people in my life. My mom is finally opening back up. It took a while, but losing your kids isn't easy. There is no way to just move on from that. The insurance money from dad's passing and selling off the business is going to keep her secure. She told me about the money she stashed as well. I don't think she planned to tell anyone about it, but the police found fifty thousand dollars in a bag in the abandoned tent near our site. She claimed it as hers and told me what had happened and how she got it. Clever woman. How it ended up in the tent is a mystery to me. We have our theories, but they are just theories.

There's a knock at the door and I place the copy of *Desperation* by Stephen King on the table. It's been through hell and is telling about that weekend. Looking over at mom because I am not sure if she was expecting company, we turn the music down. We were listening to some music and playing games. Just trying to be a family again.

"It's probably the mail carrier. He likes to check on me from time to time," Mom says cheerfully.

"Mrs. P, you naughty woman," Ale says playfully.

"Oh, Ale, I can never be you." She winks when she says this. She likes her, and Ale knows it's a joke, but my mom can be a little too much.

David stands up to answer the door, and it's in fact the mail carrier. He's a little too friendly with David, and I instantly feel jealous. I've always been a little too jealous. It's obvious the mail carrier doesn't have the hots for mom because the way he looked at David when he closed the door makes it obvious that David has a better chance with him. His eyes lingered a little too long on David and the rest of us.

"Oh, that wasn't Tommy. He must be on vacation or something."

"You know your mail carrier's name?" Ale says.

"Don't you?"

"No, I don't even get mail." She continues to tell my mom.

"Well, Tommy is nice. You should meet him." She says with an obvious look of intention.

Ale's snuggled up on the couch and rolls her eyes because my mom is still trying to set her up with someone. She doesn't approve of Ale's new relationship, and I am still working through my feelings around it.

David comes in, tossing the envelope down. Giving him a playful look, I raise my eyebrows in a tease. I know David isn't interested in anyone but me, but playing with him like this is a lot of fun.

His cast is off, and he's healed well. He's got a few scars on him, but we like to call them battle wounds.

On the table in front of us is an envelope addressed to Victor. We all look at each other, wondering if he'll open it. None of us want to be the ones to reach for it or say anything.

"I'll do it." Victor grabs the envelope and tears through it.

We all sit around waiting to hear what it says. There are two pieces of paper inside.

Victor reads them in silence. He looks up and places them carefully back into the envelope, setting it next to a book on the table. I'm glad the book I left behind made its way back to us. I guess another thing survived the weekend.

We were all there because Victor has been tracking his acceptance letter into graduate school, but Victor doesn't look ok; he just sits back down with Ale. There's something happening with him right now.

We all look at each other confused.

"There's no postmark on the envelope," David says.

I look down and David's right—there's no return address. A part of me wants to pick them up and read them myself, but Victor's response tells me everything.

Something Happened.

ACKNOWLEDGMENTS

For as long as I can remember I have wanted to be an author and publish a book. This here is the product of the many hours spent in front of the computer writing, stressing, and banging on the keyboard. The book you are holding would not have been possible without the help of the following people.

Mom, my guardian angel. You were still alive when I talked to you about plans to write a book. You always encouraged me to go for whatever I wanted and cheered me on the whole time. I can hear you cheering from your current resting place. There is so much of you in this book and in the character of Ms. P I know that if people had the chance to meet you, they would love you as much as I did. Thank you for the 40 years of life and being such a great mom, support, and best friend. I think about you always, RIP I love you.

Carlos, my number one fan, soulmate, and favorite person in the world. I honestly could not have done this without you. You were by my side the entire time and like my mom, cheered me on and lifted me up when I thought I couldn't do it. This is our book. We did this, together.

To my family, I hope you enjoy this book. We loved going camping growing up, so that was a big inspiration for the book. I hope you enjoy how I twisted our family tradition into something other people can enjoy in a terrifying way. Chris, Nicole, Robert, Dean, Dad, I love you. William, Megan,

Alissa, Adrianna, Madison, Jacob, Avery and Taylor, your uncle wrote a horror/thriller with a dash of slash. I hope you enjoy it. Ivan and Carlos, you've been awesome additions to the family I appreciate you. Kara, welcome to the family, I can't wait to get to know you more. Michelle, you came into the family during our time of grief but through that I have got to know you through shared interest, thank you for your support.

My extended family, there are too many of us but know I appreciate you all so much. Your love and support throughout my life is priceless.

The Negrete Family, Susan, Nicole, Catrina, thank you for being there for me and welcoming me into your family. You all have been some of the biggest supporters of me and I am so grateful to have you in my life. To all the nieces and nephews, you are some of the kindest people I have met.

To my Beta team: Elyse, Corina, and Alex!!! You three helped me so much in editing and working through various parts of the story. This would not be what it is without you. Your help and suggestions took this manuscript to the next level. I can't wait for your help on the next project. You three rock!!!!

To my Copy-Editing Team: Christie and Ris, thank you for taking the time to read this and offering feedback. You are not just part of this team you are my friends.

Lori, your edits polished this up in a way I am so grateful for. Your friendship has cost me a lot of money because all we do is talk about the books we want to buy, but I appreciate you so much. *Thank you for being a friend.*

Danielle Lynn author of *Fate Will Bring You Home*, watching you write your book inspired me to kick my butt into gear. I am so glad to have been able to share this journey alongside you. We did it!! We're both published authors.

Christopher M. Tantillo, author of *The Night I Spent with*

Aubrey Fisher. Thank you for your friendship. You helped throughout so much of this process, and I don't know if I would have given up if you didn't help me navigate through some of this. I am forever grateful.

Brandon T. Bernard, author of *the Mad World series.* I cannot express in words what you have done for me. Thank you for all the help in discovering ways to edit, organize and talk through all the things that were new to me during this process. You brought my cover to life and exceeded my expectations. I value our friendship so much and I am so glad that I met you.

The Bookies and Besties community thank you all for following me on this journey. I really hope you enjoy this book. I hope you find the nods to our little community inside.

I want to send one last big thank you. I couldn't have done this without you, THE READERS, ESPECIALLY THE ONES READING THIS. I appreciate every one of you. You will never know how much I appreciate the support. THANK YOU.

ABOUT THE AUTHOR

Arthur Avalos is a Chicago based Author and practicing therapist. He lives in the Lakeview neighborhood of Chicago with his two cats, Jabari and Raven, his dog Maggie, and his partner Carlos, an aspiring author's husband. In their spare time they like to go to the bookstore and film content for social media to entertain the masses but more importantly have fun with each other.

Something Happened is Arthur's first novel and hopefully will not be his last. That depends entirely on you and if you like it, and want him to write more.

For updates on future projects.